Ida Farnell

The Lives of the Troubadours

Ida Farnell

The Lives of the Troubadours

ISBN/EAN: 9783337400415

Printed in Europe, USA, Canada, Australia, Japan

Cover: Foto ©Andreas Hilbeck / pixelio.de

More available books at **www.hansebooks.com**

THE LIVES OF
THE TROUBADOURS

*TRANSLATED FROM THE MEDIAEVAL
PROVENÇAL, WITH INTRODUCTORY MATTER
AND NOTES, AND WITH SPECIMENS OF
THEIR POETRY RENDERED INTO ENGLISH*

BY

IDA FARNELL

FORMERLY SCHOLAR AT LADY MARGARET HALL
OXFORD

London
Published by David Nutt
In The Strand

1896

To the Memory of

MY BROTHER,

GEORGE STANLEY FARNELL.

"Mortz trahiritz, ben vos posc en ver dire
Que non poguetz el mon meillor aucire."

Contents

Contents

Contents

ix

INTRODUCTION.

LIVES OF THE TROUBADOURS

INTRODUCTION

THE Lives of the Troubadours, though more than once published in their original form, have never, I think, hitherto been wholly translated. It seemed to me, therefore, that an English version of them might be acceptable to those readers who, while not Provençal students, take a keen interest in the life and thought of the best ages of chivalry.

The literary activity of the troubadours extended, roughly speaking, from 1100-1250. Their poetry was at its best during the last thirty years of the twelfth century, and the early part of the thirteenth; and it was during the latter period that the desire of knowing something of the troubadours' lives seems to have made itself felt. About that time it became customary to head the collection of a troubadour's poems with the story of his life, which often served to explain otherwise obscure allusions in the poems. The writers of these Lives

were either contemporaries of the greatest troubadours or belonged to the succeeding generation,
and, judging from internal evidence, were not more
than two, or, at the most, three in number. Hugh
of Saint Circ, who claims to have written two of
the Lives, probably wrote many more besides.

Of several of them there are two versions, of
which the longer and more romantic often seems an
imaginative expansion of the older and more trust-
worthy account. As a whole the Lives may be
regarded as fairly authentic; the writers of them obtained their information from allusions in the troubadours' poems, from well-established tradition in the
case of the earlier troubadours, or from their own
personal knowledge in the case of contemporaries.
Scattered as they originally were in various MSS.,
the Lives have been in modern times collected and
edited, though not as yet critically. A complete
collection of them is to be found in Raynouard's
Choix des poésies provençales, and in 1878 appeared
a revised edition of Prof. A. Mahn's *Die Biographieen der Troubadours*, which is that from
which I have made my translations, and to which I
have referred in the course of them.

The collection of Lives in question is of great
value in many ways. It is, to begin with, the chief
monument of Provençal prose that we possess, and
there is often a peculiar charm in the naïve

simplicity of its style, in spite of its loosely-strung sentences, want of logical sequence, and occasional incoherence, faults common to all prose in its youth. Apart, however, from its style, the collection is the best, and sometimes almost the only source of information left us of the troubadours, and the manner of lives they led. It introduces us into a strangely interesting country and age; a country that was the home of chivalry, and for a hundred years, at least, the centre of such refinement and culture as then existed in Western Europe; an age when men were first shaking off the fetters of many centuries of barbarism, and finding new delight in form and beauty. From it too we learn something of those who played great parts in mediaeval history: Henry II. of England, his wife and sons, Philip Augustus of France, the kings of Aragon and Castile, the unhappy Raymond of Toulouse, Boniface and Conrad of Montferrat, and many knights and barons who were less prominent and yet important figures in the mediaeval world. The collection shows us likewise, with more or less distinctness, the struggles of the English and French kings, and the final overthrow of the Angevin rule in France; it speaks to us of the crusades, of the contests between the Christian kings of the north of Spain and the Arabs of the south; of the rise of the north Italian towns, with their feuds and jealousies; and, lastly, reveals to us, only too clearly, the desolation and misery produced by the Albigensian War, and the establishment of the supremacy of France in Provence.

All this is in itself enough to make the troubadours' Lives of high interest, but their chief value consists in the insight they give us into the manners and morals of Languedoc during the twelfth and thirteenth centuries. And here it may be well to try to discover what was the essential character of the troubadour world, as represented to us by Provençal poetry and the book before us. In opposition to the wide-spread enthusiasm for things mediaeval, which Scott and the Romantic School generally did so much to awaken, there is a certain tendency now, owing to a wider knowledge of the evils of the Middle Ages, to pass severe judgment upon them, to doubt that chivalry exercised a potent influence on conduct, and that those nobler qualities, which we are accustomed to associate with the twelfth, thirteenth, and fourteenth centuries, existed to any extent in the men of those times.

Now, in the world of Provençal poetry and of the Lives, the elements of good and evil are strangely interwoven; it is not such a world as Scott delighted in, but neither is it entirely one of barbarous, unbridled passions and unmitigated corruption.

In the beautiful country where the Langue d'Oc was spoken, memories of the old Roman civilization and institutions were still fresh, and Roman, or Graeco-Roman cities, such as Marseilles, Arles, Nimes, and Toulouse, early became centres of wealth and refinement. The three greatest sovereignties of the south of France were those of the County of Provence, the County of Toulouse, and the Duchy of Aquitaine, to which the County of Poitou was united. The most powerful ruler of Provence in troubadour times was the famous Alphonso II., who reigned over Aragon, Barcelona, Provence, Carlat, and Millau, etc. (see *infra*). Toulouse was at the height of her glory in the reign of the heroic Raymond of St. Giles, one of the chief leaders of the first crusade ; her power was later on, under Raymond VI., broken by the Albigensian War. The most renowned lord of Aquitaine and Poitou was the troubadour, William IX. (see *infra*). His grand-daughter, Eleanor, by her marriage with our Henry II., brought Aquitaine under the Angevin rule, her son, Richard Plantagenet, becoming, later, Duke of Aquitaine.

The lords of these three States were the staunch friends and patrons of troubadours, and in this their example was followed by the rulers of the multitude of small fiefs that were under them or independent of them. These small fiefs, in the

south, indeed, fostered rather than retarded intellectual growth, for each little court bade the
troubadour welcome, and cultivated poetry with
enthusiasm; and each, by the splendour of its
hospitality, promoted a social intercourse that the
less genial climates of northern countries did not
admit of.

The feudalism of Languedoc was obviously more
democratic than that of the north, and the
distinction of knighthood was at times conferred
on burghers and even peasants. The wealth and
importance indeed of the former class prevented
there being any impassable barrier between them
and the nobles; and the extreme violence of
Bertran of Born's attack upon the arrogance and
presumption of the peasants, speaks well also for
the prosperity of these as compared with the
peasants of Europe at large. In any case, and
whatever the separation of classes, poetry was a
common ground on which princes, burghers, and
even peasants might be found together; the lords
of Toulouse and Marseilles, for instance, were both
of them the friends of the merchants' sons, Peire
Vidal and Folquet, as also the Viscount of Ventadorn of the peasant Bernart.

In a country then, where these favourable con-
ditions existed, and which, though certainly not
remarkable for its piety, was peculiarly open to the

refining influences of Christianity, there flourished certain lofty and deep-rooted principles, such as are the essence of what we call chivalry: the protection, namely, of the weak and oppressed, the devotion to truth and loyalty, and to constant and noble action, and, above all, the reverence and worship of woman. A society in which such standards of life existed could not be altogether corrupt, and though it may be said that realities are one thing and ideals another, it is impossible that the general recognition of certain ideals should be wholly without influence on every-day life. The collection of Lives is by no means without instances of a lofty and spiritual connection between knight and lady, of the devotion of man to man, and of romantic generosity; and indeed there is hardly a page either in the Lives of the troubadours, or in their poetry, that does not bear witness, not only to their minds being saturated with ideas of chivalry, but to the direct influence of these ideas on their conduct.

But though it would be unjust to deny the existence of certain noble elements in the Languedoc of this period, the barbarity and corruption that ran side by side with better things is sufficiently manifest in the book before us. That which chivalry inculcated was impossible for the average man to carry out. It might prompt the Dauphin of Auvergne, for example, to maintain the cause of the troubadour, Peire of Maensac, who with his lady appealed to him for protection; it might prompt him also to a profuse and reckless hospitality, but it did not withhold him from a gross breach of faith towards the honest burgher, Peire Pelissier. In . fact, a spirit of lawless violence is found together with one of absolute Quixotism, a spirit of self-seeking with that of self-abandonment, treachery with loyalty, a pure and ethereal love with its opposite.

For the degeneration of mediaeval love chivalry itself is largely responsible, both by ignoring the accepted Christian marriage tie and by substituting for it an essentially unnatural relation between men and women. By way of compensating for all that the sordid and business-like marriages of the age failed to give, chivalry, in fact, encouraged a connection between knight and lady into which love and love alone entered; in it the lady's mission was to incite her lover to noble deeds, the lover's to strive to the uttermost to win her praise; and, while glorying, at a distance that nothing could bridge over, in the perfections of his lady, his greatest reward was the joy of service and of loving. Now, that such a relationship could be lasting or general was not in human nature, and the tie often, therefore, degenerated into one of sensuality or of self-interest, the lady, in this latter case, desiring a knight to win her fame, and the knight a lady to advance him in the world.

We must then be content to take the troubadour age as it was, and be prepared to find a standard of morals wholly different from our own. We must regard it as a time of lofty principles, and a time when a great, and, on the whole, a noble effort was made towards the dispersion of intellectual darkness; but, on the other hand, one in which the savage instincts of centuries were but ill-suppressed, and the ideals but very imperfectly realized. It is, however, of the highest importance to us that such aspirations existed. The influence of the Provençal poets, childish, narrow, ill-disciplined as they were, has lasted on through centuries, and some of the noblest sides of human life are still those that owe their origin to Provençal chivalry. The study, too, of the troubadours' Lives is a moral lesson of no small significance, as must always be conveyed by the spectacle of the struggles, failures, or partial victories of those who are reaching out, however feebly, after truth and beauty; and they and their poetry certainly teach us, if nothing else, that a want of self-control and grasp on the realities of life bears within it the early-ripening seeds of moral and intellectual decay.

Some few of the Lives given here are nothing

more than short notices of little or no intrinsic interest. I have, however, inserted them, partly for the sake of completeness, and partly because they are in most cases the only mention we possess of men of some literary importance. From the more detailed Lives it will be seen that the career of a troubadour of ability was, as a rule, a prosperous and also a varied one. If he began life poor and socially insignificant, he might, it is true, pass through an apprenticeship of poverty and of long wanderings on foot; but sooner or later he was sure to win the favour of lords and princes. Wherever he went it would be part of his profession to sing the valour of the lord and the beauty of the lady beneath whose roof he found himself. His canzones to the *châtelaines* who thus protected him might often mean nothing more than the homage of a dependent to a lady far above him; but, on the other hand, they might be the love poems of one in whose inflammable southern nature a respectful admiration had developed into a real passion.

To the translation of the Lives of the troubadours I have, though well aware of the difficulty of rendering Provençal verse into English, added some few specimens of their poems. Much of the effect produced on us by Provençal poetry is owing to the softness and beauty of the language itself, with its full vowel sounds, musical completeness, and the ease with which it lends itself to a complicated system of rhymes and metre. / Over and above this, however, the poetry, when at its best, has a beauty that can make itself felt, I think, even in translations; it is then for the roughness and imperfection of these that I now apologize, rather than for the attempt itself.

A very slight acquaintance with the troubadours impresses one with the plausibility of the remark which has been made, that the chief part of their lyric poetry might pass for the work of one man alone, so great is the uniformity of their ideas. True, however, as it is, that there was a common store of ideas, and of set expressions, from which the troubadours drew largely, several of them at least have an individuality of the most pronounced kind, and no one, for example, could fail to distinguish from one another Bernart of Ventadorn's passionate tenderness, Peire Cardinal's lofty scorn, the Monk of Montaldon's shrewd wit, and Bertran of Born's war-like intensity.

The influence of the literature of Provence on other countries will be seen to some extent in the course of this book. It was felt in the greater part of Europe, in France (that is, the northern half of modern France), England, Germany, Spain, Portugal, and, above all, in Italy. It was Provence that taught the poets of the Middle Ages the use and the beauty of rhyme; it was in Provence, as there is every reason to believe, that there arose the *tenzon*, the *alba*, the *serena*, and probably the *pastourelle*, all the chief forms of mediaeval lyric poetry in fact. As to the influence of Provence on Italy, it will be seen how, before Italy had any literature of her own, her northern states cultivated the language and literature of Provence, and gave a willing shelter to many a troubadour, while Sicily also looked to Languedoc for its models and inspiration. We have sufficient evidence of the admiration of Dante and also of Petrarch for poets such as Bertran of Born, Folquet, Arnault Daniel, and Sordello, an admiration shown both by the Italian poets' words of praise, and by their imitation of form and expression. Who could fail to recognize Provençal love, ennobled and glorified, in the adoration of Dante for Beatrice? In fact, the great Italian school of poetry, to which the Guidos, Dante, and Petrarch equally belong, is the legitimate successor and offspring of the troubadours' poetry and ethical idea.

The troubadours have left us a remarkable number of fine 'Complaints' or elegies on the death of their patrons and mistresses; they have also left us satires of striking power and boldness, but nevertheless their chief theme was love, and it is pre-eminently as writers of canzones or love-songs that they take a place in literature. The extra-ordinary sameness of their themes has ~~already~~ been touched on. The return, for instance, of Spring; the joy of all things living, in contrast to the sadness of the poet; the thousand graces of his lady, and his despair of ever winning her—such ideas form the basis of poem upon poem; equally extraordinary, however, is the variety of treatment that these ideas receive, as well as the variety of form and metre of the poems in which they appear.

The rapid development of Provençal poetry is a well-known phenomenon in the history of literature. It burst into life like a tropical plant, but only too soon began to show the faults not of youth but of a premature old age. Indeed, confronted by these faults, one is inclined to think, that even if the Albigensian War had not crushed out its strength, its decay could only have been arrested by a poet of greater genius than the troubadours could boast of among their ranks. With some notable exceptions there is in them a lack of manly vigour and of the "high seriousness" that is an essential element of the best poetry. Too often the troubadours merely play with their gift, absorbed rather in the intricacies of their own treatment of a theme than in the theme itself. Of religious enthusiasm they had little or none. The crusades which stirred the rest of Christendom to its very depths made little impression on Provence; and in the few crusading songs I have translated, it will be easily seen that the troubadour in his heart of hearts would rather kneel at his lady's shrine than at the Holy Sepulchre. For a time, however, something of the strength and sweetness that religion gives was inspired in them by their passionate worship of love, of a mistress ever perfect, and ever unattainable; 'and it is the strength and sincerity of their passion, together with a certain ethereal delicacy and child-like grace, that, apart from the beauty of their form, give a charm to the troubadours which amply atones for their lack of knowledge and profundity.' A further interest is lent to the reading of their poems by a certain pathetic consciousness on our part of the relentless cruelty with which the crusaders of the Albigensian War were to silence for ever the voices of so many sweet, child-like, and inconsequent singers who, all unforeboding of evil, rhyme on as though life were never to give them other grounds for sadness than the fading of Spring, the silence of the nightingale, and the coldness of their lady's heart.

It is undeniable, however, that Provence has given us no poet of the first order; but the same remark applies to the mediaeval literature of most countries, and the really great poets are not so many in number that we can afford to altogether neglect those of the second rank, who, though they cannot show us life in all its many-sidedness, may notwithstanding present to us certain aspects of it with no small truth and beauty.

We cannot afford to neglect altogether men whom Dante was pleased to look on as his teachers, men whose influence on the literature of France and indirectly of England has not been inconsiderable; and whose disciple, Petrarch, the teacher of Ronsard, and Spenser, and Shakspear, ruled in Italy for centuries supreme as the poet of Love. Those marvellous translations of Dante Rossetti, which give English readers so much of the grace and beauty of the early Italian poets, will show how closely these latter are connected with their Provençal masters and models.

Mr. Swinburne has been, I think, the first English poet to appreciate the exquisite form and sweet lyrical tone of the troubadours themselves. Mr. Browning has chosen the story of Sordello, one of the noblest figures in the Divine Comedy, for his philosophic poem.

These examples may surely serve as my justification.

The chief books that I have found helpful in the study of Provençal literature, and to which I can refer the reader are—

Chrestomathie provençale. K. Bartsch.

Gedichte der Troubadours. 4 vols. Edited by A. Mahn.

La Poésie des Troubadours. Raynouard.

Bertran de Born. Edit. A. Thomas.

Der Mönch von Montaudon. Edit. E. Philippson. 1873.

Peire Vidal. Edit. K. Bartsch. 1857.

Leben und Werke der Troubadours. F. Diez.

Histoire de la poésie provençale. Fauriel.

Jaufre Rudel. Edit. A. Stimming. 1873.

Guillem de Cabestanh. Edit. F. Hüffer. 1869.

Ponz de Capduoill. Edit. M. Napolski. 1880.

Folquet de Romans. Edit. R. Zenker. 1896.

Sordello. Edit. C. de Lollis. 1896.

Arnaldo Daniello. Edit. U. A. Canello. 1883.

THE COUNT OF POITIERS

Reigned from 1086-1127.

THE Count of Poitiers, who is the earliest troubadour mentioned, was, at the age of fifteen, one of the most powerful princes of his time—a man of great valour, personal charm, and wit, but also of notorious profligacy and impiety.* He bore no part in the Crusade of 1094, on which started nearly all the great lords of Languedoc under Raymond of St. Giles. In 1101, however, he yielded to the influence of the times, and, heading a large army, proceeded to the Holy Land. This army was scattered and destroyed by the Turks, William, almost alone, escaping on foot. The eight poems of his still existing are graceful but superficial; they are nearly all similar in their form, which is one of archaic simplicity. The poem translated below is of great historic interest from the fact of its being one of the earliest of Provence (and, indeed, the only one on the First Crusade), as also from its naïve confirmation of what we know of the Count of Poitiers from other sources.

OF WILLIAM IX., COUNT OF POITIERS AND DUKE OF AQUITAINE.†

Now the Count of Poitiers was one of the most courteous men in the world, and one of the greatest

---

* William of Malmesbury speaks of his taking pride in denying the existence of God; he speaks also of his witticisms, which roused shouts of laughter from those who sat at table with him.

† See Mahn's *Biographieen der Troubadours*, i.

deceivers of ladies—a valiant knight in warfare, and bounteous in love and gallantry. And he knew well to sing and to make poetry, and long time went through the world beguiling ladies. And his son had to wife the Duchess of Normandy, by whom he had a daughter, the which was wife of King Henry [II.] of England, and mother of the Young King, and of Lord Richard, and of Count Geoffrey of Brittany.

CRUSADING SONG.*

SINCE that to sing [1] I have a mind,
I'll make a song of dol'rous kind ;
I'll no more give obedience [2] blind
    In Limousin or in Poitou.

I wander forth to exile drear,
And leave behind my son so dear,
In grievous peril and in fear,
    For great the ill his foes will do.

And many a heavy sigh I heave,
To lose fair Poitou sore I grieve,
To Fulc of Anjou's care I leave
    My goodly lands and well-loved son.

* For original, see *Chrestomathie Provençale*, p. 32 (K. Bartsch).

If Fulc to succour him disdain,
And eke my royal suzerain,[3]
The base to spite him will be fain,
  And no ill deed will leave undone.

If wise and brave he should not be,
When I have passed beyond the sea,
The Angevins he needs must flee,
  And yield to Gascon miscreants.

If 'gainst my fellows any way
I've done amiss, so pardon they,
And unto Jesus for me pray,
  In Latin speech and in Romaunce.

Valour and joy I loved full well,
But now to these I bid farewell,
And wander forth with Him to dwell,
  That giveth weary sinners peace.

Gracious and gay I was of yore,
But this our Lord doth will no more,
From life's sad fardel I implore
  Full urgently a swift release.

My dear delights to God I bring,
These may He take for offering:
Pride, knighthood, many a well-loved thing,
  So He my soul with pardon cheer.

When by the pangs of death opprest
May I with many a friend be blest;
Too well I loved disport and jest,
   And ever sought them far and near.

Now must I leave disport and jest,
   Sable, *gris*, and minevere.

[1] Since that to sing. The form of the original poem is a a a b,
c c c b d d d b, etc., 12 stanzas $+\frac{1}{2}$ stanza.
[2] Obedience. By obedience he probably means that which he
has given to love.
[3] Suzerain. His suzerain was Philip I. of France.

CERCAMON

Date of his birth from 1100-1110.

CERCAMON, or Search the World, the protector of Marcabrun,
stands chronologically next to William IX., Count of Poitiers.
His four or five extant poems are insignificant, and his
'pastoretas' have perished. The allusion to his having
composed these latter is important, inasmuch as it proves
this form of poetry to have existed in Provence at a very
early period.

OF CERCAMON.*

Now Cercamon was a jongleur of Gascony, and
made 'vers' and 'pastoretas'[1] after the ancient
manner, and sought the wide world over, as far
as man can go, wherefore he was called Cercamon.

*See Mahn, lxxxi.

[1] **Pastoretas.** The 'pastoreta,' or *pastourelle*, a species of poetry that, as there seems little doubt, originated in Provence, tells of a poet of noble birth, who riding alone in the country meets a shepherdess. Her rustic beauty causes him to alight from his horse and offer her his love ; which after a resistance that is generally little more than coquetry, she in most pastourelles accepts. See M. Jeanroy's interesting account of the origin and nature of the pastourelle, in his *Origines de la poésie lyrique en France.*

MARCABRUN

1140-1185.*

MARCABRUN, probably the third poet in chronological order, was a man of great originality, who stood aloof from his contemporaries, setting the ordinary laws of chivalry at defiance and despising love and women. The majority of the poems left us of him are satirical and censorious in nature. His two most interesting ones are a pastourelle of great piquancy and sprightliness, with an original treatment of the usual theme, and the poem here translated—a romance, namely, relating to the Crusade of 1147, possessing charming grace and simplicity, but also the childishness and want of depth of the typical troubadour. The heroic and religious spirit is altogether wanting in it, and the promises of heavenly bliss are held light in comparison with the enjoyment of the present. Marcabrun was the first poet to introduce the theme of the maid forsaken by her lover for the Cross, a theme that afterwards became a favourite one.

* The exact years of the birth and death of most of the troubadours cannot be fixed, so that the dates given here and elsewhere are with some few exceptions those between which arose the poems of each troubadour respectively.

OF MARCABRUN.*

NOW Marcabrun was found cast before a grea
man's door, nor knew men ever who he was o
whence he came. Lord Aldric of Vilar nurture(
him, and afterwards he dwelt long time with on
Cercamon, a troubadour, until that he too fell t(
making poetry. And at that time he was calle(
Panperdut,[1] but thereafter Marcabrun. And, i
those days, all that was sung was called 'vers
and not 'canzone.'[2] And much was his nam(
noised abroad in the world, and much was h
feared for his tongue; for so slanderous was h
that, at the last, he was done to death by th
Castellans of Guienne, of whom he had spoke
great ill.

A DAMSEL DESERTED BY HER LOVER.†

BESIDE a fountain fair and bright,[3]
Within a garden that was dight
With greenest grass and flowers of white,
  Seated beneath a spreading tree,
Where glad birds sang of Spring's delight,
I found alone in piteous plight
  The maid that doth my true love scorn.

* See Mahn, iv.
† For original see *Chrestomathie provençale*, p. 49 (K. Bartsch).

A damsel she most wondrous fair,
And to high rank and riches heir,
But when I deemed this lady rare
  By the bird's song would gladdened be,
And the green garment Spring doth wear,
And graciously would hear my prayer,
  Anon she weepeth all forlorn.

Sore by the fountain did she grieve,
And many a heavy sigh did heave:
" My heart Thou dost of joy bereave,
  O Jesu, heavenly king ! " she cried ;
" And through Thy shame none can conceive
My sorrow, for the bravest leave
  Our country, e'en as Thou hast willed.

" To Thee my love his way doth wend—
My gentle, fair, and gracious friend—
With me fierce woes without an end,
  Weeping, and longings vain abide :
Curs'd be King Louis[4] that did send
To bid all men Christ's tomb defend—
  Whereby my breast with grief is filled."

In pity of her grievous teen
I nearer drew, " Fair maid, I ween,"
I said, "such sadness ne'er hath been,
  Why dim the beauty of thy face ?

What doth avail thee grief so keen,
Since He that giveth woods their green
Can give thee gladness as of yore?"

"My lord," quoth she, "full well I know,
God will to me great mercy show;
In heaven is endless joy I trow,
For me and other sinners base:
But *here* of that whence joy doth flow
He giveth nought—yet why this woe,
For small to me the love he bore."[5]

[1] **Panperdut.**   Pannum perditum ("Lost clout," according to
Suchier).

[2] **Vers and not canzone.**   These words are one of several
proofs of Marcabrun's antiquity. After his time, 'vers'
was an expression used vaguely of a poem that was sung
or recited, and which, if in stanzas, generally consisted of
seven of them. 'Canzone' was a name given to poems
that were mainly on love, that consisted of five or six
stanzas, and that had to be sung.

[3] **Beside a fountain fair and bright.**   The rhyming system of
the original is a a a b a a c d d d b d d c, e e e b e e c, etc.

[4] **King Louis.**   Louis VII. of France.

[5] **He bore.**   The original is here obscurely expressed. The
second "he" refers to the lover who, at the best of
times, had shown his lady nothing but indifference.

PEIRE OF VALERIA

Born about 1120, composed till beyond 1150.

LIKE Cercamon and Marcabrun, Peire of Valeria was a Gascon, and like them too was one of the earliest of troubadours. The two poems he has left us are of no literary merit.

OF PEIRE OF VALERIA.

PEIRE OF VALERIA was of Gascony, of the country of Sir Arnaut Guillem of Marsan, and he was a jongleur at the same time and season as Marcabrun; and he made 'vers' of little worth, of flowers, of leaves, and of the songs of birds, even as men were wont to make at that time. His singing was of no great worth nor was he.

GUIRAUDON THE RED

1120-1147.

THE refinement and delicacy of Guiraudon's canzones, seven of which are extant, are a considerable advance upon the archaic poems of Cercamon and Peire of Valeria. His lady, the daughter of the Count of Toulouse, went with her father to the Crusade of 1147. She was taken prisoner by the famous Monreddin, Prince of Aleppo, whom she afterwards married, and at his death ruled over Aleppo during her sons' minority.

* See Mahn, lxxxii.

NOW Guiraudon the Red was of Toulouse, the son of a poor knight. And he came to the court of his lord, Count Alphonso, for to serve him. And he was courteous and well skilled in singing, and he became enamoured of the Countess, the daughter of his lord, and the love he had for her taught him to make poetry, and he made many canzones.

✓ BERNART OF VENTADORN

✓ 1148-1195.

LITTLE is known of Bernart beyond that which his biographer gives us. He is undoubtedly the first great Provençal poet, and indeed one of the greatest mediaeval love-poets in all Europe. In him are found the best characteristics of Provençal lyric poetry, complete self-abandonment and humility, alternations of rapture and despair, perfect freshness and sincerity, a great joy in spring and nature united to a great joy in love. Love is conceived of by him as a religion exalting and purifying, and his refinement and spirituality form a strange contrast to the barbarous Europe of his day. Bernart also is one of the greatest, if not *the* greatest, masters of form and versification of Provence. His poems have a subtle and untranslatable sweetness, and an oriental languor and luxuriance of expression, which his power and freshness, however, prevent from palling upon us. His originality is incontestable; he bears no resemblance to the classics, nor to any poets more immediately preceding him.

* See Mahn, lxxxiii.

Fifty of his poems have remained to us, but in only a few of these can the lady to whom they were addressed be guessed at, for Bernart took more pains than most poets to conceal the object of his love. Some of his best lyrics are in honour of "Bel Vezer" (Fair Sight), and to Eleanor, wife of Henry II. of England.

Translations of one or two of his poems have been here attempted, but Bernart is *par excellence* a troubadour who, to be appreciated, must be read in the original.

OF BERNART OF VENTADORN.

NOW Bernart of Ventadorn was of Limousin of the Castle of Ventadorn, and was one of low degree, son to wit of a serving man, who gathered brushwood for the heating of the oven wherein was baked the castle bread. And he became a fair man and a skilled, and knew well to make poetry and to sing, and was both courteous and learned. And the Viscount of Ventadorn, his liege lord, delighted much in him, and in his singing and poetry, and ever did him great honour. And ye must know that the Viscount of Ventadorn had a wife, who was fair, and gay, and noble, and who delighted much in Sir Bernart and in his songs. And she became enamoured of him, and he of her, so that he made his vers and canzones[1] of her for the love that he bore her, and for her great worth's sake.

Long time lasted their love ere the Viscount and

*See Mahn, ii.

other men marked it. And lo! when the Viscoun
became ware of it, he withdrew his love from hin
and set watch upon his wife, and imprisoned hei
Then the lady sent unto Sir Bernart dismissing
him from her service, and bidding him depart th
land. And thereat he departed, and got him t
the Duchess of Normandy,[2] who was young and o
great worth, and who loved virtue, and honoui
and the singing of her praise. And the vers anc
canzones of Sir Bernart did greatly please her, anc
she received him at her court and gave him heart;
welcome. Long did he dwell there, singing man;
a good song of her. And he loved her and sh
him likewise. But King Henry of England tool
her to wife, and withdrew her from Normandy, anc
brought her into England, while Sir Bernart re
mained behind in grief and heaviness. Then h
departed and went unto the good Count Raymond
of Toulouse. And with him he dwelt until th
Count died ; and when the Count was dead, Si
Bernart entered the monastery of Dalon, and ther
ended his days. And this that I, Hugh of Sain
Circ, have written[4] of him did the Viscount Eble
of Ventadorn relate unto me, son of the Viscountes
that Sir Bernart of Ventadorn loved.

*TO BEL VEZER, VISCOUNTESS OF VENTADORN.**

WHENE'ER green leaves and grass appear,
  And budding flowers from branches spring,
And nightingales do strong and clear
  Uplift their voice and 'gin to sing—
Joy do they bring me, joy the flowers' sweet grace,
Joy my own heart, but most my lady's face;
And I am girt with joy on every side,
But she is joy who doth all else o'er-ride.

It marvels me that I can be,
  And ne'er my love to her reveal,
For when my lady's eyes I see,
  Their beauty all my senses steal;
Almost to her from very love I run,
And but for fear already were it done;
Ne'er was one seen of form and hue so fair,
Thus slow her faithful vassal's love to share.

To find her all alone, what bliss!
  Asleep, or else but seeming so,
Then would I steal of her a kiss,
  Since ne'er could ask it one so low;
Betwixt us few the deeds of love pardy!
Time speedeth onwards, all our best days flee;
By secret signs could we sweet converse hold,
And cunning use, instead of action bold.[5]

* For original see Mahn's *Gedichte der Troubadours*, No. 927.

CANZONE TO BEL VEZER ON HER DISMISSAL OF

*THE POET.**

In vain at Ventadorn full many a friend
  Will seek me, for my lady doth refuse me,
And thither small my wish my way to wend,
  If ever thus despitefully she use me.
On me she frowningly her brow doth bend,
For why? My love to her hath ne'er an end,
  But of no other crime can she accuse me.

The fish full heedless falleth on the prey,
  And by the hook is caught; e'en so I found me
Falling full heedless upon love one day,
  Nor knew my plight till flames raged high
    around me,
That fiercer burn than furnace by my fay;
Yet ne'er an inch from them can I away,
  So fast the fetters of her love have bound me.

I marvel not her love should fetter me,
  Unto such beauty none hath e'er attained;
So courteous, gay, and fair, and good, is she,
  That for her worth all other worth hath waned;
I cannot blame her, she of blame is free,
Yet I would gladly speak if blame there be,
  But finding none, from speaking have refrained.

* For original see *Chrestomathie provençale*, p. 59 (K. Bartsch).

I send unto Provence great love and joy,
And greater joy than ever tongue expresseth,
Great wonders work thereby, strange arts employ,
Since that I give my heart no whit possesseth.[6]

*FRAGMENT OF A POEM IN WHICH BERNART
TAKES LEAVE OF BEL VEZER.**

WHENE'ER the joyous lark I see,
That higher soars, and higher yet,
Till drunk with love's sweet ecstasy
Her sun-ward course she doth forget,
And lower sinks, with jealous fire
I burn at seeing all things gay ;
And marvel 'tis that fierce desire,
Breaks not my aching heart straightway.[7]

[1] **Vers and canzones.** See note ([2]) on Marcabrun.
[2] **The Duchess of Normandy.** Grand-daughter of William IX.
of Poitiers and Aquitaine. Upon her divorce from the
King of France she became the wife of Henry II. of
England.
[3] **Raymond of Toulouse.** The Fifth.
[4] **I have written.** For Hugh of Saint Circ (see *infra*).
[5] **And cunning use, etc.** This poem to *Bel Vezer* (Fair Sight),
for so Bernart called the Viscountess of Ventadorn, is
among the most beautiful of his earliest canzones. The
original is composed of seven stanzas of eight lines and
an *Envoi* of two lines. The rhymes, a b a b c c d d,
run throughout the poem.

*See Chrestomathie, p. 64.

[6] **My heart no whit possesseth.** The original consists of six stanzas of seven lines, and a half stanza of three lines. The rhymes, a b a b a a b, run throughout the poem.

[7] **My aching heart straightway.** The poem, of which the above stanza is the first, is one of Bernart's best, but also most untranslatable canzones. The lines are an allusion to the old superstition that the lark, being in love with the sun, flies always towards it as far as it can, till drunk with joy it loses consciousness and falls down to earth.

JAUFRE RUDEL OF BLAIA (BLAYE)

1140-1170.

THE following is one of the most beautiful of the Lives, but also, it is to be feared, one of the least authentic; it has in it all the extravagance and the delicate unearthliness that is the essence of the ideal Provençal chivalry:

> "The desire of the moth for the star,
>   Of the night for the morrow,
> The devotion to something afar
>   From the sphere of *his* sorrow."

See Mr. Swinburne's verses on Rudel in *The Triumph of Time.*

> "THERE lived a singer in France of old,
>   By the tideless, dolorous, midland sea,
> In a land of sand, and ruin, and gold,
>   There shone one woman and none but she;
> And, finding life for her love's sake fail,
> Being fain to see her, he bade set sail,
> Touched land, and saw her as life grew cold,
>   And praised God, seeing; and so died he.

"Died, praising God for His gift and grace;
  For she bowed down to him weeping and said,
'Live,' and her tears were shed on his face,
  Or ever the life in his face was shed;
The sharp tears fell through her hair and stung
Once, and her close lips touched him and clung
Once, and grew one with his lips for a space,
  And so drew back, and the man was dead.

"O brother, the gods were good to you,
  Sleep and be glad while the world endures,
Be well content as the years wear through,
  Give thanks for life and the loves and lures;
Give thanks for life, O brother, and death,
For the sweet last sound of her feet, her breath,
For gifts she gave you gracious and few,
  Tears and kisses—that lady of yours."

Few poems are left us of Rudel's, and of these the one translated is the most interesting, whether really addressed to the Lady of Tripoli, or merely one of those that gave rise to the pretty story concerning him.

OF JAUFRE RUDEL.[*]

Now Jaufre Rudel of Blaia[1] was a right noble prince of Blaia,[2] and it chanced that, though he had not seen, he loved the Countess of Tripoli[3] for her great excellence and virtue, whereof the pilgrims who came from Antioch spread abroad the report. And he made of her fair songs, with fair melodies, and with short verses,[4] till he longed so greatly to

---

[*] See Mahn, vi.

see her, that he took the Cross and embarked upon the sea to gain sight of her. And lo! in the ship there fell upon him such great sickness, that they who were with him weened he was dead therein; nathless they brought him as one dead to a hostelry in Tripoli. And the thing was made known to the Countess, so that she came unto his bedside, and took him into her arms. Then he knew that it was she, and sight and speech returned unto him, and he gave praise and thanks unto God who had preserved his life until his seeing her. And so he died in the arms of the Countess, and she gave him honourable burial in the Temple-house of Tripoli; and on that self-same day she gave herself to God, and became a nun, for loss of him, and for grief at his death. And lo, here are some of his songs.

JAUFRE RUDEL TO HIS FAR-OFF LADY.

When May-days come, full tunefully
    The birds do carol from afar,
Yet when I needs from there must be,
    Where dwelleth my sweet love afar,
As drear to me as winter's snow
Are songs, or fairest flowers that blow,
    So sad the heart within my breast.

No happiness I hope to see,
    Fail I to win that love afar;

I know of none so fair as she
  In any country near or far.
Her worth above all worth doth stand,
And captive in the Paynim's land
  I'd gladly dwell at her behest.

.   .   .   .   .   .

Ah me! What joy, what ecstasy[5]
  To seek of her a refuge far!
Mayhap too she will shelter me
  Beneath her roof, thus come from far;
Then there will be full many a kiss,
When far-off love in perfect bliss
  Doth gaily reach the long-sought rest.

.   .   .   .   .   .

The God that made all things that be,
  And formed for me this love afar,
Give me ere long the power to see
  With such great joy my love afar,
That the gay bower or garden sweet,
Where first my Lady I may greet,
  For aye may seem a palace blest.

.   .   .   .   .   .

[1] **Blaia.** Blaye, in Saintonge, on the Garonne.
[2] **Prince of Blaia.** The title 'prince' was often given then to nobles of small importance. Marcabrun, but not history, makes mention of Rudel.
[3] **Countess of Tripoli.** There were many wives and daughters of Counts of Tripoli bearing the above title, but history makes no allusion to any of these entering a convent.

⁴ **Short verses.** The original has *Paubres motz* (poor words), which Diez interprets as 'Short verses.'

⁵ **Ah me! What joy, what ecstasy.** The rhymes are in the original, a b a b c c d, a b a b c c d, etc.

THE COUNTESS OF DIA

Second half of twelfth century.

POETESSES, rare in North France, were common enough in Languedoc, specially in the second half of the twelfth century, ladies, such as the Countesses of Dia (Die) and of Provence, Claire of Anduze and Maria of Ventadorn, stepping off the pedestals that the chivalry of the age erected for them, tell in passionate words of their despair and of their love, a love that is pure and all-absorbing, and, with most of them, of a far greater intensity and headlong recklessness than that of the men.

Such a love was the Countess of Die's for the cold and indifferent Raembaut of Orange, and the grace, sweetness, and sincerity of her song to him, make it one of the most remarkable poems in Provençal literature; its subtle charm, however, has, I fear, been but ill-rendered by the translation attempted.

*OF THE COUNTESS OF DIA.**

Now the Countess of Dia, wife of Lord Guillem of Poitiers, was a fair and excellent lady. And she loved Lord Raembaut of Orange,¹ and made many a good poem of him; and behold here written some of her canzones.

* See Mahn, vii.

THE COUNTESS OF DIA TO RAEMBAUT OF
*ORANGE.**

NEEDS must I sing of one that o'er me reigneth,
E'en of my love, of whom my heart complaineth,
Whom I do prize 'bove all the world containeth,
Alas! from him kind mercy little gaineth,
 Little my beauty, wit, and far-spread fame,
For he beguileth me, my love disdaineth,
 As though I had done aught that were to blame.

'Tis strange to me that thou, my friend, dost scorn
  me,
I deem I have good reason loud to mourn me;
It is unmeet another should have shorn me
Of thy dear love, how harsh so e'er I'd borne me!
 Alas! bethink thee of that golden time
Of our first rapture—may that mem'ry warn me
 Never to lose such joy by wanton crime.

Fair virtues ever have in thee abounded,
But thy great merits leave me all confounded;
To ladies far and near thy fame hath sounded,
That none resist thee, by thy worth astounded;
 Yet thou, fair friend, I deem art passing wise,
And thou shouldst know my love is love unbounded,
 And 'fore thy memory should our parting rise.

    * See *Chrestomathie*, p. 71.

My noble lineage and my faith unfailing,
My beauty eke can ne'er be unavailing,
Wherefore with these thy stubbornness assailing,
I send this song, thee, cruel lover, hailing,
  And I would know, fair friend, whate'er betide,
Why thou dost spurn me, at my sorrow railing,
  Whether it be from Wrath or else from Pride.

Eke warn him, song, his cruelty bewailing,
  That oft great ill doth with the proud abide.[2]

[1] **Orange.**   A small State dependent on Provence, and claiming
    as its founder the legendary hero St. William.   The
    Count here alluded to was Raembaut III., who shared
    with his brother the rulership of Orange.   Of his life
    we know little, and his poems are of small merit.
[2] **With the proud abide.**   The original poem is composed
    of 5 stanzas + 1 stanza of 2 lines (a b).   The rhyming
    system is a a a a b a b, c c c c b c b, d d d d b d b,
    etc.

PEIRE OF AUVERGNE

1155-1215.

THE high esteem in which Peire of Auvergne was held, both
by himself and others, must have been owing to his great skill
in form and versification (compare the monotonous metre of
the Count of Poitiers' crusading song with the ease, richness,
and variety of Peire's "Rossinhol en son repaire," *Chrestomathie*, p. 77).   Apart from their form, however, the twenty-five
to thirty poems he has left us have little interest.   The one

most often quoted is his satire on his contemporary poets, in
which all are held up to public scorn and derision, and in
which an interesting illustration is given us of the rough-and-
ready criticism of the time. Of his love poems, the best is
undoubtedly the one given on page 77 of the *Chrestomathie*;
in it a nightingale plays the part of confidante and messenger
to the lover of the piece. The bird messenger is a common
figure in mediaeval poetry. Similarly, a sparrow is introduced
in Arnaut of Carcasses, and a parrot in Marcabrun. The
above-mentioned poem of Peire's begins somewhat in this
fashion. "Nightingale, get thee to my lady's dwelling, tell
her in what sad case I am, and bring word to me how it
stands with her, and look to it that she in nowise keep thee
with her." And the merry bird flies forth, seeking diligently
till she espies her to whom she is sent. And anon when
she sees her in her beauty, the bird begins the song wherewith she is wont to greet the night, then holds her still and
bethinks her how best to tell her tale of woe : " He that is
your loyal and faithful lover has sent me hither to pleasure
you, and if you will give me a message of comfort for him
you will have good reason to rejoice, for there is no mother's
son that loves you better. Wherefore if ye love, make no
tarriance, but enjoy it while ye may, for full soon passes it
away from you," etc.

*OF PEIRE OF AUVERGNE.**

PEIRE of Auvergne was of the diocese of Clairmont; a wise man he was and a well lettered, and
was the son of a burgher; fair and comely he was
of person, and well could sing and rhyme. And he
was the first good troubadour in the world, and he

**Mahn viii.*

who made the fairest melodies[1] ever yet made, in the 'vers' that runs:

> " De iostals breus iorns els loncs sers
>   Qan la blanca aura brunezis."
>
> (In dark days and long nights
> When the clear air is darkened.)

No canzone did he make, for in those days no poem hight 'canzone,' but 'vers.'[2] And he was greatly loved and honoured of all excellent men, and excellent barons and ladies of that time, and accounted of them the greatest troubadour in all the world, until there rose up Giraut of Borneil. Greatly did he praise himself in his songs,[3] and blame all other troubadours, saying of himself:

> " Peire d'Auvergne a tal votz,
>   Qel chanta de sobre e de sotz,
>   E il so sunt doutz e plazen ;
>   E poes es maestre de totz,
>   Ab qun pauc esclarzis sos motz
>   Qua penas nulls hom los enten."

(Peire d'Auvergne has such a voice that he can sing both high and low. His melodies are sweet and pleasant. He is master of all things, yet were it well that he should make clear his verses, the which are hardly understood of any.)

Long did he dwell with the good folk in the world, even as the Dauphin of Auvergne,[4] in whose land he was born, has told me, and thereafter he entered a monastery and died therein.

[1] **Melodies.** The original has 'son'=air, song, the diminutive of which is the Prov. *sonet*. 'Son' also means a lyric poem, accompanied by the sound (son) of the instrument.

[2] **No poem hight canzone.** See Marcabrun's life for the same remark; it points to his being among the earliest of the Provençal court poets. Dante names him among the elder poets, while Petrarch calls him "The Old."

[3] **Greatly did he praise himself.** Boasting was a common characteristic of the troubadours (see the poems of P. Vidal and others). "Touching the new and the old poetry," says Peire d'Auvergne on one occasion, "I will here make manifest my wisdom and my understanding, for mark well, all ye that are yet for to come, never before me was perfect verse composed."

[4] **The Dauphin of Auvergne.** The troubadour who quarrelled with Richard, and who composed poetry.

GUILLEM OF CABESTAING.
1181-1196.

IT is hardly necessary to dwell upon the reasons existing for disbelieving the romantic details of the following life. (See G. Paris (*Romania*, viii.), O. Beschnitt, and others for the discussion of this question.)

Cabestaing, Roussillon, and Tarascon are names found more than once in Languedoc. The names of Raymond and Soremonda appear in the documents of the time, and Guillem of Cabestaing himself is twice mentioned. The number of MSS. that are left us of his poem, "Li dous consire," do much to prove that he was a favourite character, and one whom popular imagination would readily transform into a hero of romance. The story of his love and death is entirely characteristic of the age; the husband is held up to general detestation, and the sympathies of the writer are wholly with the lover and his lady.

As to the manner of his death, similar stories are to be found in various parts of the world, all probably having their source in an old Indian "Beast fable." In Guillem's case, his songs, dwelling, as they repeatedly do, on death by love, may have suggested the connection of the fiction with him.

In his songs, only eight of which have remained to us, Guillem is the true love poet—all tenderness and submission to one far above him, and whom he has little hope to win. When driven away by slanderers from his Lady's presence, he takes, he says, perforce the pilgrim's staff, serving Love, and Love only, all the days of his life. "Very sweet to me," he cries, "is the pain she gives me, sweeter still would be the joy ; one thread of her cloak of minever, if it pleased her to grant it me, would make me happier than the greatest of favours from any other."

OF GUILLEM OF CABESTAING.*

NOW Guillem of Cabestaing was a knight of the country of Roussillon, which bordered on Catalonia and on Narbonne. And he was right goodly to look upon, renowned withal in arms and chivalry and knightly service. And, in his country, there dwelt a lady—my Lady Soremonda by name— wife of Sir Raymond of Castel-Roussillon, a knight of high descent, puissant, and proud, and cruel, and base, and hard of heart. Now Sir Guillem of Cabestaing greatly loved the lady, and made his songs of her,[1] and the lady, who was young, and

* Mahn, ix.

fair, and gay, and noble, bore him greater love than to any soul on earth; and the thing was told to Sir Raymond of Castel-Roussillon, and he, as one jealous and full of wrath, made inquiry into it, and when he knew that it was true, set watch upon his wife. And it fell upon a day, that Sir Raymond of Castel-Roussillon found Sir Guillem of Cabestaing hawking without great company, and he slew him, and caused his heart to be taken from out his body and his head to be cut off. Then he caused both head and heart to be brought unto his dwelling, and the heart he caused to be roasted and seasoned with pepper, and to be set before his wife to eat of it. And when the lady had eaten of it, Raymond of Castel-Roussillon said unto her: "Know you of what you have eaten?" And she said, "I know not, save that the taste thereof is good and savoury." Then he said to her that that she had eaten of was in very truth the heart of Sir Guillem of Cabestaing, and caused the head to be brought before her, that she might the more readily believe it. And when the lady had seen and heard this, she straightway fell into a swoon, and when she was recovered of it, she spake and said: "Of a truth, my Lord, such good meat have you given me that never more will I eat of other." Then he, hearing this, ran upon her with his sword and would have struck at her head, but the lady ran to a balcony, and cast herself down, and so died. And the news spread through Roussillon and through all Catalonia, how that Sir Guillem of Cabestaing and the lady were thus foully done to death, and how that Sir Raymond of Castel-Roussillon had set before the lady the heart of Sir Guillem. Then there arose sore weeping and lamentation in all the countries round about. And the outcry that was made of it came to the ears of the King of Aragon,[2] who was liege lord of Sir Raymond of Castel-Roussillon and of Sir Guillem of Cabestaing. And the king came to Perpignan in Roussillon, and commanded that Sir Raymond of Castel-Roussillon should be brought before him. And when he was come, he caused him to be bound, and took from him all his castles, and had them razed to the ground ; and took from him likewise all that he had, and cast him into prison, and he caused Guillem of Cabestaing and the lady to be taken, and brought unto Perpignan, and to be laid together in a tomb before the church door ; and he bade men inscribe upon the tomb the manner of their death, and likewise bade he all the knights and ladies throughout all the County of Roussillon to come thither each year and hold a solemn festival to their memories. And Sir Raymond of Castel-Roussillon died miserably in the prison of the King of Aragon.

(The following is a free and somewhat abridged translation of the longest of the three versions of Guillem's Life.)*

My Lord Raymond of Roussillon, a valiant baron, even as ye know, had for wife my Lady Margarida, the fairest lady known of in that day, and the most renowned for excellence, and worth, and courtesy. Now it happened that Guillem of Cabestaing came unto the court of my Lord Raymond of Roussillon, and offered himself to him for squire. My Lord Raymond seeing him to be fair, and gracious, and noble, bade him welcome to his court. And Guillem abode with him, and demeaned himself so that great and small loved him, and so that my Lord Raymond made him page to my Lady Margarida his wife, and then all the more did Guillem strive after worth in word and deed. Now it befell that Love, even as is his wont, assailed my Lady Margarida and fired her heart. And so greatly pleased her Guillem's speech and bearing that, upon a day, she must needs say to him: "Now tell me, Guillem, if a lady showed thee signs of love, wouldst dare to love her?" Guillem, who perceived her meaning, answered unabashed: "Yea, Lady, did I but know that the signs were true ones." "By St. John," quoth the lady, "thou hast answered bravely; but now I will try thee, and see

*See Mahn, xi.

if thou canst dissever the false signs from the true."
Then when Guillem had heard these words, he
made answer: "May it be even as ye shall please,
my Lady." Then he fell to thinking, and anon Love
moved him, and there entered into his innermost
heart those thoughts Love sends his own; and from
that hour he became Love's servant, and began to
make fair songs to honour her he loved. And Love,
who, when he wills, gives guerdon to his servants,
so sorely beset the lady with thoughts of love, that
she rested not day or night with thinking of the
excellent virtues that abounded in him. And it
happened upon a day, that the lady took Guillem
apart, and said to him: "Now tell me, Guillem,
hast thou yet discovered whether my signs of love
be true or false?" Quoth Guillem: "Lady, so help
me God, from that same hour that first I served
you, none other thought could enter into my heart,
but that you were the best and truest lady ever
born—so think I, and shall think all my life." And
the lady answered: "Guillem, I tell thee that never,
so speed me God, shalt thou be beguiled by me,
nor shalt thou pine in vain." And she stretched
forth her arms, and embraced him sweetly in that
chamber where they were, and so they became lovers.
And ere long slanderers—the which may God con-
found—began to make mention of their love, and
to guess of it from the songs that Guillem made.

And hither and thither went their talk until it reached the ears of my Lord Raymond. And full woe was Lord Raymond for losing the companion that he loved, but more for the shame of his wife.

Now it chanced upon a day, when Guillem was gone a-hawking with one squire only, that my Lord Raymond asked where he was, and a varlet told him Guillem was gone a-hawking, and one that knew told him where Guillem was; and forthwith he dight his harness secretly, and let bring his war-horse, and rode after Guillem. And when Guillem saw him come, he marvelled greatly and boded ill thereof, and came to meet him and said: "Welcome, my Lord, but why then thus alone?" And Raymond answered: "I have sought you thus to disport me with you, and have ye taken nought?" "I, my Lord, not much, for I have little found; ye wot of the proverb that says, 'He that finds little takes little.'" "Let this talk be awhile," said my Lord Raymond, "and tell me truly by the faith that ye owe me whatsoever thing I shall ask of you." "Pardy! my Lord," said Guillem, "if it is to be said I will say it." "But mark ye, I will have no shifts," said Raymond, "but require you to tell me the whole truth of that which I shall ask." "My Lord, since so ye will," said Guillem, "ask me, and I shall speak you true." Then my Lord Raymond said, "Tell me, so God help you, if ye have a lady whom ye sing and love?" "My Lord," said Guillem, "how should I sing if I did not love? Know of a truth, my Lord, that Love has me wholly in his power." "I trow well that ye love or else ye could not sing so sweetly; tell me, I pray you, who is your lady?" "Ah! my Lord, for God's sake beware of what ye ask me—is it good that a man reveal his love? Ye know that Sir Bernart of Ventadorn says,

"Duna ren maonda mos senz," etc.

(Lines in which Bernart of Ventadorn rejoices that he has never had the weakness to reveal the object of his love.)

Then my Lord Raymond said, "I plight you my word, that I will avail you as best I may," and likewise said so much to him, that Guillem spake and said, "Know then, my Lord, that I love the sister of my Lady Margarida, your wife, and ween I have her love in exchange—and now, I pray you, avail me, or leastways do me no harm." "Take my hand and plighted word that I will avail you to the uttermost," said Raymond. . . . "Let us go to her dwelling for it is nigh unto here." "So be it, I pray you," said Guillem. So they took their way to the castle of Liet, and there they were full well received of Sir Robert of Tarascon, and of my Lady Agnes his wife, sister of my Lady Margarida.

And my Lord Raymond took my Lady Agnes by the hand and led her into a chamber, and they sat them down together on a bed—and my Lord Raymond said, "Now tell me, sister-in-law, by the faith ye owe me—love ye, *par amour?* and she said: "Yea, Lord." "And whom, quoth he?" "That will I nowise tell you," answered she, "for in what does it concern you?" Nathless he besought her so earnestly that she told him she loved Guillem of Cabestaing. And this she said because she saw Guillem sore troubled, and knowing that he loved her sister, she feared lest Raymond should think ill of him. And thereat Raymond had great gladness, and the lady told the matter to her husband, the which said it was well done, and gave her his troth that she might say or do aught that could compass Guillem's escape. This did the lady, for she called Guillem to her chamber, and abode so long alone with him, that Raymond weened she must needs have granted him her love, whereat he was right well pleased and fell to thinking, that that they told him was not true. . . .

And on the morrow, they took meat at the castle amidst great merriment; and after dinner they departed and came to Roussillon. And Raymond, as soon as he might, separated him from Guillem and came to his wife and told her of that which he had seen pass betwixt Guillem and her sister.

Whereat all that night the lady was full woe. And on the morrow she let send for Guillem, and greeted him full ill, calling him false and traitorous. And Guillem cried her mercy, even as one that was guiltless of that whereof she accused him, and told her word for word all that had passed. And the lady let fetch her sister, and learnt of her that Guillem was without blame, wherefore the lady commanded him to make a song wherein he should show that he loved none other lady but her; wherefore he made this song, which says:

> " Li doutz consire
>   Qem don amors soven," etc.
> (Those sweet reveries
>   That Love doth ofttimes give.)

And when Raymond of Roussillon heard the song that Guillem had made of his wife, he caused him to come for to have speech with him without the castle; then cut off his head and put it into a flesh pot. [What now follows is almost the same as the biography translated.]

GUILLEM OF CABESTAING TO HIS LADY.*

THAT day, my lady, when I saw thee first,
  When thou didst deign to grant me such fair sight,
Anon all other longings were dispersed,
  And thou wast from that hour my sole delight;

* See Mahn's *Gedichte der troubadours*, Vol. IV., p. 140.

But one sweet smile and glance my heart was
    needing,
Such constant love upon it to impress,
That of all else I had forgetfulness.

Thy rarest beauty, and thy merry cheer,
  Thy gracious discourse, and thy loving mind—
Have wholly reft me of my reason clear,
  Which since that hour I vainly strive to find;
Thine be it then, so thou do hear my pleading,
Thine to advance thy fame and wondrous worth,
Thine too my life, thou fairest dame on earth.

No dread of suff'ring 'tis that makes me sigh,
  But I do hope that thou mayst once bestow
Some favour sweet upon me ere I die;
  And highest joy were then my bitter woe,
If once I saw thee my long sorrow heeding;
For faithful lovers must endure great pain,
Pardon all wrongs and guerdon thereby gain.

Ah, lady! would that hour were onward speeding
When in thy mercy thou wouldst not disdain
To call me lover and to ease my pain!

[1] **And made his songs of her.** The poem that, according to
    the longest account of Guillem's life, revealed the secret
    of his love to the jealous husband was that beginning:
        "Li dous consire
        Qem don amors soven."
                    (See *Chrestomathie*, p. 73.)

It is difficult, however, to see how this can have betrayed him, containing, as it does, nothing but the vaguest
allusions to his lady. It is one of his most beautiful
canzones, composed of short, fast-flowing lines, that well
express the agitations of an ardent and all-absorbing
passion.

[2] The King of Aragon. Alphonso II.

PEIRE ROGIER.

1160-1170.

IN the few poems of Peire Rogier preserved to us, there is
no special interest. Almost all of them are relating to
Ermengarde (see Life), but are frigid and didactic in style.

OF PEIRE ROGIER.*

NOW Peire Rogier was of Auvergne, and was
canon of Clairmont. And he was a man of gentle
birth, goodly and debonair, rich in all book-lore
and in natural wit, and well could sing and rhyme.
And he forsook his canonry[1] and became a jongleur,
passing from court to court, and his singing won
favour of all. And he came to Narbonne, to the
court of my Lady Ermengarde,[2] who was in those
days much honoured and prized of men. And she
welcomed him full well, and greatly honoured and
advanced him. And he loved her, and praised her

* See Mahn, xii.

in his 'vers' and canzones; and she received them, and looked favourably on them, and he was wont to call her, "You who wrong me." Long time did he dwell at her court, until men deemed him her lover. Whence blame came to her from the people of that region; and fearing that they spake of her, she dismissed him and sent him from her. Then he went his way, full sad and sorrowful, to Raembaut of Orange, even as he has said in the *sirvente* that he made of him, the which runs:

> "Seignen Raembaut per vezer
> De vos lo conort el solatz,
> Sui sai vengutz tost e viatz
> Mai que non sui per vostraver.
> Que saber voill qan men irai
> Sestals lo gabs cum hom lo fai,
> Si ni a tant, o meins, o mai
> Cum aug dir ni comtar de vos."

(Lord Raembaut, to see if there be in you comfort and joy, rather than to know your bounty, have I come hither in all speed; for I would know, ere I go forth from you, whether there be as much, or more, or less of all that good, that men speak of, in you.)

And he dwelt long with Lord Raembaut of Orange, and afterwards departed from him, and journeyed into Spain to abide with the good King Alphonso of Aragon; eke did he abide with the good Count Raymond of Toulouse, even as long as he willed. Great honour did he have of the world, while that he dwelt therein ; and in the end he entered the order of Granmon, and there did die.

[1] **And he forsook his canonry.** Peire Rogier was by no means the only troubadour who forsook the church for poetry. See Peire of Auvergne's satire on his contemporary poets, where he says of Rogier :

> " Chanta d'amor a prezen ;
> E covengral melhs us sautiers
> En la gleiz, o us candeliers
> Portar ab gran candel' arden."

(He sings openly of Love, but it would better behove him to bear a psalter in the church, or a candlestick with a great burning candle.)

[2] **Ermengarde.** One of the most distinguished women of the age, combining feminine grace and beauty with a strong masculine nature and intellect. She is spoken of as being foremost in the judgment-hall, and even as going to the field of battle ; and also as priding herself on the severity of her virtue.

ALPHONSO II. OF ARAGON.

Reigned from 1162-1196.

ALPHONSO II. was one of the most powerful rulers of his age, being, in Spain, King of Aragon and Count of Barcelona, and in Languedoc, ruler over Provence, Gavaudan, Rhodez, and Roussillon. It was his policy to maintain a close alliance with the Angevin house, the better to combat his great enemy, the Count of Toulouse, who had claims on Provence. Like his contemporary, Richard Coeur de Lion, he was the steady friend of troubadours ; and his generosity was celebrated far and wide by them. (See, however, Bertran of Born's violent assertions about him, but these history in no way confirms.)

Like Richard, too, Alphonso made poetry the amusement of his leisure hours, the making of verses having, indeed, become almost a necessary accomplishment for those of high rank, an accomplishment in which the above-mentioned princes, together with Frederic II. of Germany, the Marquis of Montferrat, the Dauphin of Auvergne, and others, showed great proficiency. Two poems of Alphonso's are left us : a tenzon of no special merit between him and Guiraut of Borneil, and a canzone. The latter has the slender matter of the average troubadour, but also the grace and harmony with which even the average troubadour could give expression to conventional ideas.

*OF THE KING OF ARAGON.**

Now the King of Aragon, the troubadour, hight Alphonso, and was the first king ever known in Aragon. And he was the son of Lord Raymond Berengar, Count of Barcelona, the which vanquished the Saracens and despoiled them of Aragon, and went unto Rome to be crowned, and returning from thence, died in Poimon, in the borough of St. Dalmas.

Thereon his son Alphonso was made king, who was father of King Peter, who was father of King James.†

RICHARD COEUR-DE-LION.
Reigned from 1189-1199.

Richard and his elder brother Henry were both generous lovers and patrons of Provençal poetry, and great favourites with the troubadours. Whether Richard composed the only

* Mahn, xiii. † See Bertran of Born—note 12.

two songs left us of him in French or Provençal can hardly
be decided.. His mother, Eleanor of Aquitaine, was a friend
and protector of troubadours; and Richard, as her son, and
as Lord of Poitiers and Aquitaine, must have been as familiar
with the one language as with the other.

Of the two above-mentioned poems, that translated by Professor York Powell, and inserted here by his kind permission,
is perhaps the more interesting. It was probably composed by
Richard while in his German prison, shortly before his release.
The second poem is the sirvente referred to in the biography,
the title *sirvente* being given somewhat vaguely to all poems
not on love. Often, but not always, the sirvente was satirical
in nature, and in Provence was much used as a weapon of
attack and defence.

DISPUTE BETWEEN RICHARD AND THE DAUPHIN OF AUVERGNE. *

NOW when peace[1] was established between the
King of France and King Richard, there was made
the exchange of Auvergne and of Quercy; for
Auvergne, that ere this was King Richard's, was
given over to the King of France; and Quercy,
that was held by the King of France, was given
over to King Richard. Now the Dauphin was
Lord of Auvergne, and his cousin, Count Guy, was
Count thereof; and they two were sore vexed and
disquieted, in that the King of France was too
nigh unto them : for they knew that he was one
of evil rule, and of great greed and niggardliness.

* See Mahn, xiv.

Aud it was so that as soon as the King of France had rule over Auvergne, he bought him a strong castle therein, Novedre by name, and despoiled the Dauphin of Usoire,[2] a rich town. Now Lord Richard, when he made war anew upon the King of France, held speech with the Dauphin and his cousin, Count Guy, and recalled to them the wrongs the King of France had done them, and promised that he would uphold them, and give them knights, and crossbowmen, and gold, if they would aid him in warring upon the King of France. And they, for the great wrongs the King of France had done them, gave ear unto Lord Richard, and sallied forth to war against the King of France. And, as soon as Lord Richard knew that the two Counts of Auvergne—the Dauphin and Count Guy, his cousin, had risen up against the King of France, behold, he made truce with him, and, passing over into England, forsook the Dauphin and Count Guy. Then the King of France gathered together a great host, and came into Auvergne; and burnt all the land of the Dauphin, and of Count Guy, and despoiled them of their boroughs and towns and castles. And they, seeing that they could in no wise withstand him, made a truce of five months with him, and accorded with one another, that Count Guy should go to England, to learn if Lord Richard would aid them, even as he had sworn

and promised them. So Count Guy passed over
into England with ten knights ; but his coming
pleased not Lord Richard, the which gave him a
rough and discourteous greeting, and bestowed on
him neither knights, nor serving men, nor crossbowmen, nor gold ; whereat the Count got him home
again, poor, and sad, and shamed. And when he
was returned to Auvergne, the Dauphin and he went
unto the King of France and made peace with him.
And lo! when they were thus at peace, the truce
between the King of France and Lord Richard
came to an end. And the French King gathered
together his great host, and entered into the land
of King Richard, and took towns, and burnt both
boroughs and castles. And Lord Richard, when
he had tidings of this, came straightway from over
the sea, and as soon as he was come, he sent to the
Dauphin and Count Guy to come to aid him, telling
them that the truce was at an end, and that they
should sally forth to war against the King of France.
And they—they would do nought of that he bade
them. Then King Richard, hearing that they would
not aid him in the war made a sirvente, in the which
he called to remembrance the oath that the Dauphin
and Count Guy had made him, and their forsaking
him at his need, because they had learnt that the
treasure of Chinon[3] was spent, and eke because
they had learnt that the French King was good in

arms, and Lord Richard bad.[4]   Likewise he said that the Dauphin was wont of old freely to give and spend, but that now he was grown niggardly for to raise strong castles, and he would fain know (he said), if it pleased the Dauphin to be despoiled of Usoire by the King of France, and that without avenging himself of it, nor bringing men-at-arms against him.   And the sirvente begins thus:

> " Dalfin ieus voill deraisner."
> (Dauphin, I will denounce thee.)

And the Dauphin made answer in another sirvente to all King Richard's sayings, and showed how he was right and Lord Richard wrong, and accused Lord Richard of the evil that he had done to him and to Count Guy, and likewise of all the evil that he had done to others.   And the Dauphin's sirvente begins thus:

> " Reis, pois de mi chantatz."
> (King, since that you sing of me.)

*LAMENT[5] COMPOSED BY RICHARD WHILE CAPTIVE.**

NEVER can captive make a song so fair
As he can make that has no cause for care,
Yet may he strive by song his grief to cheer.
I lack not friends, but sadly lack their gold!
Shamed are they, if unransomed I lie here,
    A second Yule in hold.

* See Professor York Powell's *History of England*, page 116.

My men and barons all, full well they know,
Poitevins, English, Normans, Gascons too,
That I have not one friend, however poor,
Whom I would leave in chains to save my gold,
I tell them this, but blame them not therefor
    Though I lie yet in hold.

True is the saying, as I have proved herein,
Dead men and prisoners have no friends, no kin;
But if they leave me here to save their gold,
'Tis ill for me, but worse for them, I fear,
That when I die, reproach and blame shall hear
    If I be left in hold.

Small marvel if my heart knows heaviness,
When my Lord[6] puts my land to such distress.
If he remembered what we swore of old,
The oath we took at Sens between us twain,
I know full well that I should not remain
    Many days here in hold.

Sister and Countess,[7] God give you good cheer!
And keep my Lady, whom I love so dear;
    For whom I lie in hold.

[1] **Now when peace.** Diez places the following events at abou
    the year 1196.
[2] **Usoire = Issoire.**
[3] **Chinon in Turenne, where was Henry the Second's treasure**
    then exhausted. Richard had in 1187 taken possession b
    force of Chinon and its treasures.

[4] **The French King good in arms, and Richard bad.** Richard can only in mockery have called himself ill-versed in arms, as, only a few years before, he had performed his brilliant exploits in Palestine.

[5] **Lament composed by Richard.** This poem was probably composed about the year 1193 in the Austrian prison into which Richard, on his return from Palestine, was cast by the Emperor.

[6] **My Lord.** Philip, King of France.

[7] **Sister and Countess.** Richard sent the poem to his favourite sister, Joan.

THE DAUPHIN OF AUVERGNE—ROBERT I.

Reigned from 1169-1234.

ALLUSION has already been made to the brilliancy and luxury of the small courts of Languedoc, and, amongst these courts, that of Auvergne, in spite of the Dauphin's poverty, takes a prominent place. The Dauphin's generosity was far-famed, and for this, as well as for his knowledge of poetry, his name is often quoted by troubadours. His only poems seem to have been a few satires and tenzons.

*OF THE DAUPHIN OF AUVERGNE.**

NOW the Dauphin of Auvergne[1] was Count of Auvergne; and there was no knight in all the world so wise and courteous, so bountiful and warlike as he, and none so versed in love, and gallantry, and deeds of chivalry, and none his like in learning, and understanding, and in the making of coblas,[2]

* Mahn, xv.

and sirventes, sons,[3] and tenzons,[4] and none his
like in grave and gay discourse. And by his bountiful gifts he lost the half and more of his county;
but by his prudence and thrift he knew thereafter
to win unto himself all that he had lost, yea, and
eke much more.

Now the Dauphin of Auvergne * loved the Lady
of one of his castles—the Lady Maurina by name.
And it chanced upon a day that the Lady sent
unto the Dauphin's steward, praying him for bacon,
which she would fain cook with eggs, and the
Dauphin sent her half a flitch of bacon. And the
bishop[5] came to know of it, and made thereon this
'cobla,' blaming the steward that he gave her
not the whole flitch, and blaming the Dauphin
that he caused but half to be given her:

> " Per Crist, sil servens fos meus,
> Dun cotel li dari al cor,
> Can fez del bacon partida
> A lei que lil queri tan gen.
> Ben saup del dalphin lo talen
> Que sel plus ni men no i meses,
> A la ganta li dera tres ;,
> Mas posc en ver dire
> Petit ac lart Maurina als ous frire."

> (By Christ, this steward, if he were mine,
> Right through his heart a knife I'd thrust,
> Because he gave not all the flitch

> To one that asked so courteously.
> But well the Dauphin's mind knew he,
> For if he gave an undue part,
> His master's hand would make him smart:
> Yet this I say, and tell no lie,
> Maurina had scant lard her eggs to fry.).

Now the Bishop was lover of a right fair lady—wife of Lord Chantart of Caulec, the which dwelt at Pescadoiras, and the Dauphin made this answer to the 'cobla':

> "Li evesque troban en sos breus
> Mais volon chaulet que por,
> E pesca, que li covida
> A Pescadoiras fort soven,
> Per un bel peisson que lai pren ;
> El peissos es gais e cortes,
> Mas duna re les trop mal pres,
> Car ses laissatz ausire
> Al preveire que no fais mas lo rire."

(These lines with one or two plays upon words, difficult to render into English, scoff at the Bishop's love of the Lady of Pescadoiras.)

[1] Dauphin. A title borne on account of their armorial bearings by the Lords of Viennois, and one which, on the last of them giving up the Dauphiné to France in 1343, was given to the eldest son of the King of France. About 1155 the Counts of Auvergne also assumed the title, claiming to be descended from the Dauphins of Viennois.

[2] Coblas. A word used vaguely, sometimes having the meaning of 'couplet,' sometimes that of satiric poetry, or again sometimes having the special sense of a love-poem set to some known air.

[3] **Sons.** See note (1) on Peire of Auvergne.

[4] **Tenzon.** This form of poetry was a dispute between two, or sometimes three poets, each of whom composed his share of the poem, though, indeed, tenzons exist that were evidently written by one man only. Some tenzons, as that between Hugh of Saint Circ and the Count of Rhodez, are extremely bitter altercations on material matters ; but, as a rule, they bear on subtle questions in gallantry. A similar poem is the 'Partimen,' in which a poet starts a question, and offers the choice of sides to his opponent, supporting himself the side that is rejected. After disputing through a certain number of stanzas, the poets agree to appeal to the decision of certain judges, generally ladies, and two or three in number. The following are good examples of the subjects discussed: "Is it better to love a damsel, young, fair and courteous, or a fair dame, already experienced in love?" "Twenty knights errant were riding in foul weather, and complaining among themselves because they could not find a refuge. They were overheard by two barons, who were riding in all haste to visit their ladies; one of them returned to succour the knights, the other went on his way to his lady, which of them did best?"

[5] **The Bishop.** The name of this Bishop was Robert, and he was related to the Counts of Auvergne. His disposition was a notoriously turbulent one.

PEIRE RAYMOND.

1170-1200.

LITTLE is known of Peire Raymond beyond the few details given us in his life. His career, like that of most troubadours, was one of many wanderings, and probably of many loves. He has left us about twenty songs which, though not without merit, do not place him among the more prominent troubadours. He was one of the many poets, protected by Alphonso II. of Aragon, whose glory he sings somewhat after this fashion: "Journey, Canzone to Aragon, to the King whom God maintain, for he it is that upholds all things noble, above all other kings born of woman. Even as the white blossom is above the green foliage, so is his fame uplifted and spread abroad above that of any other ; therefore, whithersoever I go his watchword is within my mouth. I proclaim his fame and do homage beside to no. Duke, King, nor Admiral."[1]

OF PEIRE RAYMOND.

PEIRE RAYMOND the Old[2] of Toulouse[3] was the son of a burgher, and, becoming a jongleur, went unto the court of King Alphonso[4] of Aragon. And the King welcomed him, and did him great honour. (And he was subtle, and wise, and knew well to sing and rhyme, making good 'vers' and good canzones and good anthems.) And he dwelt at the court of the King, and at that of the good Count Raymond of Toulouse,[5] his lord—likewise at that of Lord Guillem of Saint Lidier a long time, and then he married a wife at Pomias, and there also did he die.

[1] **Admiral.** The Arabian title, Emir, which the Crusaders introduced into Europe. In mediaeval poetry it has a higher dignity than nowadays ; and we see it, as here, ranked with King and Duke.

* Mahn, xvii.

E

² **The Old.** We are not told the reason of this surname, and
    no Peire the Young is mentioned by the MSS.

³ **Toulouse.** One of the most important of Provençal cities,
    its Counts ruling from the Garonne to the Alps ; it was
    among the first cities to foster the new mediaeval poetry.

⁴ **King Alphonso.** The II.

⁵ **Raymond of Toulouse.** Raymond V.

ARNAUT OF MARVOIL.

1170-1200.

THE circumstance in the life of Arnaut of Marvoil (or
Marveil) most dwelt on by his biographer is his unhappy
love for the Countess of Burlatz. There seems no reason to
doubt that this love was a very real and very tender one.
He is almost the only troubadour whom we know to have
served but one lady. He died young, and, to judge by his
songs, never consoled himself for his misfortunes.

His poems, of which we have over twenty, entitle him to
a high place among the troubadours. Petrarch calls him the
less famous Arnold, but notwithstanding this epithet, he is far
more often quoted by his contemporaries than Arnaut (or
Arnold) Daniel, and rightly so if we were to judge only by what
is left us of the two poets. After Bernart of Ventadorn there
is, to the modern mind, indeed, no greater love-poet among the
Provençals than Arnaut Marvoil. Warmth, tenderness, grace,
and sincerity are to be found in both, together with the oriental
extravagance, the complete subjugation to Love, and the peculiar
unearthly exaltation of the typical troubadour ; it is of such and
their loves, that Mr. Pater well says : "As in some medicated air
exotic flowers of sentiment expand among people of a remote,
unaccustomed beauty, somnambulistic, frail, androgynous, the
light almost shining through them. Surely such loves were
too fragile and adventurous to last more than for a moment."*

* See Mr. Pater's essay "On Aesthetic Poetry," in *Appreciations.*

OF ARNAUT OF MARVOIL.[*]

ARNAUT of Marvoil[1] was of the diocese of Perigord, of a castle named Marvoil. And he was a clerk of low degree, who, because he could not earn his bread by letters, took to wandering through the world; and well knew to sing and rhyme. And he loved the Countess of Burlatz,[2] daughter of the valiant Count Raymond, and wife of the Viscount of Beziers,[3] surnamed Taillefer. Now this Arnaut was of goodly face and form, and sang right well, and could read romances, and the Countess greatly honoured and advanced him. And he, loving her full well, sang her praises in his songs, but dared tell neither her nor other wight that it was he who made them, but said they were the songs of others; yet after a time, so mighty was his love, that he must needs make a song of her the which begins:

"That frank and noble bearing, that I can ne'er forget,"

and in this song he first made manifest his love to her. And the Countess shunned not his love, but hearkened to his prayers and favourably received them. And she furnished him with goodly apparel and other gear, and greatly honoured and pleasured him, and spoke him fair, so that he became emboldened to sing and rhyme of her. And, favoured

* Mahn, xviii.

by her, he dwelt at her court, esteemed and honoured of men, making many a good song on the Countess, in the which he showed forth the great good, and likewise the great ill he had of her.

Now you have heard[4] who Arnaut of Marvoil was, and how he loved the Countess of Beziers, daughter of the valiant Count Raymond of Toulouse, and mother of the Viscount of Beziers, the which was done to death by the Frenchmen, after being taken by them at Carcassone. This Countess was sur-named of Burlatz, because she was born in the castle of Burlatz; and greatly did Arnaut love her, and many a fair song did he make on her, and many a heartfelt prayer did he in all fear offer her. And she, too, bore him such great goodwill that King Alphonso,[5] who loved her, came to know of it. Then the king, marking how lovingly she bore her to Arnaut, and hearing the fair songs he made of her, became sorely grieved and jealous, so that he accused her of too great love to Arnaut; and so much did he say, and cause to be said of her, that she sent Arnaut from her, and forbade him to appear again before her, and to sing of her and of his love of her. Grief beyond all other griefs filled Arnaut's heart when he heard this, and, as one distraught,[6] he departed from her and from her court, and got him to Guillem of Montpellier, the which was his trusty friend and lord. And with him did

he abide long in tears and sadness, and with him
he made the song, which says :

> " Molt eran dous miei cossir."
> (How sweet to me was e'en my sorrow.)

TO THE VISCOUNTESS OF BURLATZ.[*]

LADY,[7] whom weeping I obey,
More lovely far than tongue can say,
Thy lover true, thy staunchest friend,
His greeting unto thee does send ;
From thee, too, craves the like, and well
Thou know'st of whom I hereby tell,
For never joy on earth I know,
Unless from thy sweet self it flow.
Longtime, oh ! Lady, I do ponder,
How best convey my meaning yonder
Where thou dost tarry—Were it best
By messenger, or me exprest ?
But messenger I dare not send,
Lest that thy wrath on me descend ;
By my own lips 'twere best then told—
But love o'er heart and mind has hold
So firm, when I thy presence seek,
I straight forget what I would speak ;
True message then my thoughts reveal,
A letter sealèd with my seal ;

[*] See for original, *Chrestomathie provençale* p. 94.

A more discreet I might not find,
Nor one more courteous, true and kind.
Love's counsel I do herein heed,
Who daily succours me at need,
Love bids me writing to implore thee
Whate'er I fear to ask before thee;
I dare not Love's command despise—
He serves him best who straight complies.
Hear what the letter does contain,
And do not thou my prayers disdain.
Oh! gracious Lady, rarely wise,
Who look'st on all with kindly eyes,
In thought, and word, and deed high bred,
In arts of courtesy the head;
Thy wondrous loveliness, thy grace,
Thy slender form, and bright-hued face,
Thy glance that with sweet love is lit,
Thy silvery laugh, and merry wit,
The goodness that in thee is seen,
Thy pleasant speech and gladsome mien,
And all thy words and actions kind—
These day and night possess my mind;
And joy and gladness flee from me,
Because thy face I may not see;
Gladness and joy from me have fled,
And wrecked my life if not bestead.
Long suffering, long anxious care,
Much wakefulness and slumber rare,

Unsated yearning, hope forlorn
Have my sad heart well-nigh outworn,
That day and night to God on high
I pray to win thee or to die.
If God thy love to me do give,
Thine ten times more than mine I live ;
For thine, oh! Lady, by my fay,
Is all the good I do or say.

That self-same day I saw thee first
Love filled my heart with raging thirst ;
And put me in so fierce a fire,
Since first it flamed it ne'er does tire ;
Has ne'er since first it flamed abated,
But grows the more in rage unsated,
As, when afar I needs must be,
Still grows the more my love to thee.

  .   .   .   .

All day I groan in this fell fight,
But bitterer far my woe by night;
For when at night to sleep I'm fain,
And think to find me eased of pain,
Alack! I toss, and turn, and start,
And think and think with heavy heart.
Thereon, to sit awhile I rise,
Then lay me down in restless wise ;
And first upon the right arm throw me,
Then straight upon the left bestow me ;

Then suddenly do lay me bare;
Then wrap me round with anxious care;
And, after such exertion vain,
Both arms I outside fling again;
And therewith, clasping hand in hand,
Turn thoughts and eyes toward that dear land,
Where thou, my Lady fair, dost dwell,
Not leaving aught that tongue can tell.

Ah! sweetest Lady, might it chance,
Whate'er the hour or circumstance,
That, once in life thy faithful slave
That rapture know, he long does crave,
Of clasping thee within his arms,
And gazing on thy peerless charms,
Kissing thine eyes, thy red lips sweet,
That mine in one long kiss should meet,
Till that I swoon with great delight—
Too much I've spoke, yet, such my plight,
Once, only once I needs must say,
What long upon my heart does weigh.

And speaking thus all speech I leave,
With drowsy lids one sigh I heave,
And sighing sink into repose.
Then wandering my spirit goes,
Makes, Lady, eager search for thee,
With whom it ever fain would be;

Quick finds the joy, for which I yearn,
When day and night for thee I burn,
And freely thy dear love possesses,
And freely thy dear self caresses.
Ah! might I ever sleep like this,
No kingly lot were such rare bliss.
'Tis better thus sleep life away
Than waking grieve the live-long day ;
And Rodocesta, nor Biblis,
Blancaflor, nor Semiramis,
Tibes, nor Seida, nor Elena,
Antigone, nor else Ismena,
Nor Isold,[8] with the hair of gold,
Did never know such joy untold,
When with their lovers they have been,
As mine is then with thee I ween.
Whereon my lips a sigh does part,
And I do waken with a start,
Open my eyes and gaze around,
To see if thou perchance be found
Hard by ; but, Lady, woe is me !
For nowhere thy loved form I see.
Turn then my face, and close my eyes,
With hands tight clasped in such wise
That slumber sweet might soothe my mind ;
But slumber sweet I cannot find,
And once more fight the battle dreary
With Love, who leaves me faint and weary.

Lady, the hundredth part, I ween,
Can ne'er be told of all the teen,
The sore travail, the torments dire
I ever suffer from Love's fire.
Through thee Love's fire alive does burn me,
And now to thee for grace I turn me;
Forgive me, if I too much dare,
And hearken, Lady, to my prayer.
Lady, of all that live the fairest,
Of all that Nature formed the rarest,
Better than I can know or say,
And sweeter than the sweet May day;
Summer shade, March sun outbreaking,
April rain the flowers awaking,
Love's fair Mirror, Rose of Beauty,
Key to honour, shrine of Duty,
House of Largesse, Queen of Youth,
Root of Wisdom, head of Truth,
Love's fair dwelling, home of Gladness,
Oh! Lady bid me leave all sadness,
Grant that thy servant I may live,
And promise me thy love to give.
Unmeet it were to ask thee more,
Thy mercy only I implore;
And, since I fealty to thee vow,
The hope to win thee give me now.
That hope to me will courage lend,
Till, with good hope, I reach life's end.

Better to die, so hope be mine,
Than without hope alive to pine.

I'll pray no more—God yield thee grace,
And never turn from thee His face.
So please thee, give me health to know,
Since love for thee has laid me low.
May Love, who conquers everything,
Eke thee a captive to me bring,
Lady !

[1] **Arnaut of Marvoil.** Arnaut was a member of the famous
Toulousain school of poetry.

[2] **The Countess of Burlatz.** The Countess was Adelaide,
daughter of Raymond V. of Toulouse. She had the title
of ' Countess,' as in Languedoc a daughter took the
feminine form of her father's title and preserved it, if
her husband were of a lower rank than she.

[3] **Beziers.** Bézier.

[4] **Now you have heard.** These words often form a preamble to
the more romantic and unauthentic parts of the biography;
for, if the first account had few details, the writer would
naturally be tempted to invent more to please the popular,
and more especially the Italian taste. In this case,
however, we know of nothing to disprove what is related.

[5] **Alphonso.** Diez considers this Alphonso to be Alphonso II.
of Aragon, while Millot declares him to be Alphonso IV.
of Castile.

[6] **As one distraught.** See the Satire of the Monk of Montaldon
on the poets of his day, where Arnaut is spoken of: " Ever
of a sorry demeanour because his Lady shows him no
mercy. And ill it is that she bids him not welcome, for

ever do his eyes cry her mercy. The better he sings the more do flow the tears."

[7] **To the Viscountess of Burlatz.** The Letter here translated is among the best of Arnaut's productions; full of passionate eloquence, sincerity, and life-like touches. Such Letters formed a special class of Provençal poetry. They were for the most part composed of octosyllabic rhyming couplets, and began and ended with the name or title of the person to whom they were addressed.

[8] **Isold.** The heroines of mediaeval romance whom Arnaut here cites on account of their love adventures, are Isold, Tristram's hapless lady, and Blanchefleur, the beautiful child, who after many trials and many wanderings is united to her lover Flore. The Greeks are Helen of Troy, Ismene and Antigone, who with the Eastern Biblis, Semiramis, and Thisbe, were known through Ovid and other Latin sources. Rodocesta is perhaps "quella Rodopeia che delusa fu da Demofoonte," and Seida possibly Criseida.

Whether or not Languedoc could once boast of a more or less extensive epic literature now lost, it is certain from the endless allusions in Provençal poetry that the troubadours were well acquainted with all the works of an epical character current in the north of France and elsewhere. Such works were derived from national sources, or borrowed from Greek or Latin, Oriental or Keltic literature.

GIRAUT OF BORNEIL.

1175-1220.

LITTLE can be said of Giraut personally, since his poems treat almost entirely of generalities. As a poet he takes one of the highest places in Provençal literature. In every respect he was the thorough troubadour, devoted to his art, and compensating by his earnestness, sincerity, and manliness for a certain lack of spontaneity and *naïveté*. His poems are mainly didactic, and those on his favourite theme—the general decay of chivalry and poetry—of great elevation and beauty. Among his productions, however, there is none more beautiful than the famous "Alba," or Morning Song, translated below. The alba, of which this is one of the finest specimens, is, as is well known, the leave-taking of two lovers who are warned of the approach of Dawn. Stationed on the towers of mediaeval castles there was, in fact, a watchman who, either by a cry or by a horn, announced the break of day, and certain hours of the night.* In the most primitive 'albas' the lovers are warned by the songs of birds, in later ones by a friend, although in some of the oldest, as this is, only the friend appears. There is little doubt that this form of poetry had its rise in Provence, from whence it passed into other countries. In German literature specially, there are many and beautiful varieties of it (see the Wächterlieder of Walther von der Vogelweide, Wolfram von Eschenbach, and others. In the dialogue between *Romeo and Juliet* beginning,

> Wilt thou be gone, it is not yet near day,
> It was the nightingale and not the lark,
>
> Act III., Scene ii.

we find the old lovers' dialogue of the albas in its most ideal form.

G. de Borneil has also written fine crusading songs, but in these, even with him, the chivalrous element, as Fauriel points out, overrules the religious one.

OF GIRAUT OF BORNEIL.†

GIRAUT of Borneil was of Limousin of the region of Essiduoill, a rich castle belonging to the Viscount

*See *Chrestomathie provençale*, page 101, "Alba," line 3, and elsewhere.   †See Mahn, xx.

of Limoges. And he was a man of low degree, but of great learning and mother-wit, who, because he was a better troubadour than any that had been before him, or that came after him, was named the "Master of Troubadours," and still is by all such as understand words of love and wisdom right cunningly set down. And greatly was he honoured by all excellent and wise men and women, who could understand the worth of his canzones. And he was wont to pass the winter in school[1] in the study of letters, and the summer in journeying from court to court, taking with him two singers[2] who sang his songs. A wife he would not, but all that he gained he gave to his poor kindred and to the church of his native town, the which was, and still is, called the church of Saint Gervais.

*ALBA.**

"Oh! glorious King, who art[3] the world's true
    Light,
All powerful God, if pleasing in Thy sight
Avail my comrade nor disdain my pleading;
Him night from me has ta'en, Thy help he's
    needing,
For soon the morn will waken.

* See *Chrestomathie provençale*, page 101, for original.

"Fair comrade, if thou'rt lost in slumber bright,
Slumber no more, shake off the dreams of night.
For in the east upon its way is speeding
That star, which in its train the day is leading,
   Full soon the morn will waken.

"Fair comrade mine, singing to thee I cry:
'Slumber no more,' the bird through woods does
     fly,
Who by her morning song would hence impel us,
O'erta'en I fear to see thee by the jealous,
   For soon the morn will waken!

"Fair comrade, haste thee to the casement high,
Day's harbingers do show them in the sky,
And these will tell thee I am true and zealous,
If not, thy loss 'twill be, for they foretell us,
   That soon the morn will waken."

   .   .   .   .   .   .

[1] **School.** One of the many schools of learning that were
then attached to monasteries and cathedrals.

[2] **Two singers.** This fact does much to prove Giraut's importance and affluence. The more powerful troubadours,
especially if they had not the gift of song, took with
them one, or, as in Giraut's case, two jongleurs to sing
and recite their poems.

[3] **"Oh! glorious King, who art."** The rhymes are: a, a, b, b, c;
a a b b c; d d e e c; d d e e c; etc. The poem is
composed of seven stanzas of five lines.

PEIRE VIDAL.

1175-1215.

PEIRE VIDAL was an extraordinary mixture of sense and folly—the fool *par excellence* of the Provençals, as also one of their most distinguished poets. He seems to have spent his long life in many wanderings, and to have known, more or less intimately, the chief princes of the age. Whether he started on the third Crusade is uncertain; but, if so, he at any rate did not get further than Cyprus. Brave, restless, impressionable, boastful, with a background of wisdom and penetration, he had all the qualities commonly attributed to the Keltic race, together with others peculiarly his own.

Vidal is one of the most prolific of the troubadours and about fifty of his poems have been preserved to us, the greater part of which form interesting reading. His canzones are simple and graceful, and devoid of the metaphysical subtleties and hard rhymes that were the snare of the style. Frequently, however, Vidal's lyrics treat not only of love but of political and other subjects, this lack of unity being a common fault in Provençal poetry, and in him more than usually conspicuous.

The first of the poems translated will give an idea of Vidal's prodigious sense of his own importance, and naïve manner of expressing that sense; the second is a version of one of his many canzones, while for Vidal's more serious and elevated work the reader is referred to the crusading song of the *Chrestomathie provençale* (page 109), which, owing to its digressions, has not been here rendered.

OF PEIRE VIDAL. *

NOW Peire Vidal was of Toulouse, and was the son of a furrier.   And he sang better than any

------

* See Mahn, xxi. and xxii.

man alive, and was a good troubadour. And he was one of the maddest of men, for he weened that all he willed came verily to pass. And no man in the world was so apt as he in the making of poems and of sweet melodies; and none so mad as he in his talk of arms, and love, and in the slandering of others. And in good sooth did a knight of Saint Giles cause his tongue to be cut out, because he made believe that he was his wife's lover; but Sir Hugh of Baux caused him to be healed of his hurt, and doctored, and, when he was healed, he passed beyond the sea, and brought home with him a Grecian woman, who was given him to wife in Cyprus.

And they had made believe to him that she was the niece of the Emperor of Constantinople; and that, through her, he should of right have the empire. Wherefore, in the making of ships, he spent all he could gain, for he weened he could win him the empire. And he bore the Imperial arms, and styled himself Emperor and his wife Empress.

And he was wont to love whatsoever good ladies he set eyes on, and to seek their love; and all made assent unto his prayers, wherefore, though one and all beguiled him, he weened he was each lady's lover, and that each one was dying for his love. And whither he went he brought with him rich chargers and rich armour, and a throne and a royal tent, and deemed himself one of the doughtiest knights in the world and the most beloved of ladies.

Now Peire Vidal, even as I have told you, loved all good ladies, and weened they loved him likewise. And it chanced that he loved Azalais, wife of Lord Barral of Marseilles, the which lord bore Peire Vidal greater good will than any man alive, for his fair poems, and for the great drolleries that he spoke and did. Moreover, they named one another "Rainier," and Peire Vidal had ever free access to him at all hours and beyond all other men. And Lord Barral knew full well that Peire Vidal loved his wife, and made merry over it, and over all the follies that he spoke and did. And all men did as much; the lady also made jest of it, as did all other ladies whom he loved, each one speaking him fair, and promising all that it pleased him to ask of them. And he, so wise he was, gave ear to all they said. And, when Peire Vidal and the lady fell out together, Lord Barral it was that made peace betwixt them, and made her promise all that was asked of her.

Now it happed upon a day that Peire Vidal knew that Lord Barral had arisen from his bed, and that the lady was alone in the chamber; so he entered into the chamber, and drew near unto

my Lady Azalais' bed, and finding her asleep,
knelt down before her, and kissed her on the
mouth.   And she felt the kiss, and weened it was
her lord, and laughing uplifted herself.   And when
she beheld Peire Vidal the fool, she began to cry
out, and to raise great uproar.   And hearing this,
her maidens hastened unto her from within, saying
"What ails you?"   And Peire Vidal went out in
haste, and the lady bade call Lord Barral, and made
her plaint unto him, because that Peire Vidal had
kissed her, and weeping prayed him to avenge her.
Then Lord Barral, even as a man of worth and sense,
made light of the matter, and fell to laughing and to
chiding his wife, for that she had noised abroad
what the fool had done.   Nathless his rebukes did
not so avail him as to hinder his wife from noising
abroad the matter, and from striving to bring ill
upon Peire Vidal, and from making great threats
against him.   Then Peire Vidal, from fear thereof,
entered into a ship and went to Genoa; and there
he tarried until he passed beyond the seas with
King Richard, for he was in sore fear lest my
Lady Azalais should seek to compass his death.
There he abode long time, and there he made
many a good song, in the which he minded
him of the kiss he had stolen of her.   And in
the one song which begins, "Aiostar e lassar," he
said :

"Assatz par que loingnar me volc de sa reio," etc.
(It well appears that she would drive me from her kingdom.)

And in another he says, " Pus onratz etz "; and in another song, which begins, " Si col paubres que iay el ric ostal," he says, " Bem bat amors ab las vergas quieu cuelh," etc.

Thus did he long dwell beyond the seas, not daring to come back again into Provence; but Lord Barral, who loved him right well, even as ye have heard say, made such great prayers unto his wife that she forgave Peire Vidal the kiss and made him gift of it. So Lord Barral sent forth his messengers unto Peire Vidal to tell him that the good-will and favour of the lady were restored to him, and to bid him come to her. And he came full joyfully to Marseilles, and full joyfully was he welcomed by Lord Barral and by my Lady Azalais. And she granted him the kiss that he had stolen of her and all was pardoned him, whereof Peire Vidal made this song which runs: " Pos tornatz sui en Proensa." (Since I am back again in Provence.)

Now* Peire Vidal, for the death of the good Count Raymond of Toulouse, was sore stricken with grief, and in his sadness clothed himself in black, and cut off the tails and ears of all his horses, and caused the hair to be shaven from his own head, and from his servants; yet did they not

* See Mahn, xxiii.

cut off their beards, or moustaches, or nails. Long time did he demean himself after the manner of a sad and foolish man. And it befell that in the time that he went thus sorrowfully, King Alphonso of Aragon came into Provence, and with him came all the honourable men of his country. Lord Blascol Romieus, Lord Garsia Romieus, Lord Martin of Canet, Lord Miquel of Luzia, Lord Sas of Antilon, Lord Guillem of Alcalla, Lord Albert of Castelveil, Lord Raimon Gausseran of Pinos, Lord Guillem Raimon of Moncada, Lord Arnaut of Castelbon, Lord Raimon of Caveira, and these all found Peire Vidal sad, and sorrowful, and arrayed as one distraught. And the king, and all the barons, who were his especial friends, began to pray him to cease from grieving, and to be of good cheer, and to make a song that they might bear back with them into Aragon. And so earnestly did the king and his barons entreat him, that he said he would take heart again, and would cease to grieve, and would make a song or do aught else that they required of him.

And he fell to loving the Loba [She-Wolf] of Penautier, and my Lady Estafania of Sardinia, and also he fell anew to loving my Lady Raimbauda of Biol, wife of Guillem Rostan Lord of Biol, the which Biol is in the mountains of Provence on this side Lombardy. Now the Loba was of Carcassonne and Peire Vidal made himself to be called Lop [Wolf] for love of her, bearing a wolf in his coat of arms. And in the mountains of Cabaret he made men hunt him forsooth with dogs, and with mastiffs, and with greyhounds, even as men hunt a wolf. And he donned the skin of a wolf to make the shepherds and dogs believe him one. Then the shepherds with their dogs hunted him and so evilly dealt with him, that he was brought as one dead to the dwelling of the She-Wolf of Penautier. And when she saw that it was even Peire Vidal, she made right merry over his folly, and laughed greatly, and also her husband; and she welcomed him joyfully, and her husband bade his servants take him and lay him in a privy chamber, and give him gentle usage, and bade a leech be sent for, and had him tended till he was healed of his wounds.

And, even as I began to tell you, Peire Vidal promised the king and his barons to sing and to make songs; and when he was healed of his wounds the king caused arms to be made for himself and Peire Vidal, and delighted much in him; and it was even at this time that Peire Vidal made this song which runs: "De chantar mera laissatz. Per ira e per dolor. (I had withheld me from singing for sorrow and woefulness.)

POEM BY VIDAL ON HIMSELF.[*]

SIR DRAGOMAN, had I a goodly steed,[2]
Soon would my enemies for mercy plead;
For even when they hear of men my name,
  They fear me more than quail doth fear hawk's
    greed;
  Nor prize their life a doit, so fierce of deed,
So stern they know me, and so great my fame.

  When donned my glitt'ring, steel-lined coat of
    mail,
  And girt my sword, Hugh's gift that cannot fail,
Whither I go, the earth doth shake with fear;
  No foes I meet that do not 'fore me pale,
  And yield me place; nought doth their pride
    avail,
So great their terror when my step they hear.

.   .   .   .

Roland and Oliver in one am I,
With Montdidier[1] in courtesy I vie;
Full often messengers do bear to me
  For my great worth and for my valour high,
  Gold rings and bands of white and sable dye,
And greetings that fill all my heart with glee.

* See *Chrestomathie provençale,* page 111.

When vanquished 'fore me jealous mockers kneel,
Who by false semblance would their craft conceal,
And by fair means or foul would joy condemn—
These verily shall learn what blows I deal,
For, be their bodies made of iron or steel,
No peacock's feather shall it profit them.

Of chivalry and love I am the flower,
Bravest among the brave—in lady's bower
Is none more courteous and more debonair,
Nor in the battle-field of greater power,
So that my enemies in terror cower
At thought of me, nor to confront me dare.

  .   .   .   .

CANZONE.[*]

GREAT joy[3] have I to greet the season bright,
And joy to greet the blessed summer days,
And joy when birds do carol songs of praise,
And joy to mark the woods with flowerets dight,
And joy at all whereat to joy were meet,
And joy unending at the pleasaunce sweet
That yonder in my joy I think to gain,
There where in joy my soul and sense remain.

'Tis Love that keeps me in such dear delight,
'Tis Love's clear fire that keeps my breast ablaze,

---

[*] For original see Mahn's *Gedichte der Troubadours*, Vol. I., page 134.

'Tis Love that can my sinking courage raise,
Even for Love am I in grievous plight;
  With tender thoughts Love makes my heart to
    beat,
  And o'er my every wish has rule complete—
Virtue I cherish since began his reign,
And to do deeds of Love am ever fain.[4]

[1] **Montdidier.** A hero of mediaeval romance of renowned
    courtesy.
[2] **Had I a goodly steed.** The original poem is of 7 stanzas
    of 6 lines, with the rhymes a, a b a a b running through
    them.
[3] **Joy.** The troubadours were fond of the effect produced by the
    repetition of one word throughout a stanza.
[4] **Am ever fain.** The original is of 6 stanzas of 8 lines, which
    have the rhymes a, b, b, a, c, c, d, d.

BERTRAN OF BORN.

Poems date from 1180. Died 1195?

BERTRAN OF BORN, both as man and poet, is one of the
most remarkable representatives of the second half of the
twelfth century, the period in which Provençal poetry reached
its fullest development.

Little is known of his domestic life beyond his long strife
with his brother Constantine over the possession of Autafort, of
which Bertran finally became sole owner. The most important
circumstance in his career, therefore, is his close connection
with the three elder sons of Henry II. of England, and the part
he took in the politics of the day, which part, whether ex-
aggerated or not, is perhaps greater than that taken by any

other troubadour. The affection that he had for the "young king,"
Henry's eldest son, seems to have been a very strong one, and
there is the ring of true sorrow in his two beautiful 'Complaints'
composed at young Henry's death, that here translated being
among the finest poems in Provençal literature. Bertran was
a zealous partisan, adhering steadily to the cause of the " young
king," and after the latter's early death to Richard's. Bertran
was also as zealous a promoter of strife. "Ever," says the
biographer, "was he fain to set strife betwixt father and son,
and betwixt brother and brother," and it was this characteristic
of his that gave him a place in Dante's *Inferno*, where he figures
as a headless trunk, holding the severed member by the hair, a
symbolical punishment, awarded as the head explains :

> " Perch' io partii cosi giunte persone
> Partito porto il mio cerebro lasso !
> Dal suo principio, ch'e in questo troncone ;
> Cosi s'osserva in me lo contrapasso." *
>
> *—Inferno*, Canto xxviii.

Space will not allow me to treat of Bertran and his poems in
detail. The translations below will give some idea, however
imperfect, of the most striking of them, and readers of Provençal
may refer to Professors Stimming's and Thomas's editions of
Bertran's poems. To speak of him generally, his life and work
are for various reasons of peculiar interest and profit to the
student of mediaeval literature. He was, to begin with, essentially a type of the undisciplined Provençal knight, and in him are
to be found the faults and virtues, the aspirations and prejudices
of his race and age. War was the very breath of his nostrils, and
his passion for it was entirely independent of its ends. Warfare
was of all-absorbing interest to him, and in spite of his one

---

* See Longfellow's translation :

> " Because I parted persons so united,
> Parted do I now bear my brain, alas !
> From its beginning, which is in this trunk,
> Thus is observed in me the counterpoise."

really fine Crusading song, religion plays but a small part in his poems. Hatred of effeminacy, sloth, irresolution, and avarice, and strong "class" prejudice, all marked features of feudalism, are to be found in Bertran in an intensified form, with other characteristics of his own. Bertran is beyond question one of the most powerful and unconventional of the troubadours. Too untutored to come under the influence of the Greeks and Romans, and too much in earnest to deal with the platitudes and subtleties of many of the Provençal poets, he speaks from the abundance of his heart of things of vital interest to him; hence the freshness, the spontaneity and unfailing vigour of his poems, qualities that, together with his great satiric force, made him feared and respected by friend and foe.

Lastly, and apart from his intrinsic merits, Bertran has a special importance resulting from the impression he produced on the mind of Dante—whose high opinion of his poetic power is conveyed to us in his *Treatise on Vulgar Eloquence* (Lib. II., c. 2), in which he speaks of him as "The great singer of arms." To his opinion of Bertran the man allusion has already been made.

OF BERTRAN OF BORN.*

NOW Bertran of Born was a castellan of the diocese of Perigord, lord of a castle called Autafort.[1] Ever was he at war with all his neighbours—with the Count of Perigord, and with the Viscount of Limoges,[2] and with his brother Constantine, and with Richard, while he was yet Count of Poitou; and he was a valiant knight and warrior, a good lover, and a good troubadour, and wise and fair-spoken, and knew to work

* See Mahn, xxiv.

both good and ill. And ever, when he would, was he lord over King Henry of England, and over his sons ; and ever did he delight in setting strife betwixt father and son, and betwixt brother and brother ; and likewise did he ever bestir himself to set strife betwixt the King of England and the King of France, and, if there were perchance a peace or truce between them, then would he, with his sirventes, strive after the undoing of that peace, and set forth how that each side was dishonoured by the making of it. And in that he set strife between them, there arose great good and likewise great ill. And he made many good sirventes, whereof great plenty are here set down, even as ye can see and hear.* Right good sirventes did he make, and never but two canzones. And the King of Aragon [3] gave for wife the songs of Giraut of Borneil to the sirventes of Bertran of Born. And he who sung for him was surnamed Papiol.[4] And Sir Bertran was courteous and debonair, and named the Count of Brittany "Rassa," and the King of England "Yea and Nay," and the young king, his son, "Sailor." [5]

Now † Bertran of Born was the lover of a lady young and noble, and of good report, the which was named my Lady Maent [6] of Montaignac, and was wife of Lord Talairan (brother of the Count of Perigord) and daughter of the Viscount of Turenne, and

<hr>

* See Mahn, xxv.   † See Mahn, portion of xxvi.

sister of Lady Maria of Ventadorn and Lady Elis of Montfort, and she was surnamed by him "Dauphin" in his songs; and even as he has therein told us, she sent him from her, saying she would have nought of his service; whereat he was full sad and sorrowful, and declared that he could never win her love again, nor find one so fair, so good, so gracious, and so wise, nor any one her peer. Then his lady counselled him to make unto himself a mistress by borrowing of each fair dame a gift, beauty, fair semblance, kind greeting, gracious speech, courteous bearing, goodly proportions, a fair form, or the like. Thus went he seeking of all fair dames one of the gifts ye have heard named, to restore to him the lady he had lost, and in the sirvente that he made thereon ye will hear named all those of whom he sought help in the making of the borrowed lady, the which runs:

"Dompna, pois de mi nous cal." †
(Lady, since you care not for me.)

Now Bertran of Born had been sent away by his lady, Lady Maent of Montaignac, and naught availed him the oaths and denials that he made, both by his songs and by plain speech, in making her believe that he loved not Lady Guiscarda.[7] Therefore went he into Saintonge to see Lady Tibors of Montausier,

* See translation below, and for original Stimming's edition of *Bertran of Born*, Song 12.

than whom was none of better report in all the world for beauty and for virtue, and for learning and courtesy. And this lady was the wife of the Lord of Chalais, and of Berbesil, and of Montausier.   And Sir Bertran made complaint unto her of Lady Maent, who had sent him from her, and would believe, neither for oath nor for denial that he could make, that he loved not Lady Guiscarda, and therefore did he pray her to take him for her knight and servitor.   Then Lady Tibors, like the wise woman she was, made this answer unto him : "Bertran, forasmuch as you have come hither unto me, I am in great joy and gladness, and hold myself greatly thereby honoured ; but, on the other hand, it ill pleaseth me that you do me honour, and offer yourself to me for knight and servitor; and ill it pleaseth me that you have said and done aught for which Lady Maent should in justice bid you leave her service, and should wax wroth against you. . But I am one of those who know how quickly change the hearts of lovers and their mistresses, and if you have nowise sinned against Lady Maent, soon shall I know the truth of it, and, if thus it be, will cause her favour to return to you ; but if the fault lie in you, nor I, nor any other lady, ought again to receive and welcome you as knight and servitor ; yet this good shall be done you, that I will maintain your cause, and will strive to set you at one."

Then Bertran was mighty well satisfied with the answer of Lady Tibors, and promised her that he would love and serve no other lady than Lady Tibors if it befell that he could not win back the love of Lady Maent. Likewise did Lady Tibors promise Sir Bertran that, if she failed to make his peace with Lady Maent, she would take him for her knight and servitor.

And it was so that ere long Lady Maent came to know that there was no fault in Sir Bertran, so she gave ear to the prayers that were made to her by Sir Bertran, and granted him permission to appear before her, and to plead his cause. And he told her how that Lady Tibors had upheld him, and all that she had promised him, whereat Lady Maent bade him take leave of Lady Tibors, and pray her to release him from the promises he had made unto her. Wherefore Bertran of Born made the sirvente, "Sabrils e foillas e flors." And he tells of the succour he went to seek of Lady Tibors, and the reception she gave him in the cobla that runs: "Domna sieu quezi socors."

Bertran of Born, even as I have told you, had a brother, Constantine of Born by name; and this same was a valiant knight of arms, but not of those that labour after fame and honour, but ever wished he ill to Bertran of Born, and good to all that wished Bertran ill. And upon a time he despoiled

Bertran of the Castle of Autafort, the which they held in common, but Sir Bertran won it of him again, and bereft him of all share therein. Then Constantine went to the Viscount of Limoges that he might maintain him against his brother; and he did maintain him, and likewise King Richard. And Richard was warring upon Ademar, Viscount of Limoges, and my Lord Richard and Ademar warred with Sir Bertran, and laid waste his land and burnt it. . . .

Now * it came to pass at the time when the young king made peace with his brother Richard, and ceased to make claim upon his inheritance, even as King Henry their father had willed, that his father gave him fixed sums for meat and drink, and for all his needs, yet no whit of land did he hold, and no man came to him for maintenance, nor for his aid in battle. Then Sir Bertran of Born, and all those barons that had aided him against Lord Richard, were sorely grieved. And the young king departed and went into Lombardy, and gave his days to tourneys and vain pleasures, leaving all these barons at war with Lord Richard. And Lord Richard laid siege to castles and to towns, and destroyed them, and took lands and burnt and laid them waste; and the young king held tourneys, and lived at ease, and slept and disported himself,

* See Mahn, xxvi.

whereat Sir Bertran made the sirvente that begins, "Dun sirventes nom cal far longor ganda." (To make sirventes I'll no longer stay.) Now the complaint that Sir Bertran of Born made herein of the young king sprang from no other cause than that the young king was the bravest and best of all the world. And Sir Bertran loved him more than any man in the world, and so likewise the young king loved and trusted him, wherefore King Henry, his father, and Count Richard, his brother, bore great ill-will to Sir Bertran. And because of the young king's most excellent worth, and because of the grief that fell on all men at his death, Sir Bertran made over him the complaint that runs, "Mon chan fenis ab dol et ab mal traire." (My singing ends in misery forlorn.)

Now in the time that Lord Richard was Count of Poitiers, ere he was yet king, Bertran of Born was his enemy, because Sir Bertran bore great good-will to the young king, the which warred at that time against his brother Richard. And the good Viscount of Limoges—Sir Ademar by name—and the Viscount of Ventadorn, and the Viscount of Gumel, and the Count of Perigord and his brother, and the Count of Angoulesme and his two brothers, and Count Raymond of Toulouse, and the Count of Flanders, and the Count of Barcelona, Sir Contoil of Estarac, a Count of Gascony, Sir Gaston of Bearn, Count of Bigorre, and the Count of Dijon, these all had Sir Bertran made to forswear my Lord Richard, and to rise against him.   And lo! all these forsook him, and made peace without him, and perjured themselves to him.   Likewise Ademar, Viscount of Limoges, that most was bound to him by love and oath, even he also forsook him and made peace without him.   Then Lord Richard, when he knew that all these had forsaken him, came before Autafort with his host and sware, saying, that never more would he go thence if Bertran gave him not Autafort, nor yielded him to his will and pleasure.   And Bertran, hearing of that my Lord Richard had sworn, and knowing that he was abandoned of these ye have heard tell of, delivered to him the castle, and yielded him to his will and pleasure.   And Count Richard met him with pardon and kissed him ; and ye are to know by a verse that he made in the sirventes that begins, " Silcoms mes avinens e non avars," (If the Count be gracious and not churlish to me,) that the Count ceased to be wroth against him, and restored to him his Castle Autafort and became his true friend.   Then Sir Bertran went forth and fell to warring on the Viscount Ademar and the Viscount of Perigord, the which had forsaken him, whence great evil came to Bertran, and great evil to them likewise.   .   .   .

Now it befell that Bertran of Born went for to see a sister of King Richard's, the mother of the Emperor

Otho, the which hight my Lady Elena,[8] and was wife of the Duke of Saxony. And the lady was fair and right courteous, and well taught, doing honour unto all by fair speech and greeting. And my Lord Richard, the which was at that time Count of Poitiers, interceded with his sister for him, and bade her speak Sir Bertran fair, and pleasure and honour him. Then she, for as much as she was right wishful of fame and praise, and knew that Sir Bertran was of high fame and excellence, and might greatly exalt her, did him such great honour that he was well content thereat, and fell to loving her, and to offering her praise and thanks. And at that season it came to pass that he was with Count Richard in his host,[9] and it was winter and the host was in grievous straits. And it was so that upon a Sunday, though the hour of noon was well-nigh past, they had neither eaten nor drunk; and being thus pressed by hunger he made the sirventes that thus begins, "Ges de diznar non fora oimais matis." (Never henceforth shall I hasten to take dinner.)

Now King Henry[10] held Sir Bertran of Born besieged within Autafort, and warred against him with his engines; for greatly did he mislike him, because he believed it was Sir Bertran that had been the mover of all the strife betwixt him and his son; and therefore was he come before Autafort to despoil him of all his heritage.

And it was so that the King of Aragon was in the host of King Henry before Autafort. And when Bertran had knowledge of it his heart was glad within him, for as much as he was his own especial friend. And it came to pass that the King of Aragon sent messengers into the castle, asking bread and meat and wine of Sir Bertran. And he gave him great plenty of them; and by the messenger that bore his gifts Bertran sent word unto the King, praying him instantly that he should cause the war-engines to be moved to another part, because the walls they bore upon were well-nigh shattered. And he, by reason of the great wealth of King Henry, told him all Sir Bertran had imparted unto him. Then King Henry bade his men to bring the engines to bear upon such parts of the walls as he knew to be well-nigh shattered, and behold! incontinently the walls were laid low, and the castle was taken, and Sir Bertran, with all his following, was led into King Henry's tent, whereat the King greeted him full ill, and spake unto him and said : " Bertran, Bertran, lo ! ye have said aforetime that never yet have ye had need of half the wits ye possess, but know ye that now ye will have need of all of them." Quoth Sir Bertran : " My lord, true it is that thus I spake, and my words were words of truth." Quoth the King : " Full well I ween your wits are now to seek." " My lord," answered Sir Bertran, "you speak true." " And wherefore?" quoth the King. "My lord," answered Sir Bertran, "on that same day that the most excellent young king, your son, died, I lost all sense and wisdom and understanding." Now when the King heard that which Sir Bertran, weeping, spake unto him, there arose within him great grief for pity of his son, and tears stood in his eyes, insomuch as he must needs swoon with sorrow. And when he had recovered from his swoon, he cried with a loud voice and said, weeping : "Bertran, Bertran, ye are very right, and meet it is that by my son's death ye lose your wits, for he loved you better than any man alive ; and I, for love of him, do set you free, and do deliver unto you your castle and your goods, and restore you to my love and favour, and give you five hundred silver marks for the harm ye have received." And Sir Bertran fell on his knees before him, offering him thanks, and the King departed with all his host.

Then Sir Bertran, when he knew what great felony the King of Aragon had done unto him, was full wroth against him.[11] And he knew how King Alphonso had served King Henry in war as his hireling; likewise was it known to him how that the King of Aragon was come of a poor family[12] of Carlades, of a castle named Carlat, the which is in Rouergne, in the lordship of the Count of Rhodey. And Sir Peire Carlat, who was lord of that castle by his great excellence and prowess, took to wife the

Countess of Millau, the which was fallen from her inheritance; and by her he had a son of great valour and excellence, who gained dominion over the County of Provence; and one of his sons, called Raymond Berenger, acquired the County of Barcelona and the Kingdom of Aragon, and was the first King that ever was in Aragon. And he went to Rome to be crowned, and returning homewards died at the town of Saint Dalmas; and he left behind him three sons—Alphonso, King of Aragon, even he that had wronged Sir Bertran of Born, and Don Sancho, and Berenger of Besandun. Likewise was it known to Sir Bertran how that King Alphonso had dealt treacherously with the daughter of the Emperor Manuel,[13] the which the Emperor had sent unto him for wife with great treasure and wealth, and with a full honourable company. And he seized upon all the treasure of the lady, and of all the Greeks that were with her, and sent them back by sea, sad and sorrowful and discomfited. And Bertran knew how Alphonso's brother Don Sancho had dispossessed him of Provence, and how he forswore himself by fighting against the Count of Toulouse for the gold which King Henry gave him. And on all these matters Sir Bertran of Born made the sirvente that begins thus: " Pois lo gens terminis floris sespandis," etc. (Since the fair flowering season begins.)

Now ye have heard that Sir Bertran of Born

minded him of the evil that the King of Aragon had done to him and others. And at the end of a great space of time, when he had heard tell of other ill deeds of the King's, he was wishful to recount them in a sirvente. And it was told Sir Bertran that there was a certain knight in Aragon, Sir Espanhol by name, that had a right strong castle named Castellot, the which he held of none; and it was in the Saracen's stronghold, from whence he made great war upon them. And the King's heart was greatly set upon this castle. And Sir Espanhol came one day into that country to do him service, and to invite him to his castle, and brought him thither in great state, both him and his men; and lo! the King, when he was within the castle, caused him to be taken, and to be cast out of it, and despoiled him of the castle.

And it is verily true that, when the King entered the service of the King of England, the Count of Toulouse put him to flight in Gascony, taking from him full fifty knights. And King Henry gave unto him all the treasure wherewith the knights should pay their ransom, and he nowise gave this treasure to the knights, but carried it into Aragon; and the knights, coming forth from prison, paid their own ransom. Likewise of a truth was there a jongleur, named Artuset, who lent him two hundred marabotins. And the King took him whithersoever he went for the space of a year, but gave him never a penny.

And it happened upon a day that Artuset, the jongleur, came to strife with a Jew; and the Jews fell upon him and wounded him sorely, him and one of his fellows. And Artuset and his fellow killed one of the Jews, whereat the Jews went to the King and besought him to avenge them, and to deliver up to them Artuset and his fellow to be slain, for the which they would give him two hundred marabotins. And the King delivered them both up to them, and received of them the two hundred marabotins. And the Jews burned them on the day of Christ's Nativity, even as Guillem of Berguedan has said in the King's despite in one of his sirventes, the which says:

> " E fetz una mespreison
>   Don om nol deu razonar,
> Quel iorn de la naision,
>   Fetz dos crestias brusar—
> Artus ab autre son par;
> E non degra aici iutgar
> A mort, ni a passion
> Dos per un iuzieu fellon."

(And he commited a sin, in the which none should seek to justify him, for on the day of the Nativity he let burn two Christians, Arthur with one, his fellow; and unmeet it is that for one base Jew two should thus be condemned to death and torments.)

Now another that hight Peire the jongleur lent him monies and horses, and that same Peire, jongleur, had spoken great ill of the old Queen of

England,[14] the which held Fontebrau, an Abbey wherein enter all noble ladies in old age; and, at the word of the King of Aragon, she caused him to be slain. And all these ugly deeds did Sir Bertran of Born call to the remembrance of the King of Aragon in the sirvente that says:

> "Quant vei per vergiers despleiar
> Los cendaus grocs indis," etc.

(When I see unfurled in the orchards the yellow and blue standards, etc.)

Now in the time and in the season that King Richard of England warred upon King Philip of France,[15] it befell that the two kings were both in the field of battle with all their men. The King of France had in his company the men of France, Burgundy, and Champagne, and Flanders and Berry; and King Richard the men of England, and Normandy, and Brittany, and Poitou, and those of Anjou, and Touraine, and Maine, and Saintonge, and Limousin. And he was upon the bank of a river called Gaura,[16] the which floweth at the foot of Niort—and one host was upon the one bank, and the other upon the other bank; and thus abode they fifteen days, each day arming them and making them ready for battle. But the archbishops and bishops, and abbots and monks were in the midst of them, and forbade the battle. And upon a certain day all King Richard's men were armed and arrayed for battle, and for passing the Gaura; and the Frenchmen armed them likewise, and arrayed them for battle. And the good men of religion came forth bearing crosses, and praying Richard and Philip to withhold them from battle. And the King of France said that he would not withhold him from battle until King Richard did him homage for all his lands on this side the sea—the Duchy of Normandy, and the Duchy of Aquitaine, and the County of Poitou ; and until he restored to him Guiort, whereof King Richard had spoiled him. And King Richard, hearing that which King Philip required of him, had great gladness, inasmuch as the men of Champagne, for the great plenty of sterlings that he had scattered among them, had sworn to him that they would not be at the battle ; and he mounted his war-horse, and set his helmet on his head, and let sound the trumpets and unfurl the banners for to pass over the water, and let order the squadrons of the barons and of his men to pass over to the battle. And King Philip, when he saw him coming, mounted his war-horse, and set his helmet on his head, and likewise all his men mounted their war-horses and armed them for the battle, save only the men of Champagne, the which set not on their helmets. And lo ! King Philip, when he saw King Richard and his men coming towards him with such great lustiness, and saw that the men of Champagne came not to the fight, was cast down and afraid, and let bring forward the archbishops, and bishops, and men of religion, all such as had prayed him to make peace and concord; and he prayed them to go to Richard to ask peace and concord of him, and he promised them to accept the peace and concord that Richard required, namely, the giving up to him of Guisort, and his claim of homage from Richard. And the holy men came to meet King Richard with crosses in their arms, beseeching him with tears that he would have pity on all the goodly men of that field that were presently to die, and promising him that if he would make peace they would cause Guisort to be given up to him, and the King to depart from his land. And the barons, when they heard of the great honour that King Philip did him, gathered around King Richard and counselled him to accept the peace and concord. And he, for the prayers of the good men of religion, and for the counsel of his barons, made peace and concord, by the which King Philip gave up Guisort unto him, and the matter of paying homage remained pending as it was before. And he forsook the field, and King Richard remained, and the two kings swore peace for ten years. And they disbanded their hosts, and sent away their hirelings. And the two kings became niggardly and covetous, and would neither call together their hosts nor spend aught, save on falcons and hawks, and dogs, and greyhounds, and buying lands and possessions, and on doing evil to their barons. And full woe were the barons of the King of France and of King Richard that they had brought about the peace, for that it had made the two kings churlish and niggardly. And Sir Bertran of Born was more angry than any other of the barons, for that he could no more delight himself in wars of his own nor of others, nor in the warfare of the two kings; for when the two kings had war together he had of King Richard what wealth and honour he listed, and was held in fear by the two kings for the sharpness of his tongue, whence he, for the wish that he had himself, and had marked in the other barons, that the two kings should return to war, made this sirvente that begins:

> "Pois li baron son irat e lor pesa."
> (Since the barons are wroth and sad.)

. . . . . .

Now when King Richard had passed beyond the sea, all the barons of Limousin and of Perigord bound themselves against him by oath, and gathered together a great power, and came before the castles and boroughs whereof King Richard had despoiled them, and fought against and took all such as defended themselves, and thus did they recover a great part of that whereof King Richard had despoiled them. Now when my Lord Richard was returned from over the sea, and was come out of prison, full wroth and sorrowful was he for the castles and boroughs whereof the barons had despoiled him. And he began to threaten them greatly, and to disherit them, and lay them low. And the Viscount of Limoges and the Count of Perigord, for the maintenance which the King of France had given and was yet giving them, set his threats at naught, and sent word to him that he was become too fierce and proud, and that they, in his own despite, would make him gracious and courteous, and condescending, and that they would, moreover, chastise him in battle. Whereat Sir Bertran of Born, as one whose only joy is in the raising of strife amongst the barons, was right glad at heart when he heard that the King threatened the barons, and that they lightly regarded him, and set his words at naught, and had sent unto him saying that they would chastise him, and would make him in his own despite gracious and courteous. And knowing that the King was sorely grieved and angered at that they said to him, and at the loss of the castles Montron and Azgen, he made one of his sirventes to cause King Richard to sally to war. . . . And the sirvente begins thus:

"Quant la novella flors par el vergan."
(When fresh flowers are seen in the gardens.)

Now when Richard had made peace with Sir Bertran of Born, and had restored to him his Castle Autafort, he took the cross and passed beyond the sea ; and Bertran remained warring upon Ademar, the Viscount of Limoges, and upon the Count of Perigord, and upon all the barons round about. And, even as ye have heard, when Richard returned, he was captured in Germany, and dwelt in prison two years, and was redeemed by gold. And when Sir Bertran of Born knew that the King was to come forth from prison, he was right glad for the great good that he knew he should have of the King, and for the harm that should come to his enemies. And, wit ye well, that Sir Bertran had written in his heart all the evil that those promoters of strife had done in Limousin, and in the lands of King Richard. And thereof he made his sirvente :

"Bem platz quar treua ni fis."
(It well pleaseth me that neither truce nor peace.)

ON THE DEATH OF PRINCE HENRY,[17] 1183.

IF all the pain, and misery, and woe,
    The tears, the losses with misfortune fraught,
That in this dark life man can ever know,
    Were heap'd together—all would seem as naught

* For original see Stimming's edition of *Bertran of Born*, page 212.

Against the death of the young English king;
  For by it youth and worth are sunk in gloom,
  And the world dark and dreary as a tomb,
Reft of all joy, and full of grief and sadness.

In dire distress, and full of bitter woe,
  Forsaken mourn the warriors renown'd,
Trouveres and jongleurs debonair, I trow,
  Too fierce an enemy in death have found,
Who bore off from them the young English king.
  To him the bountiful but niggards were;
  Nor deem that there has been or shall be e'er
On earth a loss so full of pain and sadness.[18]

Bloodthirsty Death, that bring'st us bitter woe!
  Well may'st thou boast, since that earth's noblest
     peer
To thy dark realm a prisoner must go;
  Nor was there anything to Virtue dear
That was not found in our young English king.
  More meet it were he lived, if God loved right,
  Than that should prosper many an evil wight,
Who to the just bring naught but pain and sadness.

If from this base world full of bitter woe
  Love do take wings, false are all earthly joys,
All turns to ill and sorrow here below,
  Worse follows bad, and once-loved pleasure cloys.

Be mirror to us each, young English king,
  Who wert in life of chivalry the Head ;
  Oh ! fair and loved one, whither hast thou fled
Why hast thou left us in our gloom and sadness

The Lord, who chose by reason of our woe,
  To live on earth and break sin's heavy chain,
And Death received to trample down our foe—
  That righteous Lord implore we that He deign
To pardon this our dear young English king ;
  As He true pardon is may Henry rest
  Among the holy numbers of the blest,
There where has never been nor will be sadness.

*WRITTEN BY BERTRAN OF BORN AFTER RECEIVING
KING HENRY'S PARDON,* 1184.*

IN making songs I little dally,[19]
  And all my toil I little heed ;
My arts and wiles I round me rally,
  These ever serve me at my need ;
    For by happy fate,
    Saved from grievous strait
    I 'fore Count and King
    All unscathed may sing.

* For original see Stimming's edition of *Bertran of Born*, page 162.

Since King and Count do grant me pardon,
   And cease against me to make war,
For evermore my heart I'll harden
   'Gainst Amblart, Tal'ran, Ademar.[20]
      Me as lord alone
      Autafort shall own,
      Fight for it who will
      I will rule it still.

Somewhat of war let there be left me,
   When naught but peace I see around;
Plague in his eyes that thus bereft me,
   E'en if first fault in me were found!
      Peace small joy doth give,
      One with strife I'll live,
      And none other law
      Will I hold in awe.

Little regard I time and season,
   Alike to me month, week, or day;
Nor March nor April give me reason,
   For seeking not to bring to bay
      Such as 'gainst me plot,
      Nor by force I wot,
      Three could from me gain
      Aught that's worth a grain.

While he who wills takes spade and harrow,
   And ploughs his land, I toil alone,

Lances and quarrels, darts and arrows,
 Hauberks, and helms, and steeds to own.
  Onset, tournament,
  Love with valour blent
  Joy in these I take,
  These all cravings slake.

My castles' co-heir, ill contented,
 My children's land has boldly claimed,
Had I in part thereto consented,
 E'en then I had been churlish named,
  Did I aught retain ;
  E'er he'll me constrain
  Ill with him 'twill fare,
  This I hereby swear.

  Solely will I reign
  Or Autafort disdain,
  To kingly judgment e'er
  Faith entire will bear.[21]

*BERTRAN TO THE LADY MAENT.**

LADY, who dost lightly prize[22]
 This true heart, that thou hast rent
 By thy doom of banishment,

* For original, see Stimming's *Bertran of Born*, page 148.

Whither shall I wander now?
  Plunged in sadness,
  Ne'er again shall I know gladness;
And, if I no lady find
Of a face that's to my mind,
  Fair as she that does forsake me,
  Ne'er to Love will I betake me.

Since, where'er I cast my eyes,
  None I see so full of grace,
  ˙ None so wise nor fair of face,
'Fore whose worth all men must bow,
  Whose excelling
  Graciousness is past all telling,
Then will I go borrowing
Of each lady some fair thing,
  Borrowed mistress thus creating,
  While her pardon I am waiting.

White and red, that nature dyes,
  Gives me Sembeline [23] perchance,
  And her gentle loving glance;
Boldness great I then avow,
  Naught omitting,
  So there lack no grace befitting,
Lady Elis [24] I beseech
For her frank and witty speech,
  If in this Dame Elis fail me,
  Little would all gifts avail me.

Chalais' Viscountess [25] so wise
 I would ask the favour rare
 Of her neck and hands most fair.;
This allowed me onward go,
 Ever speeding,
 And at Rochecouard make pleading,
Crave from Agnes [26] locks of gold,
Brighter ones e'en fair Isold, [27]
 She of loveliness so vaunted,
 Had not—this I say undaunted.

 . . . .

From Dame Faïdid [28] likewise,
 Would I have her teeth pearl-white,
 Gracious mien and welcome bright,
Which she does on all bestow;
 Further wending,
 My "Fair Mirror" [28] condescending
I do ask for joyous mind,
For her courteous ways and kind,
 Which have never any waning
 Love and honour for her gaining.

"Belz-Senher,"* full free of sighs
 Were I, if my love could be
 E'en as great for her as thee;
But within me there does grow

<hr>

* His Lady's pseudonym.

　　Longing tender,
　And to thee I'd liefer render
Service, though thou ne'er requite me
Than in others' charms delight me.
　　Lady, why no love bestowest,
　Since my faith full long thou knowest?

*SOME STANZAS OF THE POEM IN WHICH BERTRAN
JUSTIFIES HIMSELF TO LADY MAENT.*[29]

LOSE I my hawk in its first upward flight,
And falcon lannerets kill it in fierce fight,
　And bear it hence, and pluck it 'fore my eyes
If I not better love in grievous plight
To pine for thee, than on aught other wight
　To work my will, and win an easy prize.

　　·　　·　　·　　·　　·　　·　　·　　·

Be I joint-owner of a castle gay,
Wherein three other lords my will gainsay,
　And be we each with jealous hate on fire,
And ever need cross-bowmen in array,
Leeches and men-at-arms our call t'obey,
　If e'er to others' love I did aspire.

　　·　　·　　·　　·　　·　　·　　·　　·

Shield on my breast may I through tempest hie,
Bearing upon my head my helm awry,
　Holding short reins, that lengthened cannot be,

*See Stimming's *Bertran of Born*, page 155.

Feet in long stirrups, and small horse trotting high,
Then to an inn with surly host draw nigh,
   If lied not those that bore thee tales of me.

False jealous recreants, since that ye lie,
And to set strife betwixt us ever try,
   I counsel you that *now* you let me be!

*TO CONRAD OF MONTFERRAT ON HIS GALLANT
DEFENCE OF TYRE AGAINST SALADIN IN 1187.**

I WOT whose deeds[30] do mankind most amaze,
   'Mongst those that early rise fair fame to win,
It is Lord Conrad that on high we raise,
   Who yonder succours Tyre 'gainst Saladin,
All his recreant host affrighting ;
God grant him help, for other help delays,
Alone the toil is his, alone the praise.

   .   .   .   .

Conrad, two faltering kings right well I know,
   Who aid thee not, would'st thou their titles hear,
The one, King Philip, dreading sore his foe,
   Richard the last, who him doth likewise fear.
May King Saladin fast hold them !
Since that for God they will not strike a blow,
Have ta'en the Cross yet onwards will not go.

   * For original, see Stimming's *Bertran of Born*, page 133.

Alone for thee, Lord Conrad, by my troth
  I sing, of others little care I take,
Were't not to chide crusaders false to oath,
  Who thus their holy journey do forsake,
Reckless of our Lord's displeasure,
Battening on lux'ry and living lives of sloth,
While thou dost toil, lo! they to go are loth.

 . . . .

Good Papiol, speed with all thy might,
Thee to Savoy and Brindisi I send,
Then o'er the seas to royal Conrad wend;

When there let nothing thee affright;
Say that, though yet for him I've struck no blow,
If kings do not deceive right soon I'll go;

Yet truly if my Lady bid me stay,
So fair she is that I must needs obey.

[1] **Autafort.** A castle on the borders of Périgord and Limousin.
  The castle originally held by the family, was probably,
  however, Castle Born, situated a few miles from Autafort;
  its ruins are still to be seen.

[2] **The Viscount of Limoges.** Feudalism was nowhere more
  developed than in Limousin, where were many lords
  within narrow limits, and with ill-defined territories, who
  all vaguely recognized the suzerainty of the Duke of
  Aquitaine. Chief among these lords were the Counts
  of Angoulême, Marche and Périgord, and the Viscounts
  of Limoges, Turenne, Comborn and Ventadorn.

[3] **The King of Aragon.** Alphonso II., whose critical ability is well shown by the fact that he made the sweet and tender love-songs of Giraut of Borneil play the wife to the strong and essentially masculine sirventes of Bertran.

[4] **Papiol.** Bertran's jongleur.

[5] **"Rassa," "Yea and Nay," "Sailor."** The origin of these nicknames is obscure. "Rassa," the Count of Brittany, was Geoffrey, Henry the Second's third son ; "Yea and Nay" was Richard, and not Henry II. ; "Sailor" was "The Young King," Henry's eldest son, crowned during his father's lifetime in 1170.

[6] **Maent.** A corrupted form of Mathilda. She with her sisters, Maria of Ventadorn, and Elise of Montfort, to all of whom constant allusions are made in the troubadour poems, were the three most renowned beauties of Languedoc.

[7] **Guiscarda.** The beautiful and then the newly-married wife of the Viscount of Comborn. (See Bertran's charming song to her in Thomas's edition of *Bertran of Born*, page 117).

[8] **Elena.** Her real name was Mathilda ; her husband, Henry the Lion of Saxony, was for three years banished Germany by Frederick Barbarossa, during which time Mathilda (Henry being absent on a pilgrimage) lived at the Court in Normandy, under the protection of her brother Richard. The following episode must have taken place in the winter of 1182, when Richard, who was then on friendly terms with Bertran, summoned him to the Court then held at Argentan in Normandy. Before 1182 Bertran had known and loved the fair Maent, who probably remained ignorant of the tribute he paid to another. There is no reason, however, for supposing that his affection for the Norman Princess was a very strong one, or that it outlived the few months spent in her society. Love held a second place in Bertran's thoughts, and was little more than the amusement of his leisure hours.

[9] **In his host.** Probably Bertran was engaged with Richard in some military inspection of the troops.

[10] **Henry.** As a matter of fact Henry was not himself present at the siege of Autafort. It was Richard, aided by the King of Aragon, who, after a few days, succeeded in taking the castle in 1183. This year was the most eventful in Bertran's life. In it broke out a fierce war between Prince Henry and his brother Richard, Bertran espousing the cause of "The Young King," together with all the chief Aquitaine lords.

Richard their suzerain, sore-pressed, sought help from his father, who, on coming to his aid, made vain efforts to bring about a peace, as also to enter Limoges, the stronghold of the rebels. The "Young King" found himself in the possession of all the country round about this city, and at the head of a strong party, when Death cut him off in the moment of his prosperity, and in the flower of his age. A terrible blow was thus dealt Bertran, who, bereft of his friend and master, and abandoned by his confederates, fled to his castle, there to await the vengeance that he knew must overtake him. The passage that now follows in the 'Lives' is for simple grace and pathos one of the most interesting in the book.

[11] **Full wroth against him.** The chroniclers judge Alphonso more lightly than Bertran, and praise his generosity, yet the story of Artuset and of the victim of Eleanor were not mere inventions of our poet.

[12] **"The King of Aragon was come of a poor family."** The genealogy here given is false, as Monsieur Thomas points out, and Alphonso's descent is as follows : Gilbert, Lord of Carlat and Millau married Gerberge, sister of the Count of Provence, which latter dying without issue, left Provence to Douce, daughter of Gilbert and Gerberge. Douce by her marriage with Raymond Berengar, Count of Barcelona, united Barcelona and Provence ; her eldest son, father of Alphonso, had for his share the county of Barcelona, which by marriage he united to Aragon. The younger son inherited Provence, Carlat and Millau.

Finally, however, Alphonso II. succeeded his cousin in the rulership of Provence, Carlat and Millau, uniting them to Barcelona and Aragon.

[13] **Had dealt treacherously with the daughter of the Emperor Manuel.** Alphonso did, as a matter of fact, seek an alliance with Eudoxia, daughter of Manuel, the Emperor of the Eastern Empire ; but, as there was a long delay before Eudoxia appeared, Alphonso married Sancha of Castile, and Eudoxia, on arriving in his dominions, had to content herself with the hand of William of Montpellier.

[14] **The old Queen of England.** Eleanor of Aquitaine, who died at Fontevrault in 1204.

[15] **King Richard of England warred upon King Philip of France·** In all probability Bertran bore no part in the events here related.

[16] **Gaura.** In another edition this river is called the Gevra.

[17] **On the death of Prince Henry.** The rhymes of the poem are a b a b c d d e, which rhymes run throughout the whole of the original poem.

[18] **A loss so full of pain and sadness.** The "young king," bad son and bad brother as he was, possessed, as all the chroniclers agree in stating, singular charms of mind and person, and also a singular power of winning men's hearts.

[19] **In making songs I little dally.** The rhymes of the poem of six and a half stanzas are a b a b c c d d, and these are continued throughout the poem.

[20] **Amblart, Talaran, Ademar.** The barons who had played him false.

[21] **Faith entire will bear.** This poem, with its tone of dogged defiance and fierce joy in strife, is one of the most characteristic that we have of Bertran. There is, however, a still more famous war-song, the most powerful, indeed, in Provençal literature, but which I have not here translated, because, though commonly ascribed to Bertran, its authorship is somewhat uncertain. In it the author sings his joy when, on the approach of spring, the barons come

sallying forth to war upon each other ; when all but cowards give and take many a hard blow ; when heads and arms are hewn from their trunks, and great and small lie together on the grass ; when the brain is on fire at the war-shouts of "Aidatz, aidatz, a lor !" and at the shrill neighs of the riderless horses rushing madly through the field, etc.

[22] **Lady, who dost lightly prize.** The original poem is composed of seven stanzas and an *envoi* of four lines ; its rhymes, running throughout the poem, are a b b c d d e e f f. Bertran's love songs have not, as M. Thomas remarks, the depth and sincerity that characterize those of Bernard of Ventadorn or Giraut of Borneil. A few of them are inferior to none, however, in originality and charm, and of such the poem here translated affords a good example.

[23] **Sembeline.** The pseudonym of some unknown lady of Limousin.

[24] **Elis,** or "Alice" of Montfort, sister of Maent.

[25] **Chalais' Viscountess.** Tibors of Montausier.

[26] **Agnes.** Beyond this mention of her name nothing is known of her.

[27] **Isold.** The golden locks of Isold, Tristram's Lady, are often alluded to by the troubadours.

[28] **"Faidida" and "Fair Mirror."** Both of them are unknown ladies.

[29] **Stanzas to Maent.** The original poem is composed of seven stanzas and a half ; its rhymes which run throughout it are a a b a a b. In this poem Bertran, in the most emphatic and original fashion, justifies himself to Maent, who believed that Bertran had abandoned her for the fair young bride, Lady Guiscarda.

[30] **I wot whose deeds.** The original is composed of six stanzas, having all of them the rhymes a b a b c a a, and an *envoi* of three half stanzas with the rhymes c a a—c a a—a a.

This poem, the only Crusading song of Bertran's that we possess, was called forth by the stirring events of 1187.

It was then that the report reached Europe of Saladin's victory over the King of Jerusalem, and triumphant entry into the Holy City. All Christendom answered to the Church's call to a new Crusade, and Richard and Philip Augustus, forgetting awhile their jealousies, swore to fight in defence of the Cross. While, however, the two kings lingered on at home, each fearing to leave the other behind him, Conrad, son of the Marquis of Montferrat, entered Tyre, roused the sinking courage of its inhabitants, and compelled Saladin to retire from before it. This brilliant feat excited universal admiration, and Bertran amongst others sang Conrad's prowess. The ending of the song is graceful, but naïvely unheroic, one, in fact, in which speaks the true troubadour. No lady of Bertran's at that time existed to withhold him from the Crusade, in which, as one could easily foresee, he bore no part.

FOLQUET OF MARSEILLES.

Flourished from 1180. Died 1231.

FOLQUET, who, according to Dante, was born in Marseilles, and according to Petrarch, in Genoa, won the favour of some of the chief princes of the age—Richard of England, Raymond V. of Toulouse, Barral of Marseilles, and others. It is to Barral's wife Adelaide (Azalais) that most of his canzones are addressed, and he seems to have served her more or less steadily till the outbreak of the war against the Arabs in 1195. From that time onwards the fanatic absorbs the poet, and it is hard to recognize the Folquet of younger days in the ecclesiastic who so fiercely persecuted the Albigensian heretics, helped to establish the Inquisition in Languedoc, and heaped insults on Raymond VI. of Toulouse, the son of his former friend and patron. He is placed by Dante, however, in Paradise (*Paradiso*, Canto IX.), where he tells the Italian poet his name and birthplace.

Folquet has left us some twenty-five poems, all of which (with the exception of one written in the cloister) were composed in the early part of his life. His canzones have the love-sick despair common in troubadours. They are always graceful and harmonious, but by no means free from the metaphysical subtleties and affectations that mark the decadence of Provençal poetry. One of his finest is his 'Complaint' on the death of his master, Barral of Marseilles, two or three stanzas of which are translated below.

FOLQUET OF MARSEILLES.*

Now Folquet of Marseilles was the son of a merchant of Genoa, Master Alphonso by name, who, dying, left him passing rich. And he strove after fame and excellence, and entered the service of honourable men, having intercourse with them, and going to and fro to pleasure them; and he was held in great esteem by King Richard, and by the good Count Raymond of Toulouse, and by Lord Barral of Marseilles,[1] his liege lord. And a right good poet was he, and, withal, right goodly to look upon. Now he loved the wife of Lord Barral, his lord, and sought her love and made his songs of her, yet never by his own worth nor by his songs could he find such favour in her sight as that she made him her lover, where-

* See Mahn, xxviii.

fore he was wont to make complaint of love in his songs.

Now when the good King Alphonso of Castile had been discomfited by the King of Morocco, Miramamoli[2] by name, and had been reft by him of Calatrava, and of Salvaterra, and of the Castle of Toninas, behold! there was made great mourning and lamentation throughout all Spain, and amongst all such as heard thereof, because of the dishonour done to Christendom, and because of the harm that had come unto the good King in the discomfiture of his army, and in the loss of his lands. And full oft did the men of Miramamoli enter into the realm of King Alphonso, working therein great evil; so the good King Alphonso sent his messengers to the Pope, praying him to summon to his aid the barons of France, and of England, the King of Aragon, and the Count of Toulouse. Now Lord Folquet of Marseilles was greatly affectionate to the King of Castile, and had not yet entered into the Cistercian Order, so he made an exhortation to the barons, and to all the good people, urging them to succour the good King of Castile, showing them the honour that this succour would be to them, and the pardon it would bring them of God. And the exhortation begins thus:

> "Hueimais no i conosc razo."
> (Henceforth I know not a reason, etc.)

Now Folquet of Marseilles, even as you have heard, loved the wife of his lord, Barral, my Lady Azalais of Rocamartina, and sang of her, and made his canzones of her, but took heed that the matter was not noised abroad, forasmuch as she was his lord's wife, and that it would have been held for great baseness in him. And his lady suffered his prayers and his songs for the great praise he made of her. Now Lord Barral had two sisters of great beauty and excellence, and of these the one was named the Lady Laura of San Jorlan, and the other the Lady Mabilia of Ponteves. These both dwelt with Lord Barral, and Sir Folquet had such great liking for them that men might well ween he sought their love. Now my Lady Azalais deemed that he loved my Lady Laura, so she accused him thereof, and made many others to accuse him, till she no longer wished for his prayers and his talk, and sent him from her service, bidding him henceforth hope no further favour from her, and bidding him likewise separate himself from the Lady Laura. Then Folquet, after that his lady had sent him from her, was full sad and sorrowful, and forsook all singing, and laughter, and merriment, and long-time dwelt in great sorrow and heaviness, bewailing the mischance that had befallen him in the loss of his lady, whom he loved better than all things else, and this through one whom he nowise regarded but by courtesy. And after sorrowing in this fashion he went forth to see the Empress, the head and chief of all excellence, and of all courtesy, and of all knowledge, the which lady was wife of Lord William of Montpellier, and daughter of the Emperor Manuel.[3] And he made lamentation to her of the mischance that had befallen him, and she comforted him as best she might, and besought him not to grieve nor to despair, but for love of her to sing and to make canzones. Wherefore he, for the prayers of the Empress, made this song which runs:

"Tan mou de corteza razo."
(It (the song) arises from such a courteous motive.)

And it came to pass that my Lady Azalais died, and Lord Barral, her husband and his lord, died, and likewise died the good King Richard, and the good Count Raymond of Toulouse, and the King Alphonso of Aragon, wherefore Folquet, from sorrow for his lady, and for the Princes that were dead, forsook the world, and entered the Cistercian Order with his wife and with his two sons. And he was made Abbot of a noble Abbey in Provence called Torondet, and thereafter was made Bishop of Toulouse, where he died.

ON THE DEATH OF BARRAL OF MARSEILLES. 1192.*

E'EN as when some grievous blow [4]
   Deadeneth the heart and brain,
   And unfelt are grief and pain,
Stunned am I by bitter woe—
For my loss surpassing great
   Nowise can my heart conceive,
   None its bitterness believe
Till they meet like piteous fate.
   For Barral by cruel death is slain,
   And I to weep or laugh am fain,
Since reft of reason is my state.

Am I bound by wizard's spell,
   That all sense from me hath fled?
   No, 'tis that my lord is dead,
He that prized us passing well.
Even as the loadstone bright,
   Draweth upward iron and steel,
   So did Barral ever deal
Unto many a lowly wight;
   And he that spoiled us of the head
   Of joy, and fame to virtue wed,
Regardeth not our hapless plight.

.   .   .   .

* See Mahn's *Gedichte der Troubadours*, Vol. IV., page 136.

Needs must I resemble thee
· To the flowers, whose fate thou sharest,
That when sweetest are and fairest,
Soonest fade and cease to be ;
Then because our Lord hath died,
Let us lift to God our eyes,
And the wretched world despise,
Where as pilgrims we abide :
For fame and wisdom of the rarest
Thou God all-righteous no-wise sparest
Of those that scorn Thee in their pride.

.   .   .   .

[1] **Barral of Marseilles.** Barral of Baux, Viscount of Marseilles and Adelaide (Azalais) his wife, have already played a prominent part in the life of Peire Vidal, the first, as his generous protector, the second, as his angry lady. This Adelaide is hardly mentioned by history; in all probability she was Barral's first wife, whom he put away from him, shortly before his death, to marry a daughter of the house of Montpellier.

[2] **Miramamoli by name.** The name of the Arabian despot was Jacob Almansor, and he bore the title of Miramolin. In 1195 he had gained the important battle of Alarcos over the Christians, and followed up his victory by seizing Calatrava and other strong places.

[3] **Daughter of the Emperor Manuel.** This lady was Eudoxia, daughter of Manuel Comnenus ; betrothed to Alphonso II. of Aragon, she had on reaching Spain found him already married to Sancha of Castile. Thereupon Eudoxia retired to Montpellier, to await her father's orders, but on tidings of his death reaching her, she accepted the hand of the

Count of Montpellier (in 1181). The marriage was an
unhappy one and some years after it Eudoxia, put away
by her husband, entered a convent, where she died.
4 **E'en as when some grievous blow.** This 'complaint' is
composed of six stanzas of eleven lines, and two final
stanzas of three and four lines respectively. The rhymes
of the six first stanzas are : a b b a c d d c b b c; of the
seventh stanza : c d d, and of the eighth : c b b c.

PONS OF CAPDUOIL.
1170 or 1180-1190.

HANDSOME, noble, gay, courteous, and refined, Pons was, in
many respects, the ideal Court troubadour, and he and his
poems seem to have been deservedly popular. Most of these
latter are those of a polished man of the world, the majority
of them canzones of remarkable beauty and refinement of
form, but of little depth and originality. His three finest
poems owed their origin to some deeply-felt sorrow (undoubtedly the loss of Azalais), a sorrow, indeed, that entirely changed
the current of his thoughts. The poet of the canzones is one
who skimmed lightly over the surface of life, and never lost
his tone of airy grace and ease, while that of the beautiful
lament over Azalais, and of the spiritual Crusading songs, is
a man who has felt passionate grief, and whose only con-
solations are those of religion. There is no doubt that he
kept the resolution announced in the 'Complaint,' and forsook
love at the death of his lady, dying, indeed, not long afterwards in the Holy Land.

The poem, of which I have attempted a translation, is
amongst the best that Provence has given us. The love that
inspires it is a delicate and ethereal sentiment, and the poet's
tone of absolute humility and holy awe towards his lady is
akin to that of Dante towards Beatrice.

*OF PONS OF CAPDUOIL.**

Now Pons of Capduoil was a noble baron of the diocese of Puy Ste. Marie,[1] who made poetry and sang and violed full well. And he was valiant in battle, and learned, and courteous, and chivalrous, and fair-spoken, and of great stature and comeliness. And therewithal he was right niggardly, yet this he hid by fair demeanour and deeds of courtesy. And he loved my Lady Azalais of Mercuer, wife of Lord Ozil of Mercuer (a great Count of Auvergne), and daughter of Lord Bernart of Andusa, an honourable baron of the March of Provence. Much did he love and praise her, and many a fair song did he make of her, and loved none other while she lived ; and when she was dead he took the Cross and passed over into Syria, and there died.[2]

Now Pons of Capduoil loved that lady, even as ye have heard, and was also loved by her ; and all good people took pleasure in their love,[3] and many fair feasts, and jousts, and merry-makings were held because of it, and many a fair song was made on it. Then he, dwelling with her in such great joy and gladness, was minded to make trial of her love, like a foolish lover who neither knows great blessedness nor can bear it. For he would not believe in his own

* See Mahn, xxx.

eyes, nor in the gracious favours and honours she heaped upon him by word and deed; so he resolved within his foolish heart to make believe he loved my Lady Audiart, wife of the Lord of Marseilles, thinking that, if it grieved his lady that he held aloof from her, he might know she loved him, and if it pleased her, then his comfort would be that she had no whit loved him. He then, as a fool who does not cease from folly till evil comes of it, began to hold aloof from Lady Azalais, and to draw near and to speak well of Lady Audiart. And he said of her: "No uelh aver lemperi dalamanha, Si Naudiartz no uezian miei uelh." (I would not the Empire of Germany, if my eyes looked not on Lady Audiart.)

The Lady Azalais seeing that Pons of Capduoil, whom she had loved and honoured so greatly, had withdrawn himself from her, and drawn nearer to Lady Audiart, held him in such high disdain that she never spoke or made inquiry of him to any wight soever. And if one spoke to her of him, she would answer nothing, and went on living long in right courteous fashion, and held high court and festivals. Now during this while Pons of Capduoil went wandering through Provence, fleeing from the love of the Lady Azalais; howbeit, when he saw that she showed no sorrow thereat, and sent him neither message nor letter, he fell to thinking that he had done amiss, and turned his steps towards his own country, and desisted from this foolish trial of her love. Then grief and heaviness came upon him, and he sent humble letters and poems unto her, in the which he besought her to suffer him to appear before her, that he might plead his cause and obtain mercy of her, saying also that she should avenge herself on him, if he had in aught sinned against her. But the lady would neither listen to his prayers for mercy nor to his defence of himself wherefore he made this song of her which runs: "Aissi com cel qua pro de ualedors." (Even as one that hath many a protector.) But the song availed him nothing, so he made this other: "Qui per nesci cuidar, fai trop gran fallimen." (He who by folly doth full great ill.) This likewise did not so avail him, as that the Lady Azalais would restore her favour unto him, or would believe that he had but separated himself from her to prove whether she would be glad thereat or no; wherefore he went to my Lady Maria of Ventadorn, and the Countess of Montferrand, and to the Viscountess of Aubusson. And he brought them unto Mercuer to my Lady Azalais to ask her pardon, deeming that she would look favourably on him for the prayers of the ladies. Then Lady Azalais, for the prayers of the ladies, restored him to her favour, whereat no man in all the world was so happy as Pons of Capduoil, who said that never more would he dissemble to try his lady's love.

AMONGST all hapless mortals I am he,
　Most deeply sunk in bitter endless pain;
　Ah! sweet were Death to me, and I were fain
Cut short these days of endless misery!
　For from my life all happiness has fled,
　Since that my Lady Azalais is dead;
Borne down am I with weeping and with woe—
　Thou traitor Death! Full truly can I say,
　A better lady thou couldst never slay.

How from my grief should I uplifted be,
　If God had will'd that *me* Death first had slain!
　Ah woe is me! But now, not long in pain
Shall I outlive my love—I crave from thee,
　O Jesus, mighty One, of Truth the Head—
　Her pardon, Lord, her soul unblemishèd
Give Thou unto St. Peter and St. John;
　For therein heavenly grace does ever stay,
　Guileless it is, and this can none gainsay.

For her should all men weep right bitterly,
　For goodlier lady earth did ne'er contain;
　Like gracious bearing ne'er will be again,

* See *Chrestomathie provençale*, page 123.

And now what worth in beauty do we see?
  What worth in wit, and wisdom, fame far spread,
  Frank speech, kind greeting, courtesy high-bred?
Of what avail the fairest things on earth?
  Thou, wretched World, no more o'er me hast
    sway,
  Most vile thou art, since she has gone her way.

Now know we angels pure on high with glee
  Do welcome her, who from our midst is ta'en;
  For oft I hear, and oft wise books maintain,
"Who praised of men is, praised of God will be."
  Then well I know to Heaven's high hall she's
    sped,
  There roses and fair lilies crown her head,
And there glad choirs of angels sing her praise.
  Rightly to her, who ne'er from Truth did stray,
  In Paradise all creatures homage pay.

Oh! Lady Adelaide, since thou art dead,
All gladness from my life is vanished;
  Henceforth I bid a sad farewell to song.
And many a groan, a tear, a well-a-day,
My bitter anguish nowise do allay.

Friend Andrew, all my wishes flee away,
Now nevermore Love's call will I obey.

[1] **Puy Ste. Marie.**   Here was held a great annual festival, to which flocked all the chivalry of Languedoc.   Tournaments and contests in poetry were the chief amusements, and one of the four judges who awarded the prize for poetry was the Monk of Montaldon.   (See his life.)

[2] **And there died.**   From here begins the traditional part of the story.

[3] **And all good people took pleasure in their love.**   The love of Pons for Azalais, with its delicate moderation and immaterialism, was entirely in accordance with the laws of chivalry, and as such was generally known and approved of.   As there was no law in Provence excluding women from the possession of land, marriage there, specially, was a thoroughly business-like arrangement.   Pretexts also were readily found for repudiating a wife if a richer heiress presented herself, and love and marriage were for these reasons universally regarded as incompatible.   Love, apart from marriage, provided it remained Platonic, was, therefore, generally recognized and sanctioned.

[4] **On the death of Azalais.**   The rhymes of the original, running throughout the poem, are a b b a c c d e e; in the last stanza the first four lines are omitted.   In the *envoi* the poet addresses a friend of the name of Andrew.   Of this friend, mentioned in several of Pons of Capduoil's poems, we have no information.

RAEMBAUT OF VAQUEIRAS.

1180-1207.

OF Raembaut of Vaqueiras, one of the most distinguished of Provençal poets, we have no lack of details, for apart from the biographies, Raembaut himself, in his poems and letters, dwells with great fulness on his own life and thoughts.

The connection, alluded to in the biography, between him and William of Baux, Prince of Orange, seems to have been a very friendly one, until a dispute arose between them, caused by Raembaut's mocking William, who was attacked by fishermen, while sailing down the Rhone. Soon after this, Raembaut, though on fairly friendly terms with the Prince, left his court, and at the end of various wanderings came to that of the Marquis of Montferrat. Here, as we learn from his canzones, he loved a lady, wooed by the dissolute and turbulent Albert of Malaspina. This latter won the lady's good graces, and gave vent to his triumph in a mocking sirvente directed against Raembaut who, however, as is shown by the poem translated below, bore his defeat with sufficient independence. It was probably shortly after this episode that his connection with Beatrice began, a romantic account of which is given in the biography. His amour was put an end to by Raembaut's starting on the Crusade of 1202, and in this year, indeed, occurred Beatrice's death, which Raembaut celebrated in the 'complaint' translated below. When the poet himself died cannot be said. There is no mention of him after the death of his patron the Marquis, who was slain in a skirmish against the Bulgarians. Possibly therefore Raembaut fell fighting by his side.

Raembaut has written poems on matters relating to his patron—William of Baux; poems in honour of his first love —the Lady of Tortona, of his " Fair Knight " (Beatrice), and of the Marquis of Montferrat ; poems on the fourth Crusade, and lastly, some few poems in the form of letters. The sweetness and artistic finish of his canzones to Beatrice, make them pre-eminent amongst his works, and of these the most remarkable is the famous 'Carrussel,' three verses of which are given below. No more graceful compliment could be paid to his lady than thus representing her as having robbed other ladies of their youth, beauty, and all noble virtues, and as repulsing single-handed her assembled foes. The splendour, originality, and elaborate metre of this poem, place it, indeed, amongst the finest ornaments of Provençal literature. As for his verses on the Crusades—in them, as in those of other troubadours—the elements of chivalry and worldly glory are curiously mingled with religious zeal. In one of them he begins by exulting in his Marquis being leader of the French and Champanois; then after invoking all Christendom to the Crusade: "Rather," he says, "would I die yonder than live here, even were all Christendom mine; yet, noble Knight (Beatrice) for whom I make my song, I know not if for you I will renounce the Cross or take it up. I know not how to go nor how to stay for, such joy your beauty gives me, that when I see you I am like to die, and when I may not see you, I think to die in others' company."

His letters throw great light upon the man himself and the times in which he lived, and exhibit remarkable dexterity and boldness in the soliciting of rewards: "Noble Marquis, lord of Montferrat," runs one, "I thank God that He has brought you to great honour, for more · than any crowned head in Christendom have ye spent and conquered. I praise God for having advanced me also—a kind lord have I found in you—ye have nourished and equipped me, and made me from nothing into an honourable knight, so that courtiers smile on me, and women praise me. Moreover, I have served you ever with a right good will, and have dedicated to you all my powers, and have done in your company many a courtly deed; have wooed in many a fair place, and with arms in my hand both lost and won. I have ridden with you through all Greece, have given and taken many a hard blow, have fallen and made others to fall, have fled and pursued with you, have fought on water and on bridges, . . . have broken through serried ranks, and helped you to take prisoners . . . kings and princes. . . . With you I have pursued the Emperor from Roumania to Philopas, him that ye dethroned to crown another; and, if through you I become not rich, it will no longer seem to men that I have fought and served you as I have here shown—ye know that I speak but true, noble Marquis."

There is further a curious fragment from one of Raembaut's letters to Boniface, translated by Roscoe,* which I insert here, as being a good illustration of the chivalrous adventures of the age:

"Do you remember the jongleur Aimonet, who brought you news of Jacobina, when she was on the point of being carried into Sardinia, and married to a man she disliked? Do you also remember how, on bidding you farewell, she threw herself into your arms, and besought you, in such moving terms to protect her against the injustice of her uncle? You immediately ordered five of your bravest esquires to mount. We rode all night, after supper. With my own hand I bore her from the domain, amidst an universal outcry. They pursued us horse and foot; we fled, at full speed; and we already thought ourselves out of danger, when we were attacked by the knights of Pisa. With so many cavaliers pressing close upon us, so many shields glittering around us, and so many banners waving in the wind, you need not ask us whether we were afraid. We concealed ourselves between Albenga and Final, and, from the place of our retreat, we heard on all sides the sound of horn and clarion, and the signal-cries of pursuit. Two days we remained without meat or drink, and when, on the third day, we recommenced our journey, we encountered twelve banditti, and we knew not how to conduct ourselves; for to attack them on horseback was impossible. I dismounted, and advanced against them on foot. I was wounded by a lance; but I disabled three or four of my opponents, and put the rest to flight. My companions then came to my assistance; we drove the robbers from the defile, and you passed in safety. You, no doubt, recollect how merrily we dined together, although we had only a single loaf to eat and nothing to drink. In the

* See Roscoe's translation of Sismondi's *Literature of the South of Europe.*

evening we arrived at Nice, and were received by our friend
Piuclair with transports of joy.

"The next day you gave Jacobina in marriage to Anselmo,
and recovered for him his county of Vintimiglia, in spite of
his uncle, who endeavoured to despoil him of it."

RAEMBAUT OF VAQUEIRAS.*

RAEMBAUT[1] of Vaqueiras was the son of a poor
knight of Provence, of the Castle of Vaquieras,
one named Peirors, who passed for mad. And
Raembaut became a jongleur, and abode full long
with the Prince of Orange, William of Baux. Well
did he know to sing and to make coblas and
sirventes; and the Prince of Orange did him great
good, and great honour, and advanced him, and
made him to be known and prized of all good
folk. And afterwards, Raembaut departed from him,
and gat him to Montferrat—to the court of my
Lord the Marquis Boniface,[2] and therein dwelt full
long, growing in wisdom, in knowledge, and in
prowess. And he became enamoured of the sister
of the Marquis, the which hight my Lady Beatrice,
wife of Lord Henry of Carret, and he made of
her many fair songs, calling her therein, "Fair
Knight,"[3] and men weened she loved him well. Now
well have ye heard who was Raembaut of Vaqueiras,
and how he came to honour, and by whom; but

* See Mahn, xxxii.

now I will tell you how that when the Marquis
had dubbed him knight, Raembaut became enamoured of my Lady Beatrice, sister of the Marquis
and my Lady Azalais of Salutz. Greatly did he
love her and desire her, having care that none
should know of it, and much did he spread abroad
her fame, and many a friend did he win for her.
And she was wont to bear herself full graciously
towards him, yet he the while was dying for desire
and fearfulness, for he durst neither beseech her for
her love nor show that he strove thereafter, until, as
one sore pressed, he told her that he loved a lady
of great excellence, yet durst not make known the
goodwill and love that he bore her nor seek for
hers in exchange, in such fear was he of her great
excellence; and he besought her for God's sake
to tell him whether she held it meet, that he should
speak his mind, or should die loving the lady thus
privily. Then that noble lady—my Lady Beatrice—
when she heard this and knew the goodwill that
he bore her, having also ere now full well perceived
that he was, from great yearning for her, nigh unto
death, was moved by love and pity, and spake
and said : " Raembaut, full meet it is that the true
lover of a gentle lady should fear to show his
love, but or ever he die, I read him to tell it to
her, and pray her to take him for servant and for
lover ; and I will warrant, that if she be wise and

courteous she will in nowise hold it for an ill and shameful thing in him; rather will she prize him the more, and hold him the better man for it. Likewise I read you to speak your mind and will to her you love, and to bid her take you for her knight, since you are such as no lady in the world should scorn for knight and servant; for my Lady Azalais, Countess of Saluza, suffered Peire Vidal, and the Countess of Burlatz, Arnaut de Marvoil, and my Lady Maria, Gaucelm Faidit, and the Lady of Marseilles, Folquet; wherefore I give you counsel and license that you, by my word and surety, may beseech her for her love." Then Raembaut, hearing the counsel and assurance that she gave, and the license, that she promised him, told her that *she* was verily the lady that he so much loved, even she of whom he had sought counsel; whereat my Lady Beatrice told him that he was come in a happy hour, and that if he strove after worth, and after the doing and speaking of good things, she would indeed choose him for knight and servant. So Raembaut strove to his uttermost to increase her fame, and it was then that he made the canzone which says:

> "Eram requier sa costum eson us."
> (Now demand of me her bearing and demeanour.)

After this it befell that the Marquis, with his host,

passed over into Romania,[4] and with great help from the Church conquered the kingdom of Salonica, and then it was that Raembaut, for his valorous deeds, was made knight; and there the Marquis gave him rich lands and revenues, and there also did he die.

.   .   .   .

A POEM PROBABLY RELATING TO RAEMBAUT'S UN-FORTUNATE LOVE FOR A LADY, WHO FORSOOK HIM FOR ALBERT MALASPINA.

IN fierce unrest[5] to race and ride,
    To watch, to labour and to grieve,
    'Tis well! for these all joy I leave,
And calmly heat or frost abide.
    In iron and steel arrayed will pass my days,
    And dwell in tangled groves and bosky ways;
Sirventes and Descortz[6] shall be my song,
And still the weak I'll aid against the strong.

What though my Lady's scorn and pride
    Should my fond heart full long deceive,
    Deem not the less to fame I cleave,
Or sing the less whate'er betide;
    Nor deem I shun the deeds that win me praise,
    For virtue's call the good knight e'er obeys;
Nor will I die that death of shame and wrong
I feared when in the pass,[7] time was not long.

* For original, see Mahn's *Gedichte der Troubadours*, Vol. II., page 166.

THE "CARUSSEL" (WAR CHARIOT). [*]

FIERCE to battle sally [8]
  The dames of all the land,
Round their leaders rally,
  And like the churls make stand;
In the pass or valley
  To build a town they plann'd,
And tower;
Yet, such the fair foe's power,
She doth no wise dally
  To bring to shame the band.
The flower
Of beauty for her dower
Hath Beatrice, 'gainst whom their flag unfurling,
And at her worth full many a foul threat hurling,
They war, while smoke and dust are round them
  whirling.

And the town united
  Dig moats, and ramparts raise;
Dames, all uninvited,
  Pour in through many ways,
Though thereby be slighted
  Their beauty, youth, and praise.
I ween,
To fighting will be seen,

* For original, see *Chrestomathie provençale,* page 128.

Beatrice incited,
　　Whose virtues all amaze;
Who queen
Of beauty e'er hath been,
And, for her worth all other worth excelleth,
E'en as her sire his enemies repelleth,
So she short time, I ween, all unresisting dwelleth.

. . . .

Fast Beatrice fareth,
　　Her goodly virtues dight,
Armour none she weareth
　　Strong goeth to the fight;
Those 'gainst whom she beareth
　　Are in an evil plight;
Small fear
Hath she of far or near,
And the few she spareth
　　Betake them soon to flight,
Severe,
She hath reft them of their gear,
Their chariot of war asunder riven,
And to the commons such defeat hath given,
That they full helpless back to Troy are driven.

ON THE DEATH OF BEATRICE.

(Composed while taking part under the Marquis of Montferrat in the
Conquest of the Eastern Empire.)

NOR Spring nor[9] Winter gives me joy,
  Nor groves of oak, nor days serene,
  Prosperity is grievous teen,
My greatest pleasures breed annoy;
  My solace now is weary Care,
  My Hopes are turned into Despair;
Yet once Love filled my every wish,
Quickening me more than water fish.
  Alas! that ere from Love I went,
  For bitter is my banishment!
Like death me seems all other life,
All other comfort—toil and strife.

 . . . .

Brave warriors, the army's flower,
  Strong battering-rams and sieges bold,
  The fall of ramparts new and old,
The battle won, the scalèd tower—
  Such sights and sounds are mine, but these
  To love-sick hearts bring little ease;
Though where the fight does fiercest rage
Stern war against the foe I wage,
  And win me many a goodly prize,
  Since love has vanished from my eyes,

* See Mahn's *Gedichte der Troubadours*, Vol. IV., page 193.

This fair world seems but desolate,
And song can ne'er my grief abate.

Riches full ill my pains requite,
　Methinks more riches I did gain
　When o'er my heart Love held his reign,
And gave me rapturous delight;
　More precious far such happiness
　Than here great wealth and power possess.
Ever the more my power does grow,
The more of sorrow I do know,
　For from my life all joy has flown,
　Since my Fair Knight has left me lone,
And nought can bring to me relief,
For aye the fiercer grows my grief.[9]

.　　.　　.　　.　　.　　.　　.　　.

[1] **Raembaut.** The chief poet of Provence proper. Vaqueiras was in the neighbourhood of Orange.

[2] **Boniface.** The Second of that name. He became Marquis and King of Jerusalem in 1192 at the death of his father, the famous Conrad of Montferrat, who was murdered on the same day that he was proclaimed King of Jerusalem.

[3] **Fair Knight.** Beatrice, as the story goes, received this name in the following manner: One day her brother, the Marquis, after visiting her, left his sword behind him in her bower. Thereupon Beatrice, throwing aside her upper garment, took the sword from its scabbard and tossed it in the air, deftly catching it in its fall, and trying to wield it in knightly fashion. All this the poet saw through a cleft of the door, and hence arose the name.

[4] **Romania.** Jerusalem, having remained in the hands of the Turks ever since it had been taken by Saladin, a new Crusade was in 1198 preached by Pope Innocent III. Thibaut IV. of Champagne was chosen as leader of the Christian Army, but as his death followed shortly after the election, Boniface took his place. In 1202, therefore, Raembaut unwillingly made ready to follow his master to the Holy Land. As is well known, the conquest of the Greek Empire, and the establishment there of a Latin dynasty diverted the Crusaders from their original design of marching on Jerusalem. Baldwin of Flanders became Emperor of the great Eastern Empire, while Boniface obtained the Kingdom of Thessalonica.

[5] **In fierce unrest.** The original poem is composed of five and a half stanzas of eight lines, the rhyming system being, a b b a c c d d. The same lines are carried throughout the poem.

[6] **Descortz.** The descort was a poem made up of stanzas of varied metres and rhymes; it was used to express the want of harmony in the poet's mind when his love was unreturned.

[7] **I feared when in the Pass.** An allusion to the adventure related in the letter above where the poet and his friends hid from their foes' pursuit.

[8] **Fierce to battle sally.** Whether Raembaut conceived the idea of this poem himself, or whether it was suggested to him by some mock contest of ladies that actually took place, is uncertain.

The canzone is of unusual length being composed of nine stanzas of fifteen lines of varied length. The rhyming system is: a b a b a b c c a b c c d d d.

[9] **Nor Spring nor Winter.** The original poem is composed of six stanzas of twelve lines. The rhymes are: a b b a c c d d e e f f, and these are unchanged throughout the poem.

PEIROL.

1180-1225.

PEIROL'S love for Saill plays an important part in this biography, and, though her name hardly appears in any of his canzones, a large proportion of them are doubtless in her honour. Their love seems for some time to have kept within the bounds laid down by mediaeval chivalry. These, however, having been finally overstepped, the Dauphin, Saill's brother, interfered and brought about the poet's banishment. After this time we hear little further concerning him, though a farewell canzone to Saill exists, in which Peirol speaks of having chosen another lady. Probably things went ill with him, for the Monk of Montaldon makes a mocking mention of him, for having during thirty years worn the same garment. The biography alludes to his marriage at Montpellier, and his poems prove him to have passed some time at Montferrat. During the period of his connection with Saill the third Crusade was set on foot. The Dauphin bore no part in it, though possibly Peirol did, for in a later poem he congratulates himself on having seen the Holy Sepulchre.

About thirty of his canzones are preserved to us, together with his share in a few tenzons. His love-poems are full of tenderness and grace, with the alternations of despair and hope, and the tone of absolute subjection to love, characteristic of troubadours. "My lady slays me," he cries, "for such misdoing as would be little to her credit, if I dared to say it —she does the sin, and I the penance thereof." . . . "What shall I do then?" (he cries, speaking of the hopelessness of his love,) "I will depart from this folly—and yet not I—for I shall even bring thereby ruin upon myself, as he that has fallen to gambling, and that loses and loses in the hope to win. . . . Right high was I that now am fallen so low, for it has chanced with me, as with one that dreams of joy, and waking finds nothing. Where can I find truth? In nought that has a fair semblance, since in her I find deceit." . . . "In great heaviness am I day and night, and small is my comfort, yet, if so it might be, full fain were I to steal of her a kiss, and if she were angry thereat, how gladly would I give it her again."

In Peirol's "Contention with Love" (the poem translated) one sees in a quaintly graceful and original fashion the struggle between Love and Religion, that is so marked a feature of Provençal Crusading songs; and at the end of it is a bold satire on Richard of England and Philip of France, two of the most powerful sovereigns of the age.

PEIROL.*

NOW Peirol was a poor knight of Auvergne, of a castle named Peirol, the which lies in the Dauphin's land, at the foot of Roquefort. And he was a man right courteous and goodly; and the Dauphin of Auvergne arrayed him, and retained him in his service.

Now the Dauphin of Auvergne had a sister, wife of a great baron of Auvergne, Lord Beraut[1] of Mercuer, and she was named Saill[2] of Claustra, and was fair, and good, and far renowned. And Sir Peirol became enamoured of her, and the Dauphin interceded with her for Peirol, and delighted greatly in the canzones that Sir Peirol made of his sister, and greatly also did they pleasure the lady, insomuch that she loved him, and granted him his desires to the knowledge of the Dauphin. Nathless

*See Mahn, xxxiii.

the love of Sir Peirol and the lady was brought to such a pass that the Dauphin waxed jealous thereof, for he weened she gave him more than beseemed her, so he dismissed Sir Peirol and bade him go thence, and gave him neither raiment nor arms. Then Peirol could no longer maintain himself as knight, and so became a jongleur, and passed from court to court, receiving of the barons raiment and money and horses; and at Montpellier he got him a wife, and there brought his days to an end.

*PEIROL'S TENZON WITH LOVE.**

WHEN from weary sorrow free [3]
    Love did once my heart discern,
He to tenzon challenged me,
    Even as ye now shall learn.
"Peirol, ill it is to turn
Thus thy face from me so long,
Prithee, tell me, since from Song
And from me thou dost refrain,
How dost Honour hope to gain?"

"Love, that I have long obeyed,
    Thou dost little heed my woe,
And full long hast thou delayed,
    Promised pleasure to bestow;
See, no wrath thereat I show,

* See Mahn's *Gedichte der Troubadours*, Vol. IV., page 123.

Only this I ask of thee,
Unmolested let me be ;
Henceforth nothing else I crave,
Better gift I might not have."

" Peirol, dost thou then forget
  That fair lady, that erewhile
Thee with gracious welcome met ?
  I it was that bade her smile,
  And by many a cunning wile
Thou did'st hide thy wayward mind,
So I held thee true and kind ;
But thine am'rous songs and mien
Were but to deceive I ween."

" Love, when first she met my eyes,
  I did love my lady well,
Loved e'er since—such sweet surprise,
  Such sweet rapture o'er me fell ;
  Now I needs must break the spell,
And like me, howe'er they grieve,
Many knights their dames must leave,
These if Saladin were slain
Here in gladness would remain."

" Peirol, how so great the power
  Wherewith 'gainst the Turks ye start,
They'll not give you David's tower,
  Choose *thou* [4] then the wiser part,
  Sing and love with all thy heart.

Wilt thou go if kings delay ?
See, they think but of the fray ;
Do but mark the barons' strife,
'Tis on such they spend their life."

"Love, full long I've sin defied,
    Now I must 'gainst sin contend—
May sweet Jesus be my guide,
    And His peace amongst us send,
    That the kings' fierce strife may end !
They their succour still withhold,
And the Marquis brave and bold,
Sore in need of help doth stand,
Close beset in Paynim's land."

[1] **Beraut of Mercuer** was one of the greatest lords of Languedoc. Azalais, Pons of Capduoill's lady, married an Oisil of Mercuer.

[2] **Saill.** A contraction of Assalide. There is no mention of Claustra in the Chronicles.

[3] **When from weary sorrow free.** The original poem is composed of six stanzas (rhymes a b a b b c c d d running throughout the poem followed by a half stanza (c c d d).

[4] **"Choose thou."** The first three lines are addressed to the Crusaders in general, the line following to Peirol himself.

GUILLEM OF SAINT LEIDIER.[1]

1180-1200.

LITTLE is known of Guillem of Saint Leidier beyond the details given us in the version of his Life, translated below, and in a somewhat longer account of him, in which it is related how, upon Guillem's paying court to a beautiful Countess—the Marchioness, his lady, revenged herself on him by giving herself to Hugo Marescalc—the consequence of which was Guillem's complete estrangement from her.

Guillem of Saint Leidier is no prominent figure in Provençal literature. His canzones, however, express with considerable grace and elegance the love-sick despair of the typical troubadour, and are also free from the affectations and the straining after effect of some of the other poets of Provence.

*GUILLEM OF SAINT LEIDIER.**

GUILLEM of Saint Leidier[1] was a puissant castellan of Veillac, of the diocese of Puy Sainte Marie, and he was an honourable and stout knight of arms, and a bountiful giver of goods, and a right true lover, and right learned, and courteous, and right well loved of men. And he paid court to the Marchioness of Polomiac,[2] sister of the Dauphin of Auvergne and of the Lady Saill of Claustra, and wife of the Viscount of Polomiac; and Lord Guillem of Saint Leidier being thus enamoured of her, praised her in his canzones and called her "Bertran"—and likewise called her "Bertran,"

* See Mahn, xxxiv.

Lord Hugo Marescalc, his fellow, the which wa
privy to all the words and deeds that passe
betwixt them.   And all three called each othe
"Bertran,"[3] and all three knew great gladness.   Ye
was Lord Guillem's gladness turned to sorrow, fo
the two Bertrans full wrongfully and discourteousl
entreated him.

CANZONE TO BERTRAN.[*]

FAIR friend with joy I gin my song,
    And eke on joy I set my heart;
    Please God great joy will be my part,
Since mine will be the prize ere long.
    Though sore my fear, I will be bold,
    And hope to dwell in joy untold;
I'll not despair, whate'er betide,
But ever in such love abide.

And this my love doth make me think,
    No man of worth hath e'er been found,
    Who is not under Love's yoke bound;
Yet who from service least would shrink
    Wins for one good a dozen cares,
    One joy a thousand griefs prepares;
Sad he by others' joy must sit,
And hold his foolishness for wit.

[*] See Mahn's *Gedichte der Troubadours*, Vol. II., page 49.

[1] **Guillem of Saint Leidier.** A Guillem of Saint Leidier is
mentioned in the *History of Languedoc.* There are
several small places named St. Leidier (or St. Didier)
in the south of France. One of these is in Velay,
somewhat north of Le Puy, and it is to this Saint Leidier
that Guillem probably belonged.

[2] **The Marchioness of Polomiac.** Wife of Heraclius of Polomiac
(Polignac), a powerful baron whose castle lay near Le Puy.

[3] **"Bertran."** It was common for very intimate friends in
Languedoc to take the same pseudonym.

THE MONK OF MONTALDON.

1180-1200.

THE Monk of Montaldon is decidedly one of the most
interesting of the troubadours, as much on account of his
strong personality, as from the fact that his life throws a
most curious light on the manners and morals of the age.
Of a noble family, of which he was probably a younger member,
it was natural enough that he should have been "made a
Monk"; it was natural also being, as his poems show, endowed
with a strong taste for the good things of life, and a keen
interest in men and their follies, that he should crave a wider
sphere of action than the monastic career afforded. The
general laxity of the age, and the hope of pecuniary advantage
to the Order, induced his Superior to allow him to wander
at large, and have his full share of the pleasures and gaieties
of the southern European courts. At these courts his wit
and talents made him a conspicuous figure. He seems to
have known intimately three of the greatest sovereigns of
the age—Richard I., Philip Augustus, and Alphonso II. of
Aragon; he was the friend and boon companion of the barons,
and held a high office at the great court festivals of Puy
Sainte Marie.

As a poet the monk occupies a peculiar position. As with his predecessor, Marcabrun, love was with the Monk by no means an all-absorbing passion, and, though he turned off canzones skilfully, they were composed from necessity rather than from choice. In this he was unlike the great mass of the troubadours ; he was unlike them too in an indifference to form, curious in an age when form was everything. With little then to recommend them as regards style, versification, and depth of feeling, his poems, however, stand out among those of the time for their originality, sense, reason, power of satire, and interest of matter generally.

The Monk has left us about twenty poems, and of these one of the most interesting is that here partly translated, in which he represents himself holding converse in heaven with God the Father, who treats him with marked favour, justifies him in leaving the cloister, and declares that singing and laughter win divine approbation. The naïve irreverence of the poem is, of course, not peculiar to the Monk, but characteristic of the whole Middle Ages.

Another of the Monk's most striking poems is an imitation of Peire of Auvergne's satire on his contemporary poets. The form of both is similar, and the Monk lashes his own contemporaries no less thoroughly than Peire of Auvergne the poets of *his* day. Herr E. Philippson, who has edited the Monk's works, is of the opinion that the satire, like Peire's, was composed for the table, and sung or recited (amidst shouts of laughter probably) to men inflamed by feasting and drinking ; it is specially valuable for the hints it gives about many noted troubadours.

Much of the Monk's satire is directed against the follies and artificialities of women, specially of the old women of his time, whom he described as laying paint upon their faces to such an extent as to be rapidly exhausting its supply.

Now the Monk of Montaldon[1] was of Auvergne, of a castle named Vic,[2] that is nigh unto Orllac,[3] and he was of gentle blood, and was made a Monk of the Abbey of Orllac, and the Abbot gave him the priory of Montaldon, and there he in all things demeaned him so as best to profit the priory. And while yet he abode in the monastery, he made coblas and sirventes on all such matters as were noised abroad in that region. And the knights and barons drew him forth from the monastery, and greatly honoured him, and whatsoever it pleased him to ask of them, that gave they, and he brought all to Montaldon his priory. Much did he increase and enrich his church, wearing ever the habit of a Monk. And thereafter he gat him back to Orllac and to his Abbot, showing him how he had advantaged the priory of Montaldon, and beseeching him to graciously empower him to order his life after the good pleasure of King Alphonso of Aragon.[4] And the Abbot granted it to him, and the King bade him to eat flesh, and pay court to ladies, and sing songs, and make poetry. And behold, all this he did; and he was made Lord of the Court of Puy Sainte Marie,[5] and had the giving of the Sparrow-hawk. Long time had he

*See Mahn, xxxvi.

rule over the Court, even until it broke up. Then he departed, and gat him into Spain ; and great honour and pleasance was done him therein by all the kings, and lords, and honourable men. Now there is a certain priory in Spain called Vilafranca,[6] appertaining to the Abbey of Orllac, and he improved, and increased, and enriched it, and there brought his days to an end.

THE MONK OF MONTALDON'S VISION OF HEAVEN.[7]

WHILOM I did Heaven see,
   Whence I'm glad and free of care ;
   Loving greeting gave me there
God, who rules all things that be.
   Earth and ocean, mountain, valley :
"Monk, why cam'st thou here ?" spake he,
   "How does my Montaldon fare,
   Where thy friends around thee rally ?"

"Lord, for well-nigh two years' space[8]
   'Neath the cloisters' yoke I've lain,
   Whence the barons me disdain,
And will turn from me their face,
   E'en that here I sing thy praises ;
Randon,[9] who was never base,
   Who o'er Paris has his reign
   Lamentation for me raises."

* See *Chrestomathie provençale*, page 131.

" Monk, 'tis evil in my sight,
   That 'twixt convent walls thou art,
   And on strife dost set thy heart,
Eager for dispute and fight,
   For thy rule 'gainst neighbours striving;
Songs I love and laughter bright,
   These great worth to life impart,
Montaldon through them is thriving.

" Lord, I feared to go astray
   If to singing I inclined :
   Who delight in lies does find,
In thy favour cannot stay,
   Singing then I have forsaken,
From the world have turned away,
   On the lessons set my mind,
   Nor the path to Spain have taken."

.   .   .   .

[1] **Montaldon.** Or Montaudon was probably an insignificant priory, of which no traces were left after the Albigensian War. It is uncertain where it was situated.

[2] **Vic.** Near Aurillac in Auvergne; it is now called Vic-en-Carladès, or Vic-sur-Cère.

[3] **Orllac.** Aurillac.

[4] **King Alphonso.** Alphonso the Second.

[5] **The Court of Puy Sainte Marie.** The splendour of the festivals at Puy Sainte Marie, has been alluded to in note 1 on Pons of Capduoil. It is said that in the

middle of the lists a sparrow-hawk was fastened to a pole, and whatever knight undertook to defray the expenses of the year's festival, took down the said sparrow-hawk, and fastened it to his wrist. This bird was also the prize given to the best knight, and in the *Cento Novelle Antiche*, the Monk is spoken of as being one of the four judges appointed to award it. Herr E. Phillipson thinks that it was Robert I., the Dauphin of Auvergne, who founded the festivities, and gave the Monk his office.

[6] **Villafranca.** It is uncertain where this monastery was situated.

[7] **The Vision of Heaven.** The original is of six stanzas, all of which have the rhymes: a b b a c a b c.

[8] **For well-nigh two years' space.** The Monk, at the composition of this poem, had returned to the monastic life at Montaldon, after having for some time lived in the world. He now complains that the barons, his friends, and patrons, had, since his retirement, forsaken him.

[9] **Randon.** This can be none other than Philip Augustus of France.

ARNAUT DANIEL.

1180-1200.

OF Arnaut or Arnold Daniel nothing is known beyond the few details given us in the life ; and the anecdote there related of his dispute with the jongleur, is the only circumstance by which we can in any way decide as to the period in which he lived.

The importance of Arnaut Daniel is perhaps less from the intrinsic merit of the poems preserved to us of him, than from the fact that Dante considered him chief among Provençal poets. This opinion is expressed in the following lines from the *Purgatorio*, where the Italian Guinicelli, after pointing out Arnaut to Dante, and speaking of him as cleansing himself from the sin of voluptuousness, continues :

> "'O frate,' disse, 'questi ch'io ti scerno
> Col dito' ed additò uno spirto innanzi,
> 'Fu miglior fabbro del parlar materno,
> Versi d'amore, e prose di romanzi
> Soverchiò tutti ; e lascia dirgli stolti,
> Che quel di Lemosì credon ch'avanzi.'"

Purgatorio, Canto xxvi.*

These lines sufficiently show that Dante admired the obscure subtleties of Daniel's style, and considered him greater than the Limousin, Borneil, whom the troubadours, for their part owned as " Master."

Again, in the treatise on *Vulgar Eloquence* (*De Vulgari Eloquio*), Dante speaks of Arnaut as the Singer of Love *par excellence* (LIB. II., c. ii.): "Circa quae sola (armorum probitatem amoris ascensionem et directionem voluntatis), si bene recolimus, illustres invenimus vulgariter poetasse, scilicet Bertramum de Bornio arma, Arnaldum Danielem amorem, Gerardum de Bornello rectitudinem." He also cites several of his canzones as models, and confesses himself his imitator in the ' Sextine.' Petrarch also considers Arnaut "The great Master of Love, who still does his country honour by his novel and fair speech." It is hard for us to conceive how the eighteen existing poems

---

* See Longfellow's translation (emended):
> "'O brother,' said he, 'he whom I point out,'
> And here he pointed at a spirit in front,
> 'Was of the mother tongue a better smith.
> Verses of love and proses of romance,
> He passed them all ; and let the idiots talk,
> Who think the Lemosin surpasses him.'"

can alone have awakened such admiration. The most marked feature of these is their so-called " Hard Style," which, though not of Arnaut's invention, is more faithfully adhered to by him, than by any other troubadour. Its chief characteristics were : enigmatical expressions, strange plays on words, hard constructions, alliterations, and above all, unusual and difficult rhymes. This manner of writing Arnaut seems to have adopted on the principle that, as the style must suit the subject, a simple and easy one should be adopted for the expression of happy love, and the " Hard Style " for that of *unhappy* love. But there is a classic polish about his work and a firm logic and complete presentment of subject that bespeak a true master ; and Dante, who knew the difficulties of the style, could better appreciate its beauties than those to whom it may at first appear strange and artificial.

*OF ARNAUT DANIEL.**

NOW Arnaut Daniel was of the same country as Arnaut of Marveil, of the diocese of Perigord to wit, and of a castle named Ribeyrac. And he was gentle and learned, and delighting himself greatly in poetry, forsook his learning and became a jongleur. And he learnt a manner of making poetry with " scarce rhymes," wherefore these rhymes are difficult to understand and to learn.

Now Arnaut loved a great lady of Gascony, wife of Lord Guillem of Buovila,[1] but men deemed not that the lady ever so much loved him, as that she hearkened to his prayers, wherefore he says :

*See Mahn, xxxviii.

"Ieu sui Arnautz quamas Laura [2]
E cas la lebre ab lo bou.
E nadi contra suberna."

(I am Arnaut, who love Laura, and hunt the hare with the ox, and swim against the tide.)

Long time did he bear her this great love, making many a good song of her, and a man right courteous and debonair he was.

Now it chanced upon a time, that he was in the court of King Richard of England, and there, likewise, was a jongleur, the which bade him defiance in the making of "scarce rhymes." Then Arnaut held himself scorned thereby, and either defied the other, and both gave their palfreys in pawn thereof unto the King. And the King shut up each man in a separate chamber, and Sir Arnaut, in so great dudgeon was he, could in no wise link one word to another, but the jongleur rhymed on lightly, and made his songs speedily.

Now they had but ten days ordained them, and lo, in five more they must needs joust before the King, when the jongleur asked of Arnaut if he had finished, and Arnaut answered, "Yea, three days agone," while verily of never a word had he bethought him. And all night long the jongleur sang his song, for to know it the better; and Arnaut bethought him the while how he might set the jongleur at naught, till it fell out one night as the jongleur

sang his song that Arnaut learnt it of him, and
also the melody.   And when they were come before
the King, Arnaut said that he would rehearse him
his song, and began full lustily that which the
jongleur had made.   And straightway on hearing
it, the jongleur looked him in the face, and said,
it was *he* that had made it.   Then the King asked
how that might be, and the jongleur besought the
King to learn of him the truth.   Then the King asked
of Sir Arnaut how this thing had happened, and
Sir Arnaut told him all that had happened, and
the King delighted much in it, and made great
jest of it.   And he held them quit of their pledges,
and unto each he gave fair gifts.   And it was
given to Arnaut to sing thereof, the which sang :

> "Anc ieu non lac, mas ella ma."
> (Never did I have it, but she has, etc.)

[1] **Wife of Lord Guillem of Buovila.** A William of Bouville,
possibly the son of this lady, is mentioned in the *History
of Languedoc*. Arnaut's canzones are addressed to several
ladies, and it is not possible to distinguish from the
rest those to the Lady of Bouville.

[2] **I am Arnaut who loves Laura.** These lines are alluded to
in no flattering way by the Monk of Montaldon, who,
with the troubadours in general, thought far less highly
of Arnaut than did Dante. "Arnaut Daniel," says the
Monk, "has sung nothing all his life but a few foolish
verses that none understand, since he 'Hunted the hare
with the ox, and swam against the stream' his singing
is not worth a berry." Petrarch, however, evidently

admired the figure, since in his 177th Sonnet he borrowed it. The meaning of the obscure passage seems to be, that it is as difficult for the ox to hunt the hare, or for a man to swim up stream, as for Arnaut to win his lady's love.

GAUCELM FAIDIT.

1190-1240.

GAUCELM FAIDIT'S poems, containing as they do few personal allusions, do little to confirm the details given us in the *Life*. Among his fellow troubadours Gaucelm's reputation seems to have been anything but high; Elias of Uisel mentions him scornfully, and the Monk of Montaldon said that his singing was never heard but from Uzerche (in Limousin) to Agen (in Guienne). Most of his poems are addressed to the famous Maria, wife of Ebles IV. of Ventadorn. Probably in the last years of the twelfth century is to be placed a poem, in which, after leaving her, he craves her forgiveness. If we are to believe his canzones, he remained during this time at the Court of Boniface of Montferrat until drawn back to Limousin by his love for Maria, who, as he says, in opposition to the *Life*, granted him full forgiveness, and again accepted him as lover.

The Crusade of 1202 seems to have found him still faithful to Maria. It is then that he must have composed the Crusading-song of which a portion is translated. Probably he himself took part in the expedition, as in one canzone he speaks of himself as absent on it, but longing to be back again with his lady, and taking comfort in the thought of the grief she showed at their parting.* Gaucelm had later other love adventures, and among the last poems he composed is one in which

* See Mahn's *Gedichte der Troubadours*, Vol. I., page 40.

he compares the fickleness of the lady he then served to the steadfastness of Maria.

Some sixty of Faidit's poems are left us, most of them of great charm, tenderness, and fine finish. "And you, Love," he cries in one of them, "you that have made me such fair promises, remember now to succour me. Go to her, and go Mercy likewise with you, and I, beneath your protection will go thither also. And, if she show me love, and advance me, you and Mercy shall alone have the thanks. . . .

"Great love groweth within me for a fair flower surpassing white; she with her bright colour of crimson and ruby, and with her fair face and loving eyes, hath so sweetly pierced and wounded me, that I have given me once more to hopes of love. Ah! white, vermeil and sweet-smelling flower, I cry you mercy, and if Mercy prevail over you, yours will be the praise, and with joy and gladness ye will put me into Paradise. . . ."

In another canzone he exclaims rapturously on his lady granting him her love : "Ah! how sweetly did she whom I adore make me hers ; when kissing me upon the mouth her sweet breath robbed me of my heart. So fair she is that the birds in the meadows rejoice over her, and make their songs of her. . . ."

Of the two poems, portions of which are translated below, that on the Death of King Richard shows Faidit to have been one of the many troubadours who tasted Cœur de Lion's bounty, and whose poems represent him as the ideal hero of chivalry. In his Crusading song Faidit, also like other troubadours, blames Philip of France for the unknightly qualities of caution, sloth, and cowardice.

*OF GAUCELM FAIDIT.**

Now Gaucelm Faidit was of a town named Uzerche of the diocese of Limousin, and he was the son of a

* See Mahn, xl.

burgher, and sang worse than any man in the world, yet made many a good melody, and many a good canzone. And he became a jongleur, because at dice he had lost all that he had. And he was a man of open hand, and a full gluttonous eater, and a wine-bibber, wherefore he grew beyond measure fat. And for a right long time was he ill-fortuned in the getting of gifts and fame, for it was even twenty years and upwards that he journeyed through the world, and he and his songs received the while small favour of any.

And he took to wife a wanton, who long time went with him from court to court, the which hight Guillelma Monia, and was passing fair and skilled, but became even as big and fat as he. And she was of a rich town named Alest, in the march of Provence, and of the lordship of Lord Bernart of Andusa. And my lord, the Marquis Boniface of Montferrat, gave him goods, and raiment and equipment, and set him in great fame, both him and his songs.

Now you have heard who was Gaucelm Faidit, and how he came and stood; and of such great hardihood was he that he became enamoured of my Lady Maria of Ventadorn, the best and loveliest lady then alive. And he made his songs of her, and in his songs he sought her grace, and sang her excellence. And she suffered him for the great praise he gave her, and thus their love endured for nigh upon seven years.   And all that while she had not granted him his desires.

And it fell upon a day that Sir Gaucelm came before his lady, and told her that if she granted him not his desires, she should lose him, and he would go seek a lady from whose love he should win great favours, whereat full wrothfully he took his leave.   Then my Lady Maria sent for one named my Lady Audiart of Malamort, who was both fair and gently born, and told her what had passed betwixt Sir Gaucelm and herself, and besought her to give counsel how best to answer Sir Gaucelm, and how to keep him in her service without granting him his desires.   Then my Lady Audiart said that she would counsel her neither to keep him nor to dismiss him, but rather would she make him separate himself from her without rancour or enmity.

And hearing this my Lady Maria was passing glad, and besought her instantly that she would bring this to pass.   And right so my Lady Audiart departed, and made choice of a courteous messenger, and sent word unto Sir Gaucelm, saying that he should better prize a little bird in the hand than a crane flying in the sky.   And Sir Gaucelm, when he had heard this message, got him to horse, and went unto my Lady Audiart.   And she made countenance of great love unto him.   And he asked her why she had sent word to him of the little bird and the crane, and she told him that she had great pity of him, knowing that he loved, yet was not loved again. "Know then," quoth she, "that she whose fame you have increased is the crane, and I am the little bird that you hold in your hand, to do unto me as you list." And wit you well that I am of gentle birth, and of great riches, and young of years, and men call me passing fair; likewise have I never yet given nor promised, and never yet beguiled nor been beguiled of others; and right wishful am I of honour, and for the love of one that may win me praise and renown. I wot you are he, of whom I may have all this, and I am she that can well reward all. I would have you then for lover, and do make you gift of myself and of my love, if so be that you will take leave of my Lady Maria, making in a canzone courteous complaint of her, and saying that since she will even follow no other way, you have found an honourable and gentle lady that will cherish you. And behold, when Gaucelm had heard the fair words that she spake to him, and the prayers that she made to him, and had seen the loving countenance that she showed to him, and her great fairness withal, he was so overtaken by love that he wist not where he was. And when he was come to remembrance, he thanked her as best he might, saying how that he would do all her behests, and would depart from loving my Lady Maria, and would wholly set his mind on her. And either made other this promise : and Gaucelm departed full of joy, and he bethought him of a song, by the which men might understand that he had separated himself from my Lady Maria, and had entered the service of another. And the song runs:

> "Tant ai sufert longamen greu afan."
> (Such grievous sorrow have I suffered long.)

And my Lady Maria knew of the song, and rejoiced much at it, and likewise my Lady Audiart, for she thereby perceived that he had believed her false promises, and had withholden his love and praise from my Lady Maria.

Now after a space, it befell that Gaucelm Faidit came with great gladness for to see my Lady Audiart as one who hoped to enter straightway into her chamber. And she greeted him full well, and Sir Gaucelm knelt at her feet, telling her that he had done her behest, and had turned towards her his love, and that she should now give him that she had promised him, and should amend him all he had done for her. Then said my Lady Audiart: "Great is your excellence and your renown, and no lady is there in the world who should not deem herself happy in winning your love, for you are indeed father of all excellence; but that which I promised you I did, not because I minded to love you *par amour*, but rather to draw you forth from the prison wherein you dwelt, and from that foolish hope wherein for more than seven years you have been kept; for I knew the mind of my Lady Maria, and I knew that your desires would be in nowise accorded you, and I will be your friend and well-wisher, and all you list that it were not unseemly to be. Then Gaucelm, hearing this, was full sad and sorrowful, and fell to crying the lady mercy, that she should not slay him, nor beguile him, nor deceive him. Thereon she told him that she would neither slay him nor deceive him, but rather save him from deceit and death. And when he saw that it nothing availed him to cry her mercy, he went forth from her as one distraught, for he saw that he had been beguiled, in that he had separated himself from my Lady Maria, and that she had made him promises but with the intent to beguile him. And he was minded to return to my Lady Maria and to cry her mercy, and he made the song that runs:

> "No malegra chans ni critz
> Dauzelh mon felh cor engres."

(Neither songs nor cry of birds gladden my wretched, eager heart.)

But neither for his song nor for aught else in the world would she pardon him, nor hearken to his prayers. Now when Gaucelm, even as ye have

heard, had separated himself from my Lady Maria
by reason of my Lady Audiart, he dwelt long in
grievous woe for the deceit he had suffered, until
my Lady Maria Garida of Albusso, wife of Lord
Raynaut, Viscount of Albusso, caused him to sing
and to rejoice; for so fair did she speak him, and such
semblance of love did she make him, that he became
enamoured of her, and besought her love. And she
for to win of him fame and honour, hearkened to his
prayers, and promised to accord him that which he
sought of her. And long endured Sir Gaucelm's
prayers, and long did he praise her as best he might
And she, even as though she took no pleasure in
the praise he made of her, neither loved him nor
made semblance of love to him. . . .

ON THE DEATH OF KING RICHARD I. OF ENGLAND.

ALAS! the greatest ill that I have known,
　　The bitterest woe that time can ever bring,
Woe that I needs must endlessly bemoan,
　　Must e'en by *me* be sung, by me proclaimed;
　　For Valour's sire and chief, of deeds far-famed—
The mighty Richard, England's noble king,
Is dead. Ah, God! that death what voice can sing
　　How terrible that word! how cruel its sound!
　　How cold were he whom all unmoved it found

　　　* See Mahn's *Gedichte der Troubadours*, Vol. IV., page 139.

Dead is the king. A thousand years and more
  Have passed since e'er his like on earth was seen;
Yet such a man there never lived before,
  Of bounty and of bravery so vaunted,
  E'en Alexander, who Darius daunted,
Ne'er gave so freely as my lord, I ween;
Nor Charles nor Arthur braver knights have been;
  And of a truth, in half the world he waked
  A mighty love—the rest in terror quaked.

Alas, Sir King! how will without thee fare
  Tourneys and arms, and many a noble fight,
Many a rich feast, and gallant gift and rare,
  Since thou, their founder, desolate dost leave us?
  And how will all they fare of fortune grievous,
Who, serving thee, were raised from hapless plight,
And hoped that thou their toils wouldst rich
      requite?
  How will those fare, to whom thou ere did'st give
  Great wealth and power? Such now should scorn
      to live.

Such now will suffer grievous want and woe,
  And endless tears for thee will dim their eyes.
Pagans and Turks for death of their dread foe,
  Whom more than any mother's son they feared,
  Down-trodden erst, their haughty heads have
      reared,

That hard it were to win the Tomb for prize.
So God doth will, but willed He otherwise,
   And thou, my lord, did'st live, I nothing doubt
   That soon from Syria thou would'st drive ther
      out.

That kings and princes Syria regain,
   Thereof, alack! all hope is long since dead ;
But those that now do in thy place remain,
   Should mind them of the fame thou hadst be
      fore them,
   And of thy brothers, who full stoutly bore ther
(The young king and Earl Geoffrey, Bretagne's head
And certes he that ruleth in their stead,[2]
   A constant heart should bear, and turn his face
   From all things ill, and do the deeds of grace.
    ·   ·   ·   ·   ·   ·   ·   ·

Great Lord and God, to whom belongeth pardon,
   Thou that art God, and Man, and Life indeed,
   Grant him that pardon that his sins do need ;
His faults and failings mercifully o'erlook,
Remember that for Thee the Cross he took.

SONG ON THE FOURTH CRUSADE.[3]

   Now be to us a guide
   The Lord, who for us died,

   * See *Chrestomathie provençale*, page 145.

For whom the noble-hearted,
'Mongst whom I long abide,
I leave, and much beside—
Love, honour, wealth, and pride;
 If sad from these I've parted,
I pray He may not chide.
 Farewell, sweet Limousin,
 And those that dwell therein:
 Fair dames of gentle bearing,
 Stout knights that honour win,
 Neighbours and next of kin!
 Sad on my way I'm faring,
 And bitter tears begin
 To shed, with groans despairing.

. . . .

Now anti-Christ doth haste
Fair countries to lay waste,
 And Vice, her foes dismaying,
Sweet Virtue hath abased;
Her hand on princes placed,
Good from their hearts hath chased,
 And avarice on them preying,
Foully their names disgraced—
 He, who o'er France doth reign,[4]
Base gold had liefer gain,
 Norman or Frenchman plunder,
Than Seifeddin constrain[5]

> To yield up what hath lain
>   Too long his foul yoke under—
> Such kings full long in pain
> Will groan, or great the wonder.

.   .   .   .

[1] **On the Death of King Richard.**   The rhyming system is
a b a c c b b d d, the same rhymes in the original being
continued throughout the poem, which consists of six and
a half stanzas.

[2] **He that ruleth in their stead.**   King John of England.

[3] **Song on the Fourth Crusade.**   The original poem consists of
five and a half stanzas of sixteen lines with the following
rhymes continued through the poem, a a b a a a b a, c c
d c c d c d.

[4] **He who o'er France doth reign.**   Philip Augustus.

[5] **Than Seifeddin constrain.**   Al Adel Seifeddin, who, after the
death of his brother Saladin, extended his rule over Egypt
and Syria.

RAYMOND OF MIRAVAL.

1190-1220.

THE following biography is, for the most part, the account of
a series of love intrigues that disagreeably bring into relief
the baser side of an age that is generally regarded as the
palmy one of mediæval chivalry. The lives of the troubadours
are, in more cases than one, beautified and ennobled by a
spirit of romantic generosity, and by a passionate, though
extravagant, devotion to the service of love. But the spiritual
connection between lover and lady that chivalry permitted,
and indeed encouraged, has here degenerated into mere

licence. The lady, whom Dante conceived of as a miracle of faith and purity, is here one who, for the renown the poet can give her, leads him on to love her, and then basely betrays him and mocks him, while the lover on his side shames his knighthood by paying her back in the same coin. It is true that the absolute correctness of the details given us in Miraval's life cannot be vouched for, but they are, no doubt, sufficiently typical to illustrate the fact that, while perfect obedience to the laws of chivalry was a hard matter, even to the noblest, the average man or woman fell grievously short of the self-mastery and self-renunciation that such obedience involved.

Miraval had many friends and patrons, and of these, the one with whom he was most intimately connected was his suzerain, the luckless Raymond VI., Count of Toulouse. Miraval, indeed, shared his master's misfortunes, when in 1211 the Count was excommunicated by the Pope as a harbourer of heretics, and when Simon of Montfort brought ruin and desolation into his fertile territories. With his master, also, Miraval rejoiced in the prospect of succour from Peter II. of Aragon, and with him lamented over the brave and gallant Peter, slain while contending against Simon of Montfort, at the great battle of Muret, 1213. After this year Miraval sinks into obscurity, and beyond the fact that he was still living in 1218, nothing more is known of him. The forty-eight poems he has left us, popular as they were in his time, can have but little interest to us. Though they have a unity that much of the troubadour poetry lacks, there is in them none of the truth, warmth, and tenderness that might have given them enduring value.

*OF RAYMOND OF MIRAVAL.**

Now Raymond of Miraval was a poor knight of Carcassez, who owned but the fourth part of the

* See Mahn, xlii.

Castle [1] of Miraval, in the which there were not even forty men ; but for his poetry, and for his fair speech, and for all he knew of love, gallantry, and of the courteous deeds and words that pass between lovers, he was much loved and prized by Count Raymond of Toulouse, who called him Audiart, as likewise he the Count. And the Count gave him horses, and arms, and raiment, and all he lacked. And Miraval was lord of his house, and lord of King Peter of Aragon, and of the Viscount of Beziers, and of Lord Bertran of Saissac, and of all the great lords of the country round about. And there was no great and honourable lady who did not desire his love, and did not bestir her to win it, or to win of him good-will by familiarity with her ; for he was better skilled in making them loved and honoured of others than any man on earth, and none weened herself prized of men if Raymond of Miraval were not her friend. And Raymond of Miraval loved many ladies, and made many good songs of them, but it is not thought that any returned his love, but rather did one and all beguile him.

Now well have ye heard of Raymond of Miraval and who and whence he was ; wherefore I will presently tell you more of his deeds. Know then that he loved a lady of Carcassez, Lady Loba [She-Wolf] by name, of Penautier, daughter of Lord Raymond of Penautier, and wife of a rich and powerful knight of Cabaret, joint-owner of the castle. Now the Loba was exceeding lovely and gracious, and wishful of worth and honour, and all the barons of that region, and all the strangers that looked upon her, loved her—the Count of Foix, Sir Oliver of Saissac, Sir Peire Roger of Mirepoix, Sir Aimeric of Montreal, and Sir Peire Vidal, who made many good songs of her. But Sir Raymond of Miraval loved her more than all, and by song and speech advanced her fame as best he might, even as one who could better do it than any knight alive. Then the Loba, for the great fame he had gotten her in the world, and for the knowledge she had that he could both make or mar her fortunes, suffered his prayers, and pledged to him her love, and bound him to her with a kiss. But in all this she meant but to beguile him, for she loved the Count of Foix so greatly that she had made of him her lover; and throughout the region of Carcassez their love became known to all, whence ruin came to her, and the loss of honour and of friends, for there they held as dead all those who made lovers of noble lords; and news of the evil she had done came to the ears of Sir Raymond of Miraval, and he heard likewise how that Peire Vidal had spoken ill of her in a song which begins: "Estat ai una gran sazo," (I have been long time, etc.,) in the which he says: "Mot ai mon cor felo per lieis que mala fo." (My heart is very sore for her that was evil.) Then Miraval was above all others sorrowful, and he was at first minded to speak ill of her, and to further her ruin, but he bethought him afterwards that it were better to beguile her, even as she had beguiled him. So he began to defend, and shield, and justify her in her love of the Count. The Loba heard how that Miraval, after his great sorrow, upheld her in the evil she had done, and greatly rejoiced at it, for she feared him more than any man besides. And she bade him come to her, and thanked him weeping for his maintenance and defence of her, and spoke to him, and said: "Miraval, if ever I had fame, and honour, and lovers, and friends, and if ever I had skill, and understanding, and courtesy, through you has it come to me, and of you I hold it; and whatsoever it be that has withheld me from granting you all your desires, it was in nowise the love of any other man, but rather that which you yourself have said in one of your canzones, the which runs:

> "'Amors me fai cantar et esbaudir . . .
> Bona domna nos deu damor gequir,
> Epus tan fai quad amor sabandona
> No sen coch trop ni massa non o tir,
> Que mens en val tot fag que dessazona.'"

(Love makes me sing and rejoice ; a good lady should not forsake Love, and when once she abandons herself to Love, she should neither hurry too much nor much delay, for all things are better than unseasonableness.)

" I therefore was minded to grant you such great joy in all wisdom and prudence, and, that you might hold it the dearer, would not be over hasty in the matter ; for it is but two years and six months that I bound you to me with a kiss,[3] even as you have said in your song :

> "' Passatz so cinq mes e dui ans
> Quieu vos retengui a mos comans.' "

(Two years and five months have passed since I retained you in my service.)

" And now I see full well that you will not forsake me for the blame that has fallen upon me through the slanderous lies that my enemies have spread abroad concerning me ; wherefore I tell you that, since you thus maintain me against all, behold for your sake I divest myself of all other love, and give myself to you, soul and body, wholly putting myself in your hands, and praying you to defend me to your uttermost."

Then Miraval received her gift with gladness, and long had of her all he would, but ere this he had become enamoured of the Viscountess of Minerba,[4] a noble lady, young and fair, who had not lied, nor deceived, nor herself known deceit and treachery. Wherefore Miraval, for this lady's love, separated himself from the Loba, making this song, which says :

> " Sieu en cantar souen
> No matur ni maten,
> Nons cuietz que sabers
> Men falha, ni razos."

(If I not often apply myself to singing, deem not that the knowledge and matter thereto are lacking.)

Now ye have heard how Sir Raymond of Miraval could beguile Loba, and yet dwell with her in peace, but now I will tell you of the Lady Azalais of Boissazon, and of how she beguiled him, and afterwards of another, his neighbour, the Lady Ermengarda of Castras, whom men called "The fair one of Albi." And both were of the diocese of Albi. Lady Azalais[5] was of a castle named Lombes, wife of Sir Bernart of Boissazon, and Lady Ermengarda of a town named Castras, wife of a rich vavassour right full of years.

Now Miraval fell to loving Lady Azalais, who was young, and fair, and noble, and wishful of excellence, and praise, and honour. And when she marked his love of her, she rejoiced greatly, knowing he would make her of more worth in men's eyes than any one alive. And she demeaned herself full graciously towards him, omitting naught that can be done by woman to show her love of him. And he, to his utmost power, advanced her by speech and song, and so sounded her praise throughout that region that all the barons therein fell to loving her—the Viscount of Beziers, the Count of Toulouse, and King Peter of Aragon, to the which Miraval had so vaunted her that the King, though he had not seen her, greatly loved her, and sent her his messengers and rich jewels. And he had a mind to see her, and Miraval bestirred himself to bring it to pass. . . .

So the King came to Lombes in Albi to see Lady Azalais, and thither came also Miraval, praying the King to speak well of him to her. And the King was right well received, and greatly honoured, and full favourably looked on by Lady Azalais. And no sooner had the King sat him down beside her than he besought her to give him her love, and she promised him all that he would of her. . . .

And on the morrow the thing became known through all the castle, and all the King's court, and Sir Miraval, who thought to become rich in joy by the King's intercession for him, heard tidings of it, and, sore stricken with grief, departed from the castle, leaving behind him the King and the lady. And long did he bewail the ill-doing of the lady, and the baseness of the King, making thereon this song, which says : " Entre dos uolers soi pessiu." (Between two desires I am in heaviness.)

Now when the Count of Toulouse [6] was disherited

by warfare, and by the Frenchmen, and had lost Argensa and Belcaire, and when the Frenchmen had taken St. Giles and Albi and Carcassez, and when Bederres was destroyed, and the Viscount of Beziers dead, and when likewise all the good people of that region were either dead or had fled to the Count, with whom he called himself Audiart, lo! Miraval lived in great sorrow and heaviness, because all the good people, both knights and ladies, of whom the Count was lord and master, were dead and disherited; likewise had he lost his wife, even as ye shall hear, and his lady had betrayed him, and his castle had been taken from him.

And it came to pass that the King of Aragon came to Toulouse to speak with the Count, and to see his sister, my Lady Eleanor,[7] and my Lady Sancha. And he gave great comfort to his sister, and the Count, and his sons, and the good people of Toulouse. And to the Count he promised that he would restore to him Belcaire and Carcassonne, and to Miraval he promised his castle, and to all the good people the joy they had lost. Now Sir Miraval had purposed to sing no song until his winning back the Castle of Miraval that he had lost; but in his gladness at the promise that the King made to the Count and him, to restore that they had lost, and because of the summer time which was come, and of his love of Lady Eleanor, the Count's wife—the best and fairest lady in the world—to whom he had not yet made show of love, he made this song, which says:

> "Bel mes quieu chan e condei
>   Pos laures dossa el temps iai."

> (It is meet that I sing and rejoice, etc.)

And when he had made this song, he sent it into Aragon, that the King, for his oath's sake, should come with a thousand knights to aid the Count; wherefore the King was slain by the Frenchmen before Muret, with the thousand knights that he had with him, nor was there one who escaped with his life.

Now I have told you above of Sir Raymond of Miraval, and ye have heard who and whence he was, and how greatly he was intent on all the best and most excellent ladies of that region, . . . making them to be full greatly esteemed and praised by all the good people. Truly there were some who did naught but good to him, but there were others, also, who evilly entreated him, even as he says. . . . And truly he was ¡beguiled by those whom he afterwards knew to beguile still worse himself, . . . and it misliked him much if one said that he had not won favours of dames, and he ever gave the lie to him who spoke thus.

Now it chanced that he became enamoured of a

young and well-born lady of Albi, Lady Ermengarda of Castras, who was fair and courteous and debonair, and of good customs and pleasant speech. Now I have told you of Lady Azalais of Boissazon, and how she deceived Sir Miraval, and herself also, and now I will tell you how Lady Ermengarda knew that Miraval had been mocked by Lady Azalais, and sent for him to come to her. And when he was come she said that she grieved greatly at that which was rumoured concerning Lady Azalais, and was minded to make amends to him for it with her own love, for the wrong that had been done him. And he was easily beguiled on seeing the gracious demeanour, and hearing the gracious words, with which she offered him amends for the loss he had borne. So he said he would right gladly receive amends of her, and she took him for her knight and servitor; and Miraval began to praise and love her, and to spread abroad her fame and worth. Now the lady had understanding and wisdom and courtesy, and knew to win the hearts of men and women; and Lord Oliver of Saissac, who was a great baron in that country, loved her, and besought her to take him for her husband. Meantime Sir Miraval, seeing how greatly he had increased her fame, sought guerdon of her, and prayed her to take him as her lover. And she answered him she would liefer he should become her husband, that nothing might sever them from each other, and that, for that end, he should put away his wife from him—Lady Gaudairenca by name. Sir Miraval was right glad at heart when he heard that she would take him for her husband; and he straightway went to his castle, and said to his wife, that he would not a wife that could make poetry; that in one house one poet was enough, and that she must make ready to return to her father's house, for he would no longer hold her his wife. Now his wife looked favourably upon a certain knight, Sir Guillem Bremon by name, on whom she made her dancing songs; so when she heard Sir Miraval's words she feigned great sadness, and said she would send for her relations, but sent, instead thereof, for Sir Guillem Bremon, telling him that she would take him for her husband, and leave her dwelling with him.

Sir Guillem Bremon, hearing this, was right joyful, and took with him knights, and came to Sir Miraval's castle, and alighted at the gateway. Then Lady Gaudairenca told Sir Miraval that her relations were come for her, and that she would go forth with them. At this Miraval was right glad, but the lady yet more so. And the lady, being in readiness to depart, was brought by Sir Miraval to the gateway, and finding Sir Guillem Bremon and his company awaiting her, she greeted him full well.

And as the lady was mounting her horse, she said to Sir Miraval, that since he had put her away from him, he should give her as wife to Sir Bremon; whereat Miraval said that he would gladly do it, if so she willed. Sir Bremon drew forth a ring, wherewith to espouse her, and Sir Miraval gave her to him for wife,[8] and he rode away with her.

Now when Sir Miraval put away his wife he went to Lady Ermengarda, telling her that he had done with his wife as she commanded, and beseeching her graciously to keep her promise to him. And the lady said that he had done well, and must return to the castle to make ready for the wedding festival and for her reception, for she would soon send for him. Then Miraval departed, and made great preparations for the wedding festival; and the lady meanwhile sent for Lord Oliver of Saissac, who came full speedily to her. And she said to him that she would do all he listed, and would take him for her husband, whereat he became the happiest man in all the world. And the matter was so arranged between them that that self-same evening he brought her to his castle, and on the morrow espoused her, amidst great feasting and rejoicing.

And news reached Sir Miraval that the lady had taken Lord Oliver of Saissac for her husband. Thereat, because she had made him abandon his wife, and had promised to take him for her husband, and had likewise caused him to make all things ready for the marriage, he fell into great grief and heaviness, both for all these matters, and also for Lady Azalais and the evil that she and the King of Aragon had done. He lost then all joy and merriment, and all pleasure in song and poetry, and lived two years as one distraught. And tidings thereof went sounding throughout all the country far and near, and it came to the ears of an honourable baron of Catalonia, Sir Hugh Mataplan by name, a trusty friend of Sir Miraval's, and he made of it this sirvente, which runs : " Dun sirventes mes pres talens." (The desire to make a sirvente has seized me.) And many a knightly troubadour mocked him for the scorn shown him. Howbeit, a noble lady, Lady Brunessa by name, wife of Sir Peire Rogier of Cabaret, and wishful of praise and honour, sent greetings to Sir Miraval, and comforted him, praying him to take heart again for love of her ; and she bade him know that she would verily come to see him, if he would not come to her, and would give her love to him in such wise that he should indeed know that she would not beguile him. And thereon he made this song, which says : " Ben aial messatgier." (Blessed be the messenger.)

RAYMOND OF MIRAVAL TO HIS LADY.

LADY, if Mercy help me not, I ween [9]
That I to be thy slave am all too mean,
  For thy great worth small hope to me has given
Aught to accomplish meet for dame so rare—
Yet this I would, and nowise will despair;
  For I have heard, the brave, when backward
      driven,
Strive ever till the conquering blow they deal,
So strive I for thy love by service leal.

Though to such excellence I come not near,
Nor eke of one so noble am the peer,
  I sing my best, bear meekly Love's hard burden,
Serve thee and love thee more than all beside,
Shun ill, seek after good whate'er betide;
  Wherefore, methinks, fair dame should liefer
      guerdon
With her dear self a valiant knight and true,
Than the first lord that haughtily may woo.

Against cruel Love I ever fight amain,
As wars a vassal 'gainst his suzerain,
  That him with scanty justice would disherit;
Such vassal, seeing warlike enterprise
Avails him not, perforce for mercy cries,
  So I, the better Love's sweet joys to merit,

* See Mahn's *Gedichte der Troubadours*, Vol. I., page 32.

Seek pardon for what faults in him I find,
And pray his pride may turn to pity kind.

Her eyes so lovely yet so full of guile,
At that which makes me weep and sigh do smile,
　　That graceful form, that frank and noble bearing,
Slay me with longing—yet the dear delight
Of calling mine that lady fair and bright
I ne'er may know, nathless as her true knight
E'en unto life's last hour my faith I plight.

[1] **Owned but the fourth part of the Castle.** This part-ownership of a castle was by no means uncommon in the mediaeval life of Languedoc. Bertran of Born owned Autafort, together with his brother Constantine, and Guy of Uisel shared a castle with his brothers and cousin.

[2] **Lady Loba.** It will be remembered that this lady has already been mentioned in connection with Peire Vidal, who for love of her caused himself to be hunted as a wolf.

[3] **I bound you to me with a kiss.** As Fauriel has pointed out, the ceremonial that took place on a lady's definitely accepting a man for lover was modelled on that of a vassal pledging himself to his lord. The lover, kneeling down with clasped hands before his lady, vowed fidelity to her; she then lifted him up, gave him a ring, and kissed him, as a token that she "retained" him, as it was called. Such an union was indeed so solemn a matter as to be often blessed by a priest, or dissolved by him.

[4] **Minerba.** Minerve, in the diocese of Narbonne. According to Miraval's canzones the poet remained faithful to the Loba, and was only for a short time drawn away from her by the beauty of the Viscountess of Minerve.

[5] **Azalais.** Adelaide, wife of Bernart of Boisseson, whose castle was in Albi. Azalais, like Loba, only accepted Miraval's homage in the hope that his praises of her would spread abroad her fame. Miraval, however, had no doubt of her sincerity, judging from a canzone in which he sings of his rapture at having won her love, and says that for her sake he loves the brooks, forests, gardens, and plains, the men and women, and all those that dwell near her, good or bad, wise or foolish.

[6] **Now when the Count of Toulouse, etc.** Familiar as most readers are with the main facts of the Albigensian War, allusions to them occur so frequently in the *Lives of the Troubadours*, that a brief recapitulation of them will not, perhaps, be out of place here.

The prosperity and civilized institutions of the South of France encouraged a freedom of thought that led to the rise of sects, which denied the fundamental doctrines of the Church of Rome. The virtuous lives of the Albigensian heretics secured them the protection of Raymond VI., Count of Toulouse, and of his nephew, the Viscount of Beziers; and all went well with them till Innocent III. became Pope in 1198, and sent his legates to crush out heresy among them. The violent conduct towards Raymond VI. of the legate, Peire of Castelnau, led to his assassination by one of the Count's followers, upon which Innocent induced France (or what is now the northern half of France) to make war upon the Count of Toulouse and his nephew. In 1209 the French army, under the elder Simon of Montfort, entered their lands. Raymond, in great terror, abandoned his Albigensian subjects to the mercy of the Crusaders; but the young Viscount of Beziers, though of the orthodox faith, refused to abandon any of his subjects, and in spite of the seizure of Beziers, and the wholesale slaughter of its inhabitants, prepared for a vigorous defence of Carcassonne. His heroism, however, could not save either himself or his people from destruction ; Carcassonne was taken, and the Viscount cast by Simon of Montfort into prison, where, as was commonly believed, he was poisoned.

Simon now turned against Raymond, who, after the fatal Battle of Muret (1213), found himself deprived of the greater portion of his inheritance. Raymond died in 1222, and seven years later a peace was at last made, by which a remnant of the County of Toulouse was left to his son, Raymond VII.

[7] **Lady Eleanor.** The wife of the Count of Toulouse.

[8] **And Sir Miraval gave her to him for wife.** It is difficult to believe that the very casual manner in which Miraval handed over his wife to Bremon's keeping can, even in those days, have been considered equivalent to a betrothal or wedding. Miraval's act of putting away his wife, and the subsequent fraud practised on him by Ermengarda, roused the mockery and also scorn of the troubadours. The situation was one that would naturally expose him to this, and, moreover, as chivalry countenanced a wife in addressing poems to a lover, it was felt to be an unknightly proceeding on Miraval's part to object to her doing so. One poet (Peire Duran), in particular, besides the Hugh Mataplan mentioned in the Life, composed a sirvente, in which he chides Miraval severely for his behaviour in the matter.

[9] **Lady, if Mercy help me not, I ween.** The original poem is composed of three stanzas of *eight* lines, with the rhymes a a b c c b d d, and a fourth stanza of *seven* lines, with the rhymes a a b c c c c.

BLACATZ.

· 1200-1236.

AT no period in the Middle Ages was the taste for poetry more wide-spread in Languedoc than in that immediately preceding the Albigensian War. This being the case, and generosity being with valour the most dearly esteemed of virtues,[1] it is not surprising that princes and barons should have vied with one another in their munificence towards troubadours. The best troubadours were mostly poor knights or burghers, but the nobles also cultivated their poetic gifts enough to compose more or less elegant and pleasing verses ; and, for the rest, contented themselves with a generous encouragement of the gift in those beneath them. Royal patrons of poetry, such as Cœur de Lion and Alphonso of Aragon, have already been mentioned ; amongst the barons those most highly praised by troubadours for liberality and chivalry were Blacatz and Savaric of Mauleon.

Strangely enough, of Blacatz, in spite of his high renown, we know hardly anything. In the account of him given below we have nothing but a long list of his virtues. Cadenet, Peguillan, Sordel, and many other poets who speak of him, sing his praises in much the same strain, without touching on the incidents of his life. The famous 'Complaint' of Sordel (Sordello), however, over the death of Blacatz enables us to fix with tolerable certainty the date of his death, while in a later 'Complaint' over him, mention is made of the many ladies whom he loved. The few poems of his left to us are tenzons treating nearly all of love, and having little beyond a certain skill and finish to recommend them.

OF BLACATZ.[*]

NOW Lord Blacatz was of Provence, a noble baron, high and great, bountiful and just. And he delighted in ladies, and love, and war, and spending, and feasting, and tumult, and music, and song, and play, and all such things as give a good man worth and fame. Never was there a man who loved better to take than he to give; and he was one that helped the helpless, and defended the defenceless. And the more he grew in years the more he grew in bounty, in courtesy, in valour, in land, in riches, and in honour; and the more did his friends cherish him, and his enemies contend against him; and the better grew his wisdom, his knowledge, his poetry, his hardihood, and his gallantry.

[1] **The most dearly esteemed of virtues.** The much-vaunted liberality of the age often degenerated into a wild and reckless extravagance. Diez, in his *Leben und Werke*, gives us, among other instances of lavishness, that of a baron who, on receiving an enormous sum of money as a gift from the Count of Toulouse, at once distributed it amongst ten thousand knights. Another, Diez tells us also, causing a large field to be ploughed, sowed it with small coins, while a third ordered thirty of his horses to be led before him and burnt alive, by way of emphasizing a resolution that he had taken.

[*] See Mahn, xliii.

SAVARIC OF MAULEON.

1200-1230.

OF Savaric, a knight no less renowned than Blacatz, a full account is given both in the *The Lives of the Troubadours* and elsewhere. As one of the most powerful barons of Aquitaine, he took a prominent part in political events, fought on the side of young Arthur against King John of England, and with him was taken prisoner at Mirabel, in 1202. Won over to John's cause by being made Seneschal of Aquitaine, Savaric, in this capacity, supported the Count of Toulouse against Simon of Montfort (1211), and fought in the war, waged by John against the French King. On the accession of Henry III. to the English throne, Savaric, who stood by William Marshal, and appears next to Hubert de Burgh in the great charter of 1215, vigorously defended Niort and Rochelle against Louis VIII. of France, until finding himself unsupported by the English, he was at length obliged to give them up to the enemy. Seeing that his services were not likely ever to be requited by the English King, and that the French were steadily gaining ground, Savaric tendered his allegiance to Louis, who welcomed him gladly, and restored to him all the possessions that he had lost during the war. As Louis' vassal he marched out, willingly or not, against the Albigensian heretics, but two years later, on the French King's death (1226), he again fought in Aquitaine on the English side, without, however, achieving any great success. After the year 1227 we hear nothing more concerning him, and the date of his death is therefore uncertain.

Savaric of Mauleon has left us nothing but an insignificant fragment of a canzone, and his share in two tenzons, both of which bear on the love-intrigues related in his Life.

*SAVARIC OF MAULEON.**

NOW Savaric of Mauleon was a mighty lord of
Poitou, son of Lord Reol of Mauleon. And he was
lord of Mauleon, and of Talarnom, and of Fontenai
and of Castelaillon, and of Boet and of Benaon,
and of Saint Miquel in Lertz, and of the island of
Riers, and of the island of Nives and of Nestrine,
and of Engollius, and of many another good place.
And a fair knight he was, and a courteous, and well
nurtured, and the most bountiful of the bountiful.
Above all men did he delight in bounty, and gallantry, and love, and jousts, and singing, and playing, and
poetry, and feasting, and spending. And above all
other knights was he the faithful friend of ladies and
of lovers, and wishful of seeing good men and of
pleasuring them. Likewise was he in warfare the
most valorous man of the world, and now it fared
well with him therein, and now ill; and all the war
that he made was with the King of France,[1] and
with his men. And a great book might be made of
his good deeds by him that would write it; for he
was one that had greater condescension, and mercy,
and open-heartedness, and one that did better deeds,
and was more set on doing them, than any man I
ever saw or heard tell of.

Now Lord Savaric of Mauleon came one day to
Benagues, for to see the Viscountess my Lady

** See Mahn, xliv.*

Guillelma,[2] the which he loved and sought.   And he brought with him Sir Elias Rudel, lord of Bragairac, and Jaufre Rudel of Blaia.[3]   Now all they three sought her love, and ere this each had been taken by her for knight, yet neither knew it of the others. And all three sat them down near her, that one on her right hand, that other on her left, and the third in front of her.   And each in amorous fashion looked on her; and she, as one who had not her like in hardihood, fell to looking amorously on Sir Jaufre Rudel of Blaia, for he it was that sat in front of her; the while she took the hand of Sir Elias Rudel of Bragayrac, and pressed it full lovingly, and pressed likewise, with a smile and a sigh, the foot of my Lord Savaric.   And none wist of the favour done his fellow until they had departed from the castle, whereon Sir Jaufre Rudel told Lord Savaric how the lady had looked upon him, and Sir Elias told him the matter of the hand.   And full woe was Lord Savaric when he heard what pleasure had been done them both, and he spake naught of that he had himself received, but let call Gaucelm Faidit, and Sir Hugh de la Bacalairia, and asked of them in a 'cobla' who had won the greatest favour of her.   And the 'cobla,' in the which he asked him begins: "Gaucelm tres ioc enamorat."

Now in good sooth do I say unto you how Lord Savaric was the root of all the courtesy of the world, and how he was master of all the good deeds that can ever be thought of. Now he had long time loved and honoured a gentle lady of Gascony, my Lady Guillelma of Benagues, wife of Lord P. of Gavaret, the which was Viscount of Beraumes and lord of San Macari and of Lengo, and full truly can I say that never did a man serve lady better; and long did she requite him with naught but foolish promises, and with fair messages, and with the giving of jewels; and many a time did she cause him to come from Poitiers to Gascony by sea and by land, and when he was come she knew full well to beguile him with false reasons for not granting him his desires of her; and he loved her the while so truly that he marked not her deceit, until his friends made him ware of it. And they showed him a lady of Gascony, who was of Manchac, and wife of Lord Guiraut of Manchac, and who was young, and fair, and gracious, and desirous of fame, and of seeing Lord Savaric for the good that she heard speak of him. And Lord Savaric, when he saw the lady, liked her marvellous well, and besought her love; and the lady, for the great worth that she saw in him, retained him for her knight, and appointed a day for him to come to her, and receive that he asked of her; and he left her full glad, and taking leave of her returned to Poitiers, and ere long my Lady Guillelma of Benagues got knowledge of the matter, and knew that the lady had appointed a day for him to come to her, and receive that he asked of her. Then Lady Guillelma was right jealous and sad, for that she had not retained him to her service, and she sent him as loving a letter, and message, and greeting as she best might; and she sent word to Lord Savaric, that on that self-same day, that the Countess of Manchac had given him, he should come secretly to her at Benagues, and should have of her all he would. And know of a truth that I, Hugh of Saint Circ, who have written this matter, was the messenger that went thither, and bore the message and the writing. And at Lord Savaric's court abode the Provost of Limoges, who was a worthy man and a well-taught, and a good troubadour. And Lord Savaric, to do him honour, laid before him the whole matter, and that which each lady had said and promised to him. And Lord Savaric besought of the Provost to ask him in song which lady he would go see on the day appointed by them, and in tenzon to give him his choice therein. And the Provost challenged him, and said: En Savaric ieu vos deman quem diatz en chantan. ("Lord Savaric, I ask of you to tell me in song," etc.)

The following is the *substance* of the tenzon alluded to above, in which Savaric took part; his opponents are Gaucelm Faidit, and Hugh de la Bacalairia, and the tenzon is a good example of the many ones that bore on subtle questions in the science of

Love. It consists of six stanzas of 13 lines, the rhymes of which are: a b b a c c d d e e e f f, and three half-stanzas of 5 lines with the rhymes e e e f f.

*Savaric of Mauleon.** Gaucelm, three parts in a love-game do I lay before you, that you and Hugh may each choose the best, and leave me that ye will: behold, a lady has three suitors, and their love has such great power over her that, when all three are before her, to each she must needs make semblance of love; the one she looks at lovingly, the other's hand she softly takes in hers, and smiling presses the foot of the third. Tell me now, since thus it is, to whom she owes the greatest love.

Gaucelm Faidit. Lord Savaric, well ye know that the richest gift is received by that lover upon whom those fair eyes fix their faithful gaze; it is from the heart alone such sweetness can proceed, and therefore it is a hundred times the dearest to me. As for the giving of the hand, I hold it neither favour nor disfavour, for a like joy is bestowed by ladies on all those they greet. And to him, whose foot was pressed, I deem no love was shown, nor for such should it be taken.

Hugh de la Bacalairia. Gaucelm, ye speak what seems good to you, but know that ye argue amiss, for in the glance I see not that favour to the lover whereof ye speak, and a fool is he who holds it one;

* For original, see *Chrestomathie provençale,* page 155.

for the eyes look upon him and others, and have no power besides; but when the white and ungloved hand softly presses that of its lover, then truly does love proceed from the ground of the heart. And now Lord Savaric, who so well does find us parts, may maintain the cause of the foot, for no whit will *I* maintain it.

Savaric. Hugh, since the best ye leave to me, I will maintain it without gainsaying you. Wherefore I protest that the pressing of the foot proceeded from pure love, hidden from slanderers; and well it appears, since such favour was granted with a smile, that the love it betokened was free from all deceit. And he that holds the taking of the hand for greater love, is nothing wise; nor methinks should Gaucelm hold the glance for better, if he indeed knows as much of love as he maintains he does.

Gaucelm. My lord, ye who hold light the glance from those eyes and all their sweetness, know not that they are messengers of the heart, sent by the heart to you; for the eyes reveal to lovers that which fear would keep within the heart, wherefore they are bringers of all love's joys. But often in mere mockery a lady presses full many a man's foot, and without other intent; eke Hugh maintains what is not, for the taking of the hand has no import soever, and I deem not that it came from Love.

Hugh. Gaucelm, you and the Lord of Mauleon,

ye speak great ill of Love, even as will appear in this tenzon; for the eyes that ye have chosen, and that ye uphold for best, have betrayed full many a lover, and if a false lady would press my foot a year still would my heart remain heavy. Truly ye cannot gainsay me, that the taking of the hand has a hundred times more worth, for never, if the heart were not filled with Love, would it have sent forth the hand.

Savaric. Gaucelm and Hugh, truly ye are vanquished in this tenzon, and thereon I would have pass sentence my " Heart's Guardian " * who rules me, and Lady Maria † in whom dwell all good virtues.

Gaucelm. My Lord, no whit am I vanquished, as the sentence will show, wherefore I would also have Lady Guillelma of Benagues with her fair and courteous speech pass judgment.

Hugh. Gaucelm, my cause is the best, and I can well defend me against both of you; and one I know right sweet and fair, whom I would fain make likewise judge, but that in three we have already enough.

---

[1]**And all the war that he made was with the King of France.**
Savaric did not, in all probability, serve the King of France

* Pseudonym of a lady whom Savaric served apparently at the same time that he served Guillelma of Benagues.
† Maria of Ventadorn.

for more than two years, and then apparently only from a
sense of expediency.

[2] **Guillelma of Benagues.** A Gascon lady, wife of a baron of
Gavaret.

[3] **Rudel of Blaia.** This Rudel is not of course Rudel of Blaia,
the troubadour, who died about 1170.

HUGH OF SAINT CIRC.

1200-1240.

HUGH of Saint Circ was, as a younger member of a large
family, sent to the School, or as we should say, University
of Montpellier, to prepare himself for the religious life, and
like other troubadours, he forsook the religious for the
poetic profession. After becoming the *protégé* of Guillelma
of Benagues, it was easy for him to win the good favour of
her lover, Savaric of Mauleon ; later on he also won that
of a Count of Rhodez, and of a Count of Turenne, with both
of whom (whether from his own quarrelsome disposition or
under provocation) he entered into fierce strife. After spending
some time at the Courts of Aragon, Leon, and Castile, he
settled down in Provence, where, although the life asserts
that he knew little of love, he paid court to Claire of Andusa,
a trouveresse, who like the Countess of Die composed canzones
of great tenderness and passion. A story is told of a certain
Ponsa,* who, bitterly jealous of Claire, induced the poet to
forsake his lady for herself. Hugh then, for some time,
served Ponsa and scorned Claire, until his eyes becoming
opened to the fact, that it was his praises and not his love
that his new mistress wanted, he sought forgiveness of Claire,
which, by means of a lady who interceded for him, he finally
obtained. We last hear of Hugh of Saint Circ as dwelling

* See Diez, *Leben und Werke der Troubadours*, page 339.

at the Court of Treviso, under the protection of Alberico, Marquis of Treviso, and of his brother Ezzelin of Romano, despot of Verona. As to his work, Hugh himself states that he was the author of the *Lives* of Bernart of Ventadorn and Savaric of Mauleon; it is, as stated in the introduction, by no means improbable that he also wrote many more of the lives collected. His extant poems are forty-two in number, the majority of those published being canzones of more or less merit. The one translated below is probably dedicated to Claire, though in none of them is the name of his lady mentioned; in another pretty canzone he seems to be rejoicing at having won her forgiveness.* In it he delights in the thought of renouncing an evil love, and returning to her, " In whom all virtues are to be found. It grieves him not, nor need it her that he left her, because he has learnt thereby to love her a thousand times better. A sinful man, on humbling himself, ought to find mercy, for it is the penitent sinners that cause the greatest joy in Heaven."

In his tenzons, as the example given below will show, his tone is that of bold defiance, and one indeed that only some heavy wrong would justify his adopting towards former friends and benefactors. In his political poems he is no less out-spoken, and in them proves himself both a Guelph and a staunch upholder of the orthodox faith. In one sirvente he sternly rebukes and threatens Raymond of Toulouse for protecting a Toulousain baron whom he accuses of heresy, after which he no less sternly denounces Frederick II. of Germany, summoning the Pope and King of France to a Crusade against him. In another poem that is among the last we have of him, he exclaims against the atrocious crimes of Ezzelin of Romano and rejoices at his loss of power.

* See Mahn's *Gedichte der Troubadours*, Vol. II., No. vi.

OF HUGH OF SAINT CIRC.

Now Sir Hugh of Saint Circ was of Quercy, of a town named Tegra, son of a poor vavasour, named Sir Arman of Saint Circ, by reason that the castle whence he was, is named Saint Circ, the which lies at the foot of Santa Maria of Rocamador, and was destroyed and overthrown in war. Now this Sir Hugh had many brothers older than himself, who would fain have made a clerk of him, and who sent him to the School at Montpellier, and lo, while they weened that he was learning wise books, he was learning canzones and vers, and sirventes and tenzons, and coblas, and the deeds and sayings of all the honourable men and women, who were then in the world or ever had been. And with this knowledge of his he became a jongleur; and the Count of Rhodez, and the Viscount of Turenne, and likewise the good Dauphin of Auvergne advanced him greatly by the vers, and the coblas, and the tenzons that they made with him. And he dwelt long in Gascony, poor, and journeying now on foot, and now on horse. And long did he abide with the Countess of Benagues, and through her he won the goodwill of Lord Savaric of Mauleon, the which gave him raiment and equipment. And long did he dwell with him in Poitou and in his

* See Mahn, xlv.

lands, and thereafter he dwelt in Catalonia, and in Aragon, and in Spain with the good King Alphonso of Aragon, and with King Peter, and thereafter he went into Provence and dwelt with the barons there, and then into Lombardy and into the March of Tervisana (Treviso), and in Tervisana he espoused a fair and noble lady. Much did he learn of others, and willingly did he teach that he learnt to others. And right many songs, vers, coblas, and melodies did he make; howbeit his canzones were few, for he never knew love, though with his fair words he could feign it, and could tell in his canzones how he had sped with ladies. And well he knew with his vers and with his sayings to make or mar their fortunes, yet after he had taken a wife he left the making of these canzones.

HUGH OF SAINT CIRC TO HIS LADY.[*]

THREE foes and two right cruel lords oppress me,[1]
  Who day and night strive how they best may slay
    me;
The foes—my eyes and heart, which sore distress me
  With love of one who ever will gainsay me;
  One lord is Love, beneath whose yoke I lay me,
Who claims from heart and soul obedience meek;
The other *thou*, whose love full long I seek,

[*] See *Chrestomathie provençale*, page 157.

To whom, though I should die, I nowise dare
My love reveal, and my fond heart lay bare.

What help have I, for bootless 'tis to borrow
  Some joy from others, if thou mock my pleading?
What help have I, to whom a bitter sorrow
  Is joy, from any other source proceeding?
  What help have I? Thy love my heart is leading,
While now it follows me, and now it flees;
What help have I, for nowhere find I ease?
  What help have I—how can I freedom gain,
  If thou, sweet Lady, wilt not me retain?

How can I bear this life of bitter anguish?
  And yet I cannot win me rest by dying;
How can I bear through love of thee to languish,
  One little hope my hopelessness belying?
  How can I bear for ever to be sighing,
Of joy bereft, if joy thou wilt not give?
How can I bear in jealousy to live
  Of those, who freely in thy presence dwell,
  And eke of those of whom all men speak well?

How can I live for ever broken-hearted,
  Sighing both day and night with hopes unsated?
How can I live, for when I'm from thee parted
  My words and deeds as nought by men are rated?
  How can I live, who nothing else am fated

To heed but thee, but thee and thy fair face,
Thy pleasant speech, and bearing full of grace?
  How can I live? to God my prayers rise
  That I may soon find favour in thy eyes.

.   .   .   .

*TENZON BETWEEN HUGH OF SAINT CIRC AND THE
COUNT OF RHODEZ.*[*]

"SIR COUNT, 'twere good that ye no more[2]
Should dwell through me in doubt and fear,
For nowise deem that I am here
  Aught of your mercy to implore:
Of others need I nothing gain,
Whilst lack of gold does you constrain;
  I have to beg of you small wish or need
  Rather great kindness 'twere your wants to feed."

"Hugh of Saint Circ, it grieves me sore
To see you, who were e'en this year
Naked, and poor, and sad of cheer,
  Till plenteous gifts from me ye bore;
Much more ye cost me to maintain
Than noble knights or archers twain;
  Yet if perchance I offered you a steed
  This well I know ye'd take, so God me speed."

* See *Chrestomathie provençale*, page 160.

[1] Three foes and two right cruel lords oppress me.   The
    original poem is composed of 5½ stanzas.   At every third
    stanza, consequently here at the third and fifth ones,
    new rhymes, though in the same order, a b a b b c c d d,
    are introduced.   The half-stanza forms the *Envoi* (b c c
    d d), and the poem is directed to the Countess of Provence,
    to whom, as the poet says, he is commanded to send it
    by his Lady.

[2] Sir Count, 'twere good that ye no more.   The tenzon is
    composed of two stanzas, having each the rhymes, a b b a
    c c d d.

AIMERIC OF PEGUILLAN.

1205-1270.

TWO accounts of Aimeric are to be found in the *Lives*, the
second, in addition to the details given in the first, containing
a further expansion of the love episode, and a mention of the
report that the poet died a " Heretic."   Aimeric has left us
over fifty poems, and these, together with the *Lives*, enable
us to form a fairly complete idea of his career.   His long life
was one of singular brilliancy and prosperity, and the most
splendid courts of France, Spain, and Northern Italy gave
him a ready welcome.   For several years he was the favoured
guest of Alphonso (III.?) of Castile, whom he only left to
enter under the protection of the Marquis of Montferrat ; he
also tasted the bounty of Raymond VI. of Toulouse, of
Guillem of Berguedan, of the Marquises of Malaspina and
Este, and other princes.   Wandering thus from court to
court, he naturally had various love intrigues ; many ladies, in
fact, are celebrated in Aimeric's canzones, but more especially
one whom he speaks of as winning him by nothing more than
allowing him to kiss her ungloved hand, and whom he afterwards lost, he says, by his own folly.   These canzones are,

for the most part, very pleasing and graceful, Aimeric's love of simile being in none of them carried to excess.

Aimeric of Peguillan, besides canzones, composed many poems in praise of some of the greatest princes of his age, as also 'complaints' over their deaths. Among the former the most interesting is perhaps one on the Emperor Frederick II., for whom the poet's enthusiastic admiration is expressed after this fashion: "Whilom* when died King Alphonso of Castile, and his fair and gracious son, and good King Peter of Aragon, and the Marquis of Este, I thought that Fame and Bounty had also died, until a physician sent by God came to heal men of their hurts. That physician physics us according to our needs, and does not take, but rather gives rewards. Never was physician like to him—so wise, so fair, so valorous, and good. . . . Henceforth, although before I doubted, I will now believe all they tell us of Alexander and his brave deeds.

"That wise physician whereof I speak to you is the son of the good Emperor Henry, and has the name of Emperor Frederick, and the heart, and understanding, and wisdom, and brave deeds, and well will he physic his friends, and good counsel and shelter will they find in him. Rightly is he named Frederick, for his words are good, and his deeds great and mighty." . . .

Another 'complaint' is one over the death of Raymond Berenger, the last Count of Provence of the Barcelona House. His youngest daughter and heiress, Beatrice, had been forced into marrying Charles of Anjou, brother of Louis IX. of France —a marriage that established the French rule in Provence, and at which Aimeric laments somewhat as follows: "Alas,† men of Provence, how great is your misery and shame; ye have lost your merriment and joy, your laughter and your fame, and have fallen into the hands of those of France; better had it

---

* See *Chrestomathie provençale*, page 162.

† See Mahn's *Gedichte der Troubadours*, Vol. II., page 183.

been for you if ye had died. . . . Ah ! wretched and dishonoured ones, what will now avail you your towns and fortresses, if ye belong to France, and dare neither for right or wrong bear shield and lance !" . . . Dante cites a poem of Aimeric's (*De Vulg. Eloq.* ii. 6) among other *illustres cantiones.*

OF AIMERIC OF PEGUILLAN.[*]

SIR AIMERIC of Peguillan was of Toulouse, and was the son of a burgher, who was a merchant and sold stuffs. And Aimeric learnt canzones and sirventes, but ever sang right ill. And he became enamoured of one of his neighbours, the wife of a burgher, and this love taught him to make poetry, so that he made many a fair song of her. And strife arose betwixt Sir Aimeric and her husband, the which did him dishonour. And Sir Aimeric avenged himself of it by striking him on his head with a sword, wherefore it behoved Sir Aimeric to depart from Toulouse, and enter into banishment. And he passed into Catalonia, and Sir Guillem of Berguedan gave him welcome; and upon the first song that Sir Aimeric made, advanced him and his poetry so much that he gave him his palfrey and his raiment, and made him known to King Alphonso of Castile, the which did him honour, and gave him gold and raiment. And he abode long in those countries, and after came into Lombardy,

* See Mahn, xlvi.

where all good people greatly honoured him, and
in Lombardy also he died.

CANZONE.

Lady, for thee I dwell in grievous pain.
"Sir, thou'rt unwise, small thanks from me thou'lt
    gain."
Lady, pardy, let me not love in vain.
"Sir, all thy prayers unheeded will remain."
Good lady, mine is love that cannot wane.
"Sir, more than all men else I thee disdain."
Lady, for this, grief o'er my heart doth reign.
"I, sir, am merry nor from joy refrain."

Lady sans mercy, I must go my way.
"Sir, prithee go, it boots not to delay."
Lady, not I, Love holds me 'neath his sway.
"Against my will, good sir, he bids thee stay."
Lady, cruel answers my fond words repay.
"Sir, worse than all I hate thee, by my fay."
Then, lady, wilt thou ne'er my grief allay?
"Sir, verily 'twill be as thou dost say."

Love, thou hast heap'd on me indignity.
  "Friend, there is naught else I can do for thee."
Love, thou requitest ill my loyalty.
  "Friend, by such means thou best mayst healèd be."

* *Chrestomathie provençale*, page 159.

Love, wherefore such a lady givest thou me?
"Friend, one of better worth I made thee see."
Love, from my sorrow I would fain be free.
"Friend, to some other refuge thou must flee."

Love, verily small kindness dost thou show.
"Friend, thou dost wrong to treat me as thy foe."
Love, why would'st part us, why would'st lay me
    low?
"Friend, I do grieve to see thee die of woe."
Love, do not deem that elsewhere I can go.
"Friend, then thou needs must bear full many a
    blow."
Love, dost thou think some favour she'll bestow?
"Yea, friend, serve, suffer, and great joy thou'lt
    know."

PEIRE CARDINAL.

1210-1230.

As a great moral satirist Peire Cardinal's place in Provençal
literature is unique. A deep-seated scorn for corrupt human
nature, an intense religious earnestness and loftiness of purpose,
an originality and variety in the treatment of his favourite
theme—the general perversion of mankind—make him one
of the most powerful and impressive, if not the most attractive,
of troubadours. The contrast between him and the generality
of his contemporaries is complete. Towards love and women
his attitude is indifferent, if not contemptuous ; his carelessness
also with regard to form, and the frequency with which he

imitated the verse of others, is all the more remarkable, in that perfection of style and originality of metre were what other troubadours esteemed most highly. In his poems he not unfrequently shows a consciousness of composing for those who can but ill understand him ; he seems, in fact, to have had as little in common with the world around him as Dante himself, but unlike Dante he had not for any man or woman that overpowering reverence or love which might have softened for him the stern realities of life, and inspired him with faith in humanity.

We have little information concerning Peire Cardinal's life beyond that given us in the following account of him. His poems treat mostly of generalities, but fix the period in which he lived, and prove him to have been a staunch friend of Raymond VI. of Toulouse, and, in consequence, steadily opposed to the French. The satire of Peire's forty to fifty extant poems is almost exclusively directed against the Church and Aristocracy; and as he for the most part attacks these two great bodies in the mass, there is in his poems an absence of local colouring and allusion that lessens their historical value, and also at times a want of vividness that lessens their literary tone. The poems may be divided into those against (1) the Church; (2) the Nobles; (3) Vice in general, especially lying, treachery, religious hypocrisy, avarice, and luxury; (4) Exhortations to Virtue; (5) a few invectives against private persons ; (6) three poems on love, which finish by attacking rather than defending it.

*OF PEIRE CARDINAL.**

Now Peire Cardinal was of Velley, of the city of Puy Notre Dame—of an honourable and gentle stock, and the son of a knight and a lady. And

* See Mahn, xlviii.

being yet little he was sent by his father to the Canonry of Puy, for to make of him a canon; and he learnt letters, and knew well to read and to sing. And when he was full grown he became enticed by the vanities of this world, for he felt himself gay, and young, and handsome. And many a fair discourse and fair song did he make, albeit his canzones were few; and he also made many a cunningly devised sirvente, in the which were many goodly sayings, and fair ensamples for him that would heed them, for greatly did he rebuke the foolishness of this world, and chide all false clerks, even as his sirventes do testify. And he came to courts of kings and noble barons, bringing with him his jongleur for to sing his sirventes. And he was much honoured and cherished by my lord the good King James of Aragon, and by honourable barons; and I, master Miquel of la Tor, scribe, do declare that Sir Peire Cardinal when he passed from this life was nigh upon a hundred years old; and I, the aforesaid Miquel, have written these sirventes in the city of Nismes.

A SIRVENTE AGAINST THE CLERGY.[1]

VULTURES fierce and kites, I ween,
Scent not rotting flesh so well

* See *Chrestomathie provençale*, page 173.

As the priests and friars keen
  Scent the rich where'er they dwell;
Soon the rich man's love they gain,
Then if sickness, grief, or pain
  Fall on him, great gifts they win,
  Robbing thus his kith and kin.

Priests and Frenchmen ever seek
  All ill to praise for love of gold;
By usurers and traitors eke
  Is this world of ours controll'd;
Lies and fraud to men they've taught,
And confusion 'mongst them brought;
  Order[2] none can be discerned
  That this lesson has not learned.

Know ye what on them will fall,
  Unto whom great goods belong?
One will spoil them of their all,
  Death, a robber fierce and strong,
Fells them, strips them, thrusts them down,
In four poor ells of linen brown,
  To a dwelling dark and low,
  Where great misery they'll know.

Man, great folly thou dost do,
  God's commandment why transgress?

He, thy righteous Lord and true
  Brought thee out of nothingness.
He that 'gainst the Lord would strive
  Thereby does but little thrive;
    And will win the same reward
    As Judas that betrayed our Lord.

God of Mercy and of Truth,
  Saviour, Thou our footsteps lead,
May poor sinners by Thy ruth
  Be from Hell's fierce torments freed;
Break from them sin's heavy chain,
'Neath the which they groan in pain,
    And if they their faults confess
    Grant them Thy forgiveness.

*AGAINST A BARON, WHO HAD COMMITTED ROBBERY
ON CHRISTMAS DAY.*[*][2]

GREAT is the Feast, but that man keeps it ill
  Who lifts men's cattle, and at will does slay;
And one I will not name, his pot does fill
  With flesh ill-gotten, e'en on Christmas day.
Such flesh, I say, is no wise sweet and sound,
  Unlawful too, since law it does gainsay;
Less wit than in a suckling may be found
  Has he that honours Christmas in such way.

* See Mahn's *Gedichte der Troubadours*, Vol. II., page 209.

If but a sheet he steal, with head bent low
  The poor man crouches, and a thief is named,
While through the world full haughtily may go
  The robber baron, robbing all unshamed.
The churl for nothing swings, a grievous fate,
  As if another's stallion he had claimed;
The rich thief hangs the poor, for nowise straight
  As is an arrow is their course ill-famed.

At will I sing and fiddle, none give heed,
  And none but I my singing reads aright;
As well may men the subtle meaning read
  Of nightingales' sweet songs, poured forth at night.
Yet mine is not the language of Anjoù,
  Breton or Norman it is no wise hight;
But they no more can 'twixt the false and true
  Distinguish, such through sin their grievous plight.

The following are a few prose versions of passages taken from Peire Cardinal's Sirventes:

"Priors I see that are fighters and jousters, and ill it seemeth to Saint Denis that he and other saints should be shamed by them. . . . The Church in her greed would fain be shod and clothed in the best; if ye hold an honourable fief of her prelates, they will take it of you, nor readily restore it till

ye give them a sum of gold or make a harder
bond with them. . . . If Black Friars may
win salvation of God by much eating, and by the
keeping of women; White Friars by fraudulent
encroachments, Templars and Hospitallers by pride,
canons by lending money at usury—if these come
thus to salvation, for fools I hold Saint Peter and
Saint Andrew, who suffered for God such grievous
torments. . . . Kings, emperors, dukes, counts,
and knights were wont to rule the world; but now
I see clerks holding dominion over it by robbery,
deceit, hypocrisy, force, and exhortation; greatly it
vexeth them if men give them not their all, and
this men must needs do howsoever they delay. In
the refectory it misliketh me to see rogues sitting
at the high table; an ill thing it is that they venture
thither, and that men do not chase them forth, yet
of *one* thing I must absolve them [the clerks], never
have I seen the *poor* rogue sitting beside the rich
man. The Alcaydes and Almansors need not fear
that abbots and priors will come to assail them, and
seize upon their lands, for this it would sorely vex
them to do. Nay, they are intent only on possessing
them of the world, and on overthrowing Frederick
[Frederick II. of Germany], yet till now they have
gained little in their strife with him." "The priests
call themselves shepherds, but are in truth murderers;
by their clothing they have the semblance of holiness,

yet therein they mind me of Sir Isengrim,[4] who upon a day would enter into a sheepfold, but for fear of the dogs put on sheep's clothing wherewith he beguiled the sheep, and thereon swallowed up all such as pleased him."

On women and love Peire Cardinal thus expresses himself: "I trust not in woman's vows, nor would I have her oath, for if ye put in her hands a *marabotin* for speaking the truth, and a *barbarin* for lying, it is the barbarin that will win. . . . Love taketh not from me food or drink, causeth me not to feel heat or cold, to gape or sigh, to rage at night-time, or to be downcast and sore pressed; never did I hire messenger for it, nor have been betrayed by it, for I have separated myself from it as I have done from dice."

The only *fable* existing in Provençal literature proper is one by Peire Cardinal on the general vice and folly of mankind,* in which he tells us how a storm of rain fell upon a certain city, which storm caused madness to those who were exposed to it. All the inhabitants of the city felt its effects but one man, who was sleeping within doors at the time. This latter awoke when it was no longer raining, and on going forth amongst men found them all seized with madness. Some of these, Peire tells us, the sane man finds tearing their clothes, some throwing

* See *Chrestomathie provençale*, page 175.

stones; one man deems himself a king and goes richly clad, another springs over benches, some threaten, others curse, weep, laugh, rave, and such like. The sane man looks around him bewildered, marvelling greatly at their folly. They, however, marvel still more at him, thinking him out of his wits in that he does not demean himself like them, concluding thus that *they* are sound of mind, and that he is unsound. They straightway lay fast hold upon him; one strikes him on the cheek, and one on the neck, so that he falls overcome to the ground. Pushed and trampled on he seeks to escape, and at last after much fighting reaches his dwelling beaten, covered with mire, half dead, and in great joy at his escape. Peire Cardinal then himself explains the fable: "This world is the city that is full of madmen; for the best wisdom is that of loving and fearing God, and keeping His commandments, and such wisdom is now nowhere to be found. The rain that fell upon them is covetousness, which with Pride and Evil hath encompassed all men. . . . The friend of God, wherever he be, observeth that all are mad, in that they have lost the wisdom of God; while they likewise deem him mad, because he hath forsaken the wisdom of the world."

[1] **Sirvente against the clergy.** Peire Cardinal, in the surprising audacity of his attacks on the Church and her

institutions, may be compared with his great German contemporary, Walther von der Vogelweide ; like Vogelweide also, he is the friend of the poor, and a staunch adherent of Frederick the Second in his struggle against the Pope. The poem is of five stanzas, and in the metre of the translation.

[2] **Order.** Religious order.

[3] **Against a baron.** The poem is composed of five stanzas of eight lines, and concluded by a couplet (rhymes, a b a b c b c b).

[4] **Isengrim.** The name given to the Wolf in the *Roman de Renard.* Isengrim is the embodiment of strength and ferocity, as the Fox of cunning.

SORDELLO.

1225-1250.

THE name of Sordel, or Sordello, is a household word among us, and the noble lines in Dante's *Purgatorio*, with the profound and complex character in Browning's poem, cannot but inspire one with a wish to know something of the Sordello of actual life. Yet, on turning to the scanty records, and to the poems left us of him, we are at first somewhat disconcerted. One of the biographies[1] represents him as a false-hearted traitor, false both to the husband who gave him shelter, and to the wife whom he seduced. Some of his canzones are those of a skilful, but somewhat ironic and cynical rhymer, whose chief merit, as has been remarked, is that of saying agreeably what everyone already knows, and whose chief source of pride is the exceeding number of ladies whom he has won and betrayed. Nor should we greatly esteem his valour if we are to regard as a true expression of his sentiments—a poem, in which he begs his lord, the Count of Provence, to excuse him from accompanying him on the Crusade (of 1248), and confesses his fear of the perils to which the expedition would expose him.

Yet this same Sordello is the noble poet, whom Virgil and Dante find sitting in majestic solitude, and the recognition of whom causes them such joy. That his nobility of soul was a mere conception of Dante's we can in no way suppose, and one is therefore brought to the conclusion, that the sins and follies recorded of him were in after years atoned for, and also that the poems of his preserved to us were only a portion, perhaps the least worthy portion, of the work he accomplished. This latter conclusion is, indeed, borne out by Dante's declaring in his *De Vulgari Eloquio*, that Sordello was of great eloquence, in poetry as well as in speech.

There are three poems, however, that even without Dante's praise of Sordello, would sufficiently testify to his power. The first, which Dante obviously refers to in the *Purgatorio*, where he makes Sordello the guide to the Dale of Kings is a 'complaint.' The second is a long didactic poem, the *Ensegnamen d'Onor*, or Lesson of Honour, a work of considerable interest, some learning, and at times much pithy vigour. It is full of the sentiment of noble pride and reason that inspired Dante in the Convito, and especially in the canzone that treats of true nobility. A third poem is on the death of his friend and rival Blacatz, and its originality and force are in the most striking contrast to the elegant insipidity of some of the canzones, while the splendid audacity of its attack upon the great sovereigns of the age, is without parallel even among the troubadours. Sordello has also left us various very bitter sirventes against individual contemporaries, amongst others, a series of poems against a rival troubadour, who, in his turn, speaks of Sordello as a man who "for his misdeeds had needs flee from Lombardy . . . a false, wanton jongleur, living on his jongleur tricks." We know Sordello on unimpeachable evidence as the friend and counsellor of Charles of Anjou, as a person of sufficient consequence for the Pope to insist upon his being promptly released from captivity. Of his death by violence tradition speaks; and Dante seems to confirm the report by the position he allots him in Purgatory. The Lady Cunizza (sister of Eccelin da Romano, the Ghibelline tyrant), whom Sordello carried off, is also noticed by Dante, and given a place in the Heaven of Venus (*Paradiso*, IX. 13).

> " O anima lombarda,
>   Come ti stavi altera e disdegnosa,
>   E nel muover degli occhi onesta e tarda!
> Ella non ci diceva alcuna cosa;
>   Ma lasciavane gir, solo guardando
>   A guisa di leon, quando si posa.
> Pur Virgilio si trasse a lei pregando
>   Che ne mostrasse la miglior salita:
>   E quella non rispose al suo dimando;
> Ma di nostro paese, e della vita
>   Ci chiese. E'l dolce Duca incominciava:
>   Mantova. E l'ombra, tutta in sè romita,
> Surse vêr lui del luogo ove pria stava,
>   Dicendo: O mantovano, io son Sordello
>   Della tua terra. E l'un l'altro abbracciava."

Purgatorio, VI. 61-75.

> (—" O Lombard soul,
> How lofty and disdainful thou didst bear thee,
> And grand and slow in moving of thine eyes,
> Nothing whatever did it say to us,
>   But let us go our way, eyeing us only
>   After the manner of a couchant lion;
> Still near to it Virgilius drew, entreating
>   That it would point us out the best ascent;
>   And it replied not unto his demand,
> But of our native land and of our life
>   It questioned us; and the sweet guide began:
>   ' Mantua,'—and the shade all in itself recluse,
> Rose tow'rds him from the place where first it was,
>   Saying, ' O Mantuan, I am Sordello
>   Of thine own land,' and one embraced the other.")

Longfellow's translation.

*SORDELLO.**

NOW Sordello was of Sirier in Mantua, son of a poor knight, named Sier El Cort. And he delighted in the learning of canzones, and the making of poetry. And he had intercourse with the good people at court, and learnt all he could, and made coblas and sirventes. Then he came into the court of the Count of Saint Boniface, the which honoured him full well. And in manner of pastime, he fell to loving the Count's wife, and she loved him likewise. And it happened that strife arose betwixt her brothers and the Count, who became estranged from her; wherefore her brothers, Sir Icellis and Sir Albric,[2] caused her to flee from the Count with Sir Sordello; the which dwelt with them in great bliss, and afterwards departed into Provence, where he had great honour of all good people, and of the Count and Countess, who gave him a good castle, and a noble wife.

ON THE DEATH OF BLACATZ.[3]†

I SING Sir Blacatz' death, by sorrow sore con-
    strain'd,
And meet it is I mourn with sighs and tears un-
    feign'd,

* See Mahn, xlix.
† See *Chrestomathie provençale*, page 205.

For lord and friend I've lost; no better earth
    contain'd.
Since by his death we lose all fame and worth
    unstain'd,
So foul the ill, that I have needs from hope re-
    frain'd,
Yet hope would come if, ere his heart of blood
    be drain'd,
The cowardly barons ate of it, and thereby gain'd
That courage high and firm that ever in it reign'd.

First let there eat of it, for sore I deem his need,
The Emperor of Rome,[4] if he in very deed
Would rule the Milanese, who, full of hate and greed,
Seek to rule *him*, and all his Germans little heed;
And then, if he would win Castile's fair realm, I
    read
The King of France[5] upon that noble heart to feed;
Yet eat he will not if his Mother 'gainst it plead,
For his poor fame well shows, that she his heart
    does lead.

Fain would I see the English King[6] upon it fare,
Who then a stouter heart within his breast would
    bear,
To win the land, whose loss his honour does impair,
The land that for his sloth the French as theirs
    declare;

Then I would give the Castile King[7] a double
    share,
Who, though he hold two kingdoms, one does merit
    ne'er;
Yet, if he eat, to tell thereof he must not dare,
Since, if his mother knew't, the rod she'd nowise
    spare.

    .   .   .   .

Likewise, 'twere well the Count of Toulouse[8] on it
    fed,
To mind him of that land that he abandoned;
If by another's heart he be not strengthened,
That land he'll ne'er regain, for his own heart is
    dead;
Then the Provençal Count[9] should taste that heart
    blood red,
For small the worth methinks of peer disherited,
Full valiantly he fights and sorely is bestead,
Yet eat he must, or 'neath his burdens bow his head.

Ill will the barons brook the honest words I've said,
Know they like scorn to theirs, within my heart
    is laid.

    .   .   .   .

[1] **One of the biographies.** The other biography tells how
    Sordello forsook Cunizza, and secretly married the Lady
    Otha of Strasso, sister of his friends, Sir Henry, Sir William,

and Sir Walpertin of Strasso. This so offended them that, fearing their vengeance, he went to the Court of Provence.

Sir Icellis and Sir Albric. Eccelin and Alberico of Romano.

[3] **On the death of Blacatz.** The original sirvente is composed of five stanzas of eight lines, and two final couplets, the latter of which is addressed to his lady. The rhyming system is that of the translation.

[4] **The Emperor of Rome.** Frederick II.

[5] **The King of France.** Louis IX., who had in fact legitimate claims on Castile, but who, acting probably on the advice of his mother Blanche of Castile, did not enforce claims that he knew would be most unwelcome to the Castilians.

[6] **The English King.** Henry III., who during Louis' minority did not attempt to recover the Angevin inheritance that his father had lost.

[7] **The Castile King.** We do not know the story that Sordello is referring to, nor his reasons for reproaching the King.

[8] **The Count of Toulouse.** Raymond VII., who only made peace with the Crusaders, at the sacrifice of a large portion of his inheritance.

[9] **The Provençal Count.** Raymond Berengar of Provence, the last Count of the Barcelona House, who was at that time at war with several of his towns.

BERTOLOME ÇORGI.

1250-1270.

THE northern states of Italy had, ever since the development of Provençal poetry, given the most hospitable welcome to troubadours, and paid full homage to their genius ; and when this poetry was crushed out in Languedoc itself, by the Albigensian War, it was in Northern Italy that it found a last refuge, being there fostered by men such as Sordello, Boniface Calvo, and Çorgi (or Giorgi), who, though natives of Italy, composed in the Langue d'Oc.

Çorgi himself was a Venetian, and perhaps a merchant, who, during the long strife between Venice and Genoa, was seized, while on a journey, by some Genoese, and imprisoned in Genoa for seven years. Of his extant poems (about twenty-five in number) several were composed during this imprisonment. One of these, alluded to in his *Life*, was in defence of his native city against the Genoese poet, Boniface Calvo, a sirvente which, far from alienating the two poets, led to a close bond of friendship between them. Another of his more remarkable works, composed while in prison, is full of bitter indignation at the deaths of Conradin and Frederick of Baden, who were executed in 1268 by orders of their adversary, Charles of Anjou.

Hopes of freedom came to Çorgi when Saint Louis started on his second crusade against the Turks. Requiring, as he did, to be provided with ships by Venice and Genoa, Louis sought to bring about a peace between the two towns—a peace which, as Çorgi thought, would lead to the release of all prisoners on both sides. He therefore hailed the approaching crusade with a song of rejoicing, congratulating the King of Navarre and the Count of Toulouse on bearing Louis company. Only a short time afterwards, however, he wrote a bitter poem of complaint against Louis, who, in the treaty of temporary peace that he caused to be made, had omitted to provide for the freedom of the captive poet, though this was done in a later treaty. Çorgi's poems are perhaps better in form than matter. A southern lusciousness of style and metre characterize the original of the one translated below, the soft double rhymes, of which there are so many in Provençal, giving it a musical sweetness, impossible to render in another language. The same also may be said of an ' Invocation to Saint Margaret' to be found in the *Chrestomathie provençale.*

OF BERTOLOME ÇORGI.*

Now Sir Bertolome Çorgi was a gentleman of the city of Venice, and was one of wisdom and of natural wit, knowing well to sing and to make poetry. And there came a time when he took to wandering through the world, and the Genoese,[1] who were warring with the Venetians, laid hands on him, and brought him captive to their land. And while he abode thus in prison, Sir Boniface Calvo made the sirvente written here above, the which begins:

> "Ges no mes greu sieu non sui ren prezatz,"
> (I care not if I am but little praised,)

wherein he blamed the Genoese that they let themselves be subdued by the Venetians, and spake great villainy of them; whereat Sir Bertolome Çorgi made another sirvente, written below, the which begins:

> " Molt me sui fort dun chant meraveillatz,"
> (Greatly have I marvelled at a song,)

wherein he excused the Venetians, and blamed the Genoese, so that Sir Boniface held himself put to rebuke for that he had said, and lo, through this they turned one to the other, and became fast friends; and for about the space of seven years Sir Bertolome abode in prison ; and when he was let loose he gat

* See Mahn, 1.

him to Venice, and the Commons there sent him as castellan to a castle named Coron, and there also did he bring his days to an end.

PRAYER TO THE VIRGIN.[2]

SANCTA MARIA, all maidens exceeding,
God's own belovèd, mankind to him leading,
Look down in pity, give ear to my pleading,
    Mercy, sweet lady!

Mother, most holy—oh! do not disdain me,
God's gracious pardon I pray thee to gain me,
Fruit and eke fruit-tree of virtue, maintain me,
    Mercy, sweet lady!

.   .   .   '   .   .   .   .   .

With thy sweet pity, I pray thee, befriend me,
Free me from evil, thy happiness send me,
And from Hell's torments I pray thee defend me,
    Mercy, sweet lady!

Mother of Jesus, by doubt sore distressèd,
May I have guidance of thee ever blessèd,
Who God's high favour hast ever possessèd,
    Mercy, sweet lady!

* For original, see *Chrestomathie provençale*, page 277.

Toward thee I turn me, in prayer persevering,
What may befall me, thee ever revering,
If but thy grace do avail, nothing fearing,
    Mercy, sweet lady!

O, gentle Virgin, thou life of perfection,
Thee do I long for with heartfelt affection,
On the sea grant me thy gracious protection,
    Mercy, sweet lady!

Maiden most holy, thy grace we are craving,
Star of the ocean, our souls from death saving,
Man's sail and oar art thou, life's tempest braving,
    Mercy, sweet lady!

[1] **The Genoese and Venetians.** The war between Venice and Genoa had broken out in Palestine in 1256 over the possession of a church there. The strife between them grew very fierce, and on one occasion the whole Genoese fleet was destroyed by the Venetians.

[2] **Prayer to the Virgin.** The original is composed of eight stanzas of four lines. The rhymes (a a a b) vary in each stanza.

GUIRAUT OF CALANSO.

First half of 13th Century.

GUIRAUT of Calanso's poems prove him to be a troubadour of merit, in spite of the somewhat contemptuous allusion to him in the *Life*. Among his most interesting canzones is that of which two stanzas are translated below; in it is an allegorical description of the lower or third part of love, love being divided by the poets of the day into three parts—the divine, the natural, and the sensual; which latter is represented as a beautiful woman of irresistible power. The poem was probably very well known—since Guiraut Riquier, one of the most distinguished of the later troubadours, has given a detailed explanation of it.

OF GUIRAUT OF CALANSO.* [1]

GUIRAUT of Calanso was a jongleur of Gascony, and a right learned man he was, and subtle in the making of poetry. And of the days in which he lived he made canzones of great cunning, but ill-pleasing and discourteous. And he and his canzones were ill liked in Provence, and small fame had he among the courteous.

A CANZONE ON LOVE.†

So slight her form, that she may ne'er be seen,
So fast she runs that bootless 'tis to fly,
So hard she strikes that none her power abye;
  Her steely dart deals thrusts full sweet and keen,
The which no coat of mail can e'er withstand,
So true her aim—then straightway with strong hand
  She bends her bow, lets fly a shaft of gold,
  Thereon a head of steel full sharp and cold.

* See Mahn, li.
† See *Chrestomathie provençale*, page 165, stanzas two and three.

A golden crown she bears upon her head;
Sees nought but him at whom she aims her dart,
Nor ever shoots amiss, so great her art,
 And lightly moves and fear around does spread;
And she was born of joy and of delight,
And all the wrong she does, will pass for right;
 She feeds on gladness, deals and parries blows,
 To great and small alike no mercy shows.

[1] **Canzone on Love.** The original poem is composed of six
  stanzas, with the rhymes a b b a c c d d running through
  them, followed by two stanzas of three lines each, with the
  rhymes c d d, c d d.

RICHARD OF BERBESIU.
First half of 13th Century.

RICHARD of Berbesiu is one of the later and less important
troubadours, the most remarkable feature about his poems
being a striving after effect, which led him, as his biographer
tells us, to introduce far-fetched similes, taken from the Natural
History of the time, talking as Lyly, the Euphuist in a
later age:

"Of stones, stars, plants, of fishes, flies,
Playing with words and idle similes."

*RICHARD OF BERBESIU.**

Now Richard of Berbesiu was a knight of the
Castle of Berbesiu of Saintonge, of the diocese of
Saintas, and came of a race of poor vavasours, and

* See Mahn, lii.

a good knight of arms he was, and fair of person withal. And he was better skilled in the making of poetry than in the expounding or rehearsing of it. Full ill did he speak before men, and the more good folk he saw, the more did his wits go astray, and the less did he know. And ever he needed that another should lead him forth ; yet well could he sing, and make good poetry, and fair melodies. And he became enamoured of an honourable lady,[1] wife of Lord Jaufre of Taunai, an honourable baron of that region. And the lady was gentle, and fair, and gay, and pleasant, and right wishful of fame and honour—the daughter of Lord Jaufre Rudel, Prince of Blaia, and when she knew he was enamoured of her, she made him fair semblance of love, so that he was emboldened to make his prayers to her— and she, with fair semblance of love, and as one who greatly desired a troubadour that should sing of her, received his prayers, and hearkened to them ; and he fell to making his canzones of her, and in all his songs he called her " Better than lady." And Sir Richard was ever wont in his canzones to delight greatly in similitudes of beasts and birds, and of the sun and of the stars, that the matter of them might be more novel than aught conceived or spoken by other poets. Long did he sing and rhyme of her, yet never was it thought that she granted him his desires.

[1] "And he became enamoured of an honourable lady." In the *Leben und Werke der Troubadours* Diez gives us an account of a romantic old Italian story, which he considers to be taken from a Provençal original, and the hero of which is a certain Alamanno. Now, by Alamanno is meant Bertran de la Manon, but as a canzone is attributed to this latter, which is undoubtedly composed by Richard of Berbesiu, Alamanno seems here to be put by mistake for Richard himself, and the details of the story are as follows : The poet is known to be in love, but has, so far, not revealed the name of the lady he serves. Certain knights, anxious to extract the secret from him, make use of the opportunity afforded them of doing so at a great feast, held at Puy Notre Dame. As was often done of evenings as men sat feasting together, they fell to boasting of their successes in love, and this, as they hoped, led on the poet to boast of *his* lady, and finally to speak her name. Secrecy being one of the first laws of chivalry, the offence is of the gravest, and his lady therefore dismisses him in anger. In his despair the poet becomes a hermit, and for a long time lives in the depths of a forest. At length, however, he hears from some knights, who chance to pass by his dwelling, that a great festival is to be held at Puy. Seized with a longing to take part in it, he borrows a suit of armour, appears as one of the champions, and wins the chief prize. On ·raising his helmet he is at once recognized, and all knights press round him, clamouring for a song. "I may in no wise sing," answers the poet, "till my Lady grant me her pardon." To this the lady, however, answers : "I will not pardon him until he has caused a hundred barons, a hundred knights, a hundred dames, and a hundred damsels to cry for mercy to be shown him, without knowing the reason thereof." Thereupon the poet, who was a man of resources, forthwith composes a fine canzone, which he sings before a

great assemblage of lords and ladies. "Even as an elephant," runs the canzone, "when he falleth cannot rise till other elephants uplift him by their voices, so is it with me. Deign then to cry me mercy, and to lift me up." The song, of course, has the effect of inducing the required number of knights and ladies to pray for his forgiveness, and the story ends happily with the reconciliation of the two lovers.

GUILLEM OF BALAUN.
First half of 13th Century.

GUILLEM of Balaun is a poet of lesser fame, and the only really remarkable thing in connection with him is the following romantic tale, of his attempt to prove his lady's love. A somewhat similar story is told, as we have seen, about Pons of Capduoil, and we have also more than once found a reconciliation brought about by the intercession of friends. The story is interesting, inasmuch as it throws a curious light on the age in which it was written; but the barbarity of some of its details is unpleasant to modern taste.

GUILLEM OF BALAUN.

NOW Guillem of Balaun was a noble castellan of the country of Montpellier—a right excellent knight he was, and a good poet withal, and he became enamoured of a noble lady of the diocese of Gavaudan, named my Lady Guilhelma of Javiac, wife of Peire, lord of Javiac. Much did he love her, and

* Mahn, liii.

serve her in song and speech; and she too loved him so well that she granted him all he would of her. Now Sir Guillem had a comrade, named Sir Peire of Barjac, valorous and good and handsome. And in the castle of Javiac he loved a gracious lady, named Viernetta, who took him for her knight and accorded him all he would of her. And it happened that Sir Peire fell out with his lady, insomuch that she roughly dismissed him, whereat he went away more sad and dolorous than ever in his life before. And Sir Guillem gave him great comfort and bade him not despair, promising to make them at one so soon as he should return to Javiac. And a long and weary time did it seem to Sir Peire, ere his return thither. And so soon as Sir Guillem was come to Javiac he made them at one, whereat Sir Peire was even gladder than when first he won his lady: and this he himself told to Sir Guillem. Then Sir Guillem said he would fain know whether the joy of recovering a lady's love were indeed as great as that of first winning it; so he feigned himself sore vext with my Lady Guilhelma, and withheld from sending her message or greeting, neither would he dwell in her neighbourhood. Then the lady sent him a messenger bearing full loving letters, wherein she said she marvelled that he withheld himself from her, and sent her no message; and he, like a foolish lover, would not hearken to the letters, and sent away the messenger full churlishly. Then the messenger, making great dole, returned unto his lady, to tell that which had happened. Then the lady was full sorrowful, and she charged a knight of the castle, the which knew of all that had passed betwixt them, to go to Sir Guillem of Balaun, to inquire of him why he was thus wroth with her, and to tell him that, if she had done aught amiss, he should avenge it on her, and she would amend it according to his desire. The knight went to Sir Guillem and was ill received, and when he had said his say, Sir Guillem told him he would not speak the cause of his wrath, for he knew well it was such that it might not be amended nor forgiven. The knight returned and told my Lady Guilhelma that which Sir Guillem had said, whereat she fell into despair, and said that never more would she send him messenger nor prayer, nor justification, and from henceforth she held everything for naught, and long remained of this mind.

Now it chanced upon a day that Sir Guillem fell to thinking of the great joy and blessedness which he was losing by his folly, so he mounted his horse and came to Javiac, and lodged with a burgher, for he would not come to court, and said that he was making a pilgrimage. My Lady Guilhelma came to know that he was in the town, and at nightfall, when all men were abed, she came forth from the castle with a dame and a damsel, and went unto his lodging, and bade them show her where he was, and she came into the chamber where he was lying, and fell upon her knees before him, and lowered her wimple for to kiss him, and besought him pardon for the wrong she had not done; and he would neither receive nor pardon her, but with blows and buffets drove her from before him. And the lady went back, passing sad and heavy to her lodging, and was minded never more to see him nor to speak with him; and repented her of that which Love had made her do. And he also made great dole at the folly he had committed, and he arose betimes, and came to the castle and said, that he would speak with my Lady Guilhelma to ask her pardon. And the Lady Guilhelma when she heard of it refused herself to him, and bade them cast him roughly from the castle. Then Sir Guillem went forth sad and tearful, while the lady abode in grief and repentance at the dishonour that had been done her. Thus did Guillem of Balaun endure a full year, and in all that while the lady would neither see him nor hear talk of him, wherefore he made the despairing song that begins:

"Mon vers mou merceian."
(My song begins with prayer for grace.)

Now Sir Bernart of Andusa, the most excellent knight of that country, came to know how it stood with them, and he gat him to horse, and came to Balaun, and asked Sir Guillem how it might be that he had so long withheld from seeing his lady. And Sir Guillem told him of all the matter, and of the folly that had seized upon him; and Sir Bernart, when he heard it, held it for sport and jest, and said he would make peace betwixt them; and great joy came to Sir Guillem on hearing that Sir Bernart would be their go-between. Sir Bernart departed and went to Javiac, and told the lady how it stood with Sir Guillem, and how he was sad and sorowful for the folly he had imagined within himself, and told her that the scorn he had made of her was but to prove her. And the lady made answer that she was greatly at fault for so humbling herself before him. And Sir Bernart told her that it would the more beseem her to be the first to pardon, in that she was right and Sir Guillem wrong; and as instantly as he could, did he beseech her to pardon him for the sake of God's Mercy, and avenge herself thereafter as she would. And the lady answered that since he willed it she would grant pardon, if so be that Sir Guillem, for the fault he had committed, would tear away the nail from his little finger, and would bring it her with a song, blaming himself for the folly he had done.

Sir Bernart of Andusa, seeing that he could do naught else, took leave of her, and went unto Sir

Guillem and delivered him the lady's answer. Then Sir Guillem, hearing of the pardon that was assured him, made right merry, and gave thanks to him that he had thus wrought upon his lady. Right so forth he let bring a learned leech, and caused him to tear away the nail, suffering the while great pain; and he made his song and came to Javiac, he and Sir Bernart with him. My Lady Guilhelma came forth to meet them, and Sir Guillem knelt down before her, seeking mercy and pardon of her, and presenting her the nail. And she took pity on him and made him rise, and they three entered together into a chamber, and there she pardoned him, and kissed and embraced him. And he rehearsed to her his song, and she heard it gladly; and henceforth either loved other more than ever before.

. . . .

GUY OF UISEL.

First half of 13th Century.

Guy of Uisel, his brothers and cousin, though owning, as we are told, many castles, dwelt peacefully in one of them. Three of them were troubadours, while the fourth sang that which the others composed. A few graceful 'pastoretas' of Guy of Uisel's are preserved to us, and also a few tenzons, written by his cousin and one of his brothers.

GUY OF UISEL.

GUY of Uisel was a noble castellan of Limousin, and he and his brothers, and his cousin Sir Elias, were lords of Uisel, a mighty castle, and many others had they likewise. And one of his brothers hight Ebles, and the other Peire, and the cousin Elias. And all they four were poets; and Guy made good canzones, and Elias good tenzons, and Ebles bad † tenzons, and Peire sang all that they made. Sir Guy was canon of Montferran and of Briude, and long loved the Countess of Montferran and the Lady Margarida of Albusson, wife of Sir Rainaut, Viscount of Albusson; and of these he made many good canzones, until the Pope's legate bound him by oath to make no more of them, wherefore he forsook both singing and poetry.

ELIAS OF BARJOL.

First half of 13th Century.

AMONG the twelve canzones Elias of Barjol has left us, one is worthy of mention as being evidently in imitation of that by Bertran of Born, in which the latter creates a lady for himself out of the graces and virtues borrowed from *many* ladies. Elias in the same manner creates a knight for his mistress by borrowing virtues from the most famous knights of Provence, amongst whom appear the names of the Dauphin of Auvergne, Pons of Capduoil, and Raymond of Miraval.

---

* See Mahn, liv.　　　　　　† Bad—satirical, malicious.

*ELIAS OF BARJOL.**

Now Sir Elias of Barjol was of the Agenois, of a castle named Perol. The son of a merchant was he, and sang better than any man that was at that season. And he became a jongleur, and joined the company of another jongleur that hight Oliver, and they two roamed long time from court to court. The Count Alphonso of Provence caused them to abide with him, and gave them at Barjol wives and land, wherefore men called them Elias and Oliver of Barjol. And after the Count was dead in Sicily, Sir Elias became enamoured of the Countess Garsenda,† the Count's wife, and while she lived he made of her many a fair and good song, and afterwards entered the hospital of St. Benedict at Avignon, and there also did he die.

CADENET.

First half of 13th Century.

Cadenet, judging by the number of his extant poems, was one of the most productive of the lesser troubadours. He composed a few 'pastoretas' (pastourelles), but the majority of his poems are canzones, and the lady whose praises he chiefly sang in them, was Eleanor, wife of Raymond VI. of

---

* See Mahn, lv.

† Garsenda was a princess of great virtue who after her husband's death became Regent of Provence.

Toulouse, and daughter of the famous Alphonso II. of Aragon. This lady inherited her father's taste for poetry, and was, like him, a friend and protector of poets, who, of course, in return for her bounty, united in praise of her beauty and many virtues. Besides canzones and pastourelles, we have a remarkably bitter so-called 'Half-sirvente,' by Cadenet, directed against a Count of Burlatz, who, irritated by the blame of one of the troubadours, banished them all from his court. One of his latest poems is a religious one, in which he bids farewell to the world, and exhorts his patron Blacatz to do likewise.

*OF CADENET.**

NOW Cadenet was of Provence, of a castle named Cadenet, which is on the banks of the Durance, in the county of Forcalquier, and he was the son of a poor knight. And when he was yet a child, the castle of Cadenet was destroyed and plundered by the people of the Count of Toulouse, and the men of that land were killed or captured. And Cadenet was led bound into Toulouse, by a knight named Guillem of Lantar,[1] who nurtured him and kept him in his house. And he became brave, and fair, and courteous, and could sing and discourse right well, and learnt to make coblas and sirventes. Then he departed from the lord that had nurtured him, and went from court to court, and became a jongleur, calling himself *Baguas*.[2] Long time did he go through the world, with but little good

* See Mahn, lvi.

fortune, until he came into Provence where none knew him, and there he took the name of Cadenet, and began to make canzones good and fair. And Raymond Leugier of Dosfraires [Deux frères] in the diocese of Nice gave him harness and advanced him; likewise Lord Blacatz honoured him and did him much good. And long time did he live in passing great fame and happiness, and afterwards he entered the Order of the Hospitallers, wherein also he died. And all these his deeds do I know by hearsay and by eyewitness.

[1] **Guillem of Lantar.** A baron of that name is several times mentioned in the chronicles.
[2] **Baguas.** Scoundrel or debauchee.

PERDIGON.

First half of 13th Century.

THE Albigensian War, in its political aspect, may be regarded as a struggle between the great feudal lords on the one side, and the clergy supported by France on the other. As might easily be supposed, the troubadours were, throughout, the steady friends of the barons, at whose courts they had ever found a generous welcome : and they therefore directed the full violence of their hatred against the Church, and their national enemies —the French. The one notable exception among them was Perdigon, for Folquet, at the time of the war, had long ceased to be numbered with the troubadours. Perdigon, the son of a poor fisherman, had previously won the favour of King Peter

of Aragon, the Dauphin of Auvergne, William of the Baux
—Prince of Orange, and other great Provençal rulers, and had,
under their protection, long enjoyed great honour and prosperity.
At the beginning of the war, William of the Baux, eager for the
ruin of his great suzerain, the Count of Toulouse, espoused
the cause of the orthodox, and in this, whether from a
spirit of religious fanaticism, or from a base hope of personal
gain, Perdigon followed him with enthusiasm. He accompanied
Folquet in his expedition to Rome, and, when permission had
been obtained from the Pope to preach a crusade against
Raymond, urged on the Crusaders by his fiery songs to their
work of slaughter; he was present at the terrible massacre at
Beziers, and also at the Battle of Muret, at which was slain
his former benefactor, Peter of Aragon. It is satisfactory,
however, to know that Perdigon's ingratitude met its just
reward. His last years were full of bitterness; his old friends
shrank from him, and upon the death, in the year 1218, of his
patrons Simon of Montfort and William of the Baux, he found
himself utterly alone, and glad to take shelter from the general
hatred in a Cistercian monastery.

Perdigon's political poems have been lost, and his canzones,
which have been preserved to us, are of no special merit.

*OF PERDIGON.**

NOW Perdigon was a jongleur, and knew right well
to viol, and to make poetry and to sing; and he
was of the diocese of Gavaudon, of a village named
Esperon, and was the son of a fisherman. And by
his poetry, and by his sure wit he rose to such
fame and honour, that the Dauphin of Auvergne

* See Mahn, lviii.

made him one of his knights, and gave him land
and revenues. All good folk did him honour, and
long did he dwell in great joy and happiness; but
great changes came to him, for death despoiled him
of his good days, and gave him evil ones, and he
lost friends, and mistresses, and praise, and honour,
and wealth. After this he went to Rome with the
Prince of Orange, the Lord William of the Baux, and
Folquet of Marseilles—Bishop of Toulouse, and the
Abbot of Cistel, to bring evil on the Count of
Toulouse, and to ordain a crusade, and to disinherit
the good Count Raymond. And Raymond's nephew
the Count of Beziers died, and Carcassez[1] and the
Albigeois were destroyed; and King Peter of Aragon,
with one thousand knights and twenty thousand
other men, were slain before Muret. And in all
these deeds Perdigon bore his part; and in his
songs he exhorted all men to take the Cross, and
gave praise to God because that the Frenchmen had
slain and discomfited King Peter of Aragon, the which
had arrayed him, and made him gifts, wherefore he
lost fame, and honour, and wealth, and those that had
enriched him and were yet alive would neither see
him, nor hear of him. And all those of his fellow-
ship were slain in war, the Count of Montfort,
Lord William of the Baux, and those that had joined
the Crusade; and Count Raymond recovered his
inheritance, and Perdigon dared not go or come,

and the Dauphin of Auvergne stript him of the land and revenues that he had given him. Then he got him to Lord Lambert[2] of Montel, son-in-law of Lord William of the Baux, and besought him to gain him entrance into a House of Cistel, named Silvabela, and he gained him entrance into it, and there he died.

[1] **Carcassez.** The old county, of which Carcasonne was the capital.

[2] **Lambert of Montel.** A baron, who had allied himself by marriage with the House of Montfort.

GUY OF CAVAILLON.

First half of 13th Century.

Guy of Cavaillon was a faithful friend to Raymond VII. of Toulouse, in defence of whose cause he wrote a very bitter poem against William IV. of the Baux, who had gone over to the side of the French in their attacks on Raymond, and been made King of Arles. In mocking allusion to William's falling into the hands of the burgher whom he had robbed, and to his capture by some fishermen, Guy bids this "Half prince, who got himself crowned King" to have a care to leave his state well protected, since he is so often taken prisoner. In another poem he speaks of himself as being besieged by the French in a castle called Castelnou (New Castle), and reproaches one of his brothers-in-arms for not coming to his aid.

*GUY OF CAVAILLON.**

NOW Guy of Cavaillon was a noble baron of
Provence, lord of Cavaillon. And he was a bountiful, courteous and gracious knight, and well loved
of ladies, and of all folk soever, and a good knight
of arms, and a good warrior, and he made good
tenzons and coblas of love and of merriment.
And men weened that he was the lover of the
Countess Garsenda,† wife of the Count of Provence,
the which was brother of the King of Aragon.

ALBERTET.

First half of 13th Century.

AMONG Albertet's poems is a sirvente of singular originality,
in which he declaims against Love, and professes himself
proof against the charms of the fairest women of his day,
some of whom he mentions by name. He also bore part in
a tenzon, the subject of which was the rival merits of the
Catalans (amongst whom are included those whose language
was the Langue d'Oc),[1] and the French, or those who spoke
the Langue d'Oil. Albertet's opponent declares himself for
the French, and boasts of their valour, generosity, and good
cheer, while the Catalans, he says, feast strangers on nothing
but songs. Albertet defends his countrymen, the Catalans,
with whom, he says, chivalry had its rise, and at whose tables
is that merriment without which all dishes are tasteless.

* See Mahn, lix.
† The Countess that Elias Barjol also loved.

ALBERTET.

Now Albertet was of Gapensois, the son of a jongleur named Asar, the which made good canzonets. And Albertet made many canzones with good melodies, but words of little worth, and greatly was he liked both far and near for the good melodies he made. And a good jongleur was he at court, and merry and debonair amongst all men, and he dwelt long at Orange, and thereafter went to Sisteron, where he died.

[1] **Langue d'Oc.** A geographical line, running at the northern border of Dauphiné, Auvergne, Limousin, and Perigord, divided in the Middle Ages the people who spoke the Langue d'Oil, or French language, from those who spoke the Langue d'Oc or Provençal. Languedoc included also Catalonia and Savoy, and a small portion of the southwest of Switzerland. The troubadours called their language 'Romans,' '*Limousin*,' and, later on, 'Provençal.'

AIMERIC OF BELENOI.

1190(?)-1240.(?)

AIMERIC of Belenoi, though not to be placed among the greater troubadours, nevertheless won the praise of Dante,[1] who quotes a line from him. His most interesting poems are a fine 'complaint' over the death of a Count of Roussillon; a Crusading song, though on which crusade is uncertain; and a sirvente in which he takes up the cause of Love against its enemy, Albertet.

* See Mahn, lx.

*AIMERIC, OF BELENOI.**

SIR AIMERIC of Belenoi was of Bourdelois, of a castle named Lesparra—nephew of Master Peire of Corbiac,[2] and first he was a clerk, but afterwards he became a jongleur, and made songs good, and fair and pleasant of a lady of Gascony, named Gentil of Ruis, and for her sake he remained long in that country, and thereafter he went into Catalonia, where he dwelt till he died—and behold here written some of his songs.

[1] **The Praise of Dante**—See *De Vulgari Eloquio*, Lib. II., cap. 6. 12.

[2] **Peire of Corbiac**—A troubadour of little importance.

ELIAS CAIREL.

First half of 13th Century.

THE most interesting of the poems of Elias Cairel is one addressed to William IV. of Montferrat about the year 1224, urging upon the Marquis to attempt the recovery of Thessalonica, which had been taken from his younger brother.

OF ELIAS CAIREL.†

Now Elias Cairel was of Sarlat, of a town of Perigord, and was a worker in gold and silver, and a

* See Mahn, lxi.   † See Mahn, xii.

designer of arms, but became a jongleur. Ill did he sing, and ill did he make poetry, and ill did he viol, and yet worse did he speak, but well wrote both words and melodies. Long did he abide in Romania, and when he departed from thence he returned to Sarlat and their died.

Another manuscript. Elias Cairel was of great learning and of great subtlety in the making of poetry, and in all that he would do or say. And he roamed over the greater part of the habited world, but because of his scorn of the barons, and of the age, he was not favoured as his work merited.

FOLQUET OF ROTMAN.

First half of 13th Century.

FOLQUET of Rotman, as his poems prove, spent the greater part of his life in Italy, where he sought the protection of the Emperor Frederick II. and William IV. of Montferrat. He wrote two Crusading songs, one of which is an exhortation to Frederick II. to lead his army to Palestine without delay.

*OF FOLQUET OF ROTMAN.**

FOLQUET of Rotman was of Viennois, of a borough named Rotman, a good jongleur he was, and accomplished at court and of great merriment. And greatly was he honoured of all good folk, and he

* See Mahn, lxiii.

made sirventes after the manner of a jongleur,
wherein he praised the stout and blamed the
cowardly; and he made many good coblas.

GUILLEM FIGIEIRA.

First half of 13th Century.

THE importance of Guillem Figieira consists chiefly in the
long and passionate sirvente, in which he denounces Rome
and her iniquities. A native of Toulouse, in which he dwelt
during the Albigensian war, his sympathy in the misfortunes
of his lord and country filled him with a deadly hatred of
the Church that had smiled on the atrocities practised by
the Crusaders; and it is this hatred, or rather this righteous
indignation of his, that inspires the sirvente in question, the
sustained strength and artistic finish of which make it one
of the most remarkable productions of Provençal literature.

Amongst Figieira's other poems is to be mentioned a very
forcible denunciation of the immorality of the priests, and also
two sirventes in praise of Frederick II., of whom, as might be
expected, he was an ardent admirer.

*OF GUILLEM FIGIEIRA.**

GUILLEM FIGIEIRA was of Toulouse, and was the
son of a tailor, and eke himself a tailor. And when
the French had taken Toulouse he came to dwell
in Lombardy. And he knew right well to sing,
and to make poetry, and became the jongleur of
citizens. He was not one that might dwell among

*See Mahn, lxiv.

R

barons and among gentlefolk, but made himself cherished of the riotous and wantons, and of inn-keepers and tavern-keepers. And ever when he saw a good man from the court coming to where he abode, he was vexed and grieved, and ever strove to abase him, and to lift up the dissolute.

THREE STANZAS OF THE SIRVENTE ON ROME.[1]

> Lo, a song I sing
>   With melody that pleases,
> Hence vain dallying,
>   Since speech my bosom eases.
> Him that thus would sing
>   I wot swift vengeance seizes;
> Nathless I will rise
> 'Gainst that Head of lies,
> Rome, whom all despise,
>   Foul source of all diseases
> Whereof virtue dies.

.   .   .   .

> Rome, deceiver dread,
>   Who gold alone reverest,
> From thy sheep unfed
>   Full close the wool thou shearest.

* See *Chrestomathie provençale*, page 199.

He, whose blood was shed,
 And to mankind is dearest,
He whom now I seek
Break thy rav'nous beak.
Rome, as traitress sleek
 And liar thou appearest
To Latin and to Greek.

Rome, on flesh of weak[2]
 And foolish men thou feedest,
Blind ones guidance seek,
 Whom in the ditch thou leadest;
God's commandment eke
 Methinks thou little heedest;
Since by lust of gold
Pardons thou hast sold
Unto sinners bold;
 Rome, great strength thou needest
Sin's burden to uphold.

[1] **The sirvente on Rome.** The sirvente of which these verses
 form part is of unusual length, twenty-three stanzas in
 all; each one is of eleven lines with the rhymes
 a b a b a b c c c b c. Throughout the poem the rhyme c
 of a stanza is introduced as a, into the following one,
 but otherwise each stanza has its own rhymes.

[2] **Rome, on flesh of weak.** The literal translation of the
 opening lines of this stanza is: "Rome, thou gnawest
 the flesh and bones of foolish men," a sentence not easy
 to render in verse. The above stanzas are perhaps those

that best admit of verse translation, the *substance* of some of the others is as follows :

"Rome, verily thou wast too eager in promoting vile exhortations against Toulouse, like one in raging madness didst thou gnaw the hands of great and small, yet if the noble Count live but two more years, France shall sorely rue thy arts and wiles. . . . Rome, I comfort me in that ere long great ruin shall seize thee, if the righteous Emperor [Frederick II.] does that he should. Rome, may the true Redeemer soon let me see it come to pass. . . . Rome, so fast is thy grip, that what thou clutchest may hardly escape thee : yet if thou lose not soon thy power, soon will the world be in an evil pass, and slain and vanquished. Rome, it is thy Pope that works this wonder. . . . Rome, I am passing sad to see thy power increase, for therein great misfortune threatens us all, for thou art the refuge and source of deceit and shame ; thy shepherds are false traitors, and they that prize them do great folly.

Rome, from the foul heart thou bearest in thy bosom springs up the sycamore, that strangles the whole world with its sweetness ; the wise man trembles on seeing the deadly venom thou bearest in thy breast. Rome, it is from *thy* heart that there flows that whereof most men are full. . . . Rome, with hypocrisy thou layest thy net, and many an evil morsel thou devourest, reckless of the sore need of others. Thou hast the semblance of an innocent lamb, but within thou art a ravenous wolf, a crowned serpent, begotten of a viper ; therefore does the devil give thee succour as to his familiar friend.

LANFRANC CIGALLA.

First half of 13th Century.

A LANFRANC CIGALLA, probably the troubadour, is mentioned in the *Annals of Genoa* as being judge there in the year 1243. Amongst his poems are three sirventes of interest: one in condemnation of Boniface, Marquis of Montferrat, for having deserted Frederick II., another in praise of Saint Louis, and a third against the obscene poetry then in vogue.

*OF LANFRANC CIGALLA.**

LORD LANFRANC CIGALLA was of the city of Genoa. And he was a gentle man and wise, and was both judge and knight, but lived rather the life of a judge than of a knight. And he was a great lover of ladies and of poetry; and he was a good poet, and made many good canzones, and sang full readily of God, and behold here written some of his canzones.

GUILLEM OF MONTAGNAGOUT.
Died 1270?

ANOTHER manuscript than that translated below speaks of Guillem as belonging to Toulouse, and not Provence, and this is the more likely to be the case, in that his poems treat of subjects bearing on Toulouse, one, namely, in praise of the efforts that Raymond VII. made to regain the lands lost in the Albigensian War, and another against the Inquisition then established in Toulouse and other places.

* See Mahn, lxv.

*OF GUILLEM OF MONTAGNAGOUT.**

GUILLEM OF MONTAGNAGOUT was a knight of Provence, and was a good troubadour, and a great lover; and he loved my Lady Jauseranda, of the Castle of Lunel, and made for her many good songs.

BERTRAN OF LAMANON.
Second Third of 13th Century.

BERTRAN OF LAMANON was a powerful baron of Provence, who lived in the reign of Raymond Berengar IV. of Provence, and appears as the hero of a tale in the *Cento Novelle*. Bertran wrote a poem on Sordello's dirge over Blacatz, in which he says that he wonders at Sordello's folly in dividing the heart of Blacatz among people unworthy of it; Bertran, for his part, would divide it among the women whom Blacatz loved.

OF BERTRAN OF LAMANON.†

NOW Bertran of Lamanon was of Provence, the son of Sir Pons of Brugeiras. A courteous knight he was, and fair of speech, and made many a good and merry cobla and sirvente.

BERTRAN OF BORN, THE YOUNGER.
First half of 13th Century.

THE story of John's marriage to Isabel of Angoulême, and the subsequent rebellion of his barons, is here given, as will

* See Mahn, lxvi.   † See Mahn, lxvii.

be seen, merely in explanation of a sirvente composed, as the biographer says, by the younger Bertran of Born, son of the greater poet of that name.   History bears witness to the veracity of the following account in all its essential points.   John's marriage, the year after his accession to the throne, with the bride of Hugh the Brown, Earl of Marche, led, in fact, to a rebellion on the part of Hugh and a large number of Poitevin barons, who straightway appealed to the King of France for aid.   In answer to this appeal Philip sent them young Arthur of Brittany; he and the barons of Poitou, however, while besieging Queen Eleanor, who was in the Castle of Mirabel, were surprised and defeated by John. In the spring of the following year (1203) Arthur, who had been sent by John to a prison in Rouen, died—put to death, as was the general belief, by his uncle's orders.   The rebellion now became of a most wide-spread nature.   Philip in 1204 invaded, and finally conquered Normandy, and in the following year Anjou, Maine and Touraine also fell into his hands.

The sirvente * in question was probably composed in the spring of 1205, some months before Philip had possessed himself of all the great Angevin inheritance; its author was bitterly opposed to French rule, and enraged at the supineness of John; and the substance of some of his stanzas is as follows :

"When I see the year growing young again, and leaves and flowers showing themselves, Love gives me the mind and courage to sing, and I will therefore make a biting sirvente, which I will send as a gift to King John, that he may be shamed by it.   And good cause had he for shame, would he but mind him of his forefathers, for without resistance he has given up Poitiers and Tours to King Philip; wherefore all Guienne weeps for King Richard, who spent much gold and silver to defend that land, whereof King John recks nothing; he the while thinks but of the tourney, and

---

* See Stimming's *Bertran of Born*, page 221.

the chase, and hounds, and hawks, and ease; wherefore
Honour forsakes him, and he is despoiled while yet alive of
his inheritance. . . . Barons, towards you I turn now in
rebuke; I blame the folly that ye have, and full woe am I
that I must needs speak thus. Ye have let your fame be
trampled in the mire, and ye have learnt a sort of folly that
makes you fear no chastisement." .

OF KING JOHN OF ENGLAND.[*]

NOW this is the purport of this sirvente. When
King Richard was dead there remained behind him
one of his brothers, John, surnamed Lackland, because there was no land apportioned unto him.
And he was made King of England, and Duke
of Aquitaine, and Count of Poitou. And so soon
as he was made King and Lord of Aquitaine and
Poitou, he betook him to the Count of Angoulême,
who had a right fair daughter—a maid of some
fifteen years. And the maid had been affianced by
Lord Richard to Hugh the Brown, Count of Marche,
the which was nephew and vassal of Lord Geoffrey
de la Seingna. And the Count of Angoulême had
promised him his daughter, and he received him
for his son, for no other son nor daughter had he.
Now King John said to the Count of Angoulême
that he would have his daughter for wife, and
caused her to be given him, and straightway
espoused her, and gat him to horse, and went with

* See Mahn, lxviii.

his wife into Normandy. And full woe was the Count of Marche when he knew that the King had robbed him of his wife, and he made complaint of it to all his kinsmen and friends. And all were sore wroth because of it, and took counsel together over the going to Brittany to possess them of Arthur, Count Geoffrey's son, whom they would make their lord. And of right could they do this, seeing that he was son of Count Geoffrey that was born before King John. So they made Arthur their liege lord, and swore him fealty, and brought him into Poitou, and took from the King all Poitou, but it were a few castles and strongholds he had therein.

And he the while abode with his wife in Normandy, and went not from her day or night, neither eating, nor drinking, nor sleeping, nor waking, and took her with him as he hawked and hunted. And the barons went on taking all his land; yet truly it happened that a great misadventure overtook them, for they had besieged his mother in a castle named Mirabel, and he, confirmed therein by others, brought secret succour to her, and came so stealthily that none had tidings of it until he was with them in the fort; and he found them sleeping, and took all captive—Arthur, and his barons, and those that held with him. And for jealous love of his wife (for he might not live without her) he gave up Poitiers, and returned into

Normandy, and left his prisoners bound to him by oath, and by the giving of hostages. And he passed into England, taking with him Arthur, and Lord Savaric of Mauleon, and the Viscount of Castel Airaut. And he let drown his nephew Arthur,* and Lord Savaric of Mauleon and the Viscount of Castel Airaut he put into the Tower Corp, where never man ate nor drank.

And when the King of France knew that King John had passed into England with his wife, he straightway entered into Normandy with a great host of men, and despoiled him of all the land. And the barons of Poitou rose against him, and took from him all Poitou, save only La Rochelle. Then Lord Savaric of Mauleon, like a man valiant and wise and noble, achieved by subtle devices his escape out of his prison, and took the castle, in the which he was captive. And King John made peace with him, and let him go free, and gave into his keeping all such parts of Poitou and Gascony as had not been taken from him. And thither betook himself Lord Savaric, and fell to making war upon all King John's enemies, and took from them all Poitou and Gascony, while the King dwelt at ease with his wife in England, and gave no aid to Lord Savaric of Mauleon, either with men or money ; wherefore Bertran of Born the Young—

* Arthur was in reality imprisoned at Rouen, and not taken to England.

son of the Sir Bertran of Born that made those other sirventes—because of Lord Savaric's sore need, and for the outcry that the men of Aquitaine and of the county of Poitou made of it, made this sirvente:

"Cant vei lo temps renovelar."

(When I see the season growing young again.)

DAUDE OF PRADAS.

13th Century.

DAUDE of Pradas, a troubadour of little importance, has left behind him about twenty canzones, a poem on the right treatment of birds of prey, and a didactic poem on the cardinal virtues.

*OF DAUDE OF PRADAS.**

Now Daude of Pradas was of Rouergue, of a town named Pradas, that lies four leagues from the city of Rhodez. And he was a canon of Magalona [Maguelonne], and a wise man of learning, and of native wit withal. And he knew full well the nature of birds of prey. And he made canzones because he had a mind to make poetry, and not because Love moved him to it, wherefore they found no welcome amongst men, and were not sung nor liked.

* See Mahn, lxxi.

THE LADIES CASTELLOZA, TIBORS, LOMBARDA, MARIA OF VENTADORN, AND AZALAIS OF PORCAIRAGUES.

OF these five ladies Maria of Ventadorn is by far the most celebrated. She lived in a neighbourhood fertile in poets, and at a court renowned for its splendour and hospitality, and had therefore ample opportunity for displaying her charms of mind and person. These must have been very great, for no other lady's name occurs as frequently as hers in Provençal poetry. While, however, the canzones of trouveresses such as the Countess of Die, and Claire of Andusa vie with those of the troubadours in grace and tenderness, other ladies, as, for example, Maria, seem to have betaken themselves to the composition of verses merely as an occasional recreation.

*OF LADY CASTELLOZA.**

MY Lady Castelloza was of Auvergne, a noble lady, wife of Truc of Mairona; and she loved Sir Arman of Breon, and made of him her canzones. And she was a lady right fair, right gay, and right well taught.

OF LADY TIBORS.†[1]

MY Lady Tibors was of Provence, of a castle held of Lord Blacatz and named Sarrenom. Courteous she was, and gracious, and well taught, and withal full learned and skilled in the making of poetry. And she was amorous and full well loved of others,

* See Mahn, lxxvi.   † See Mahn, lxxvii.

and full honoured by all the good men of that
country, and by all excellent ladies full greatly
striven for, and full well obeyed.   And she made
these coblas and sent them to her lover:

"Bels dous amics, ben vos puesc en ver dir."
(Fair, sweet friend,[2] full truly can I say to you).

OF LADY LOMBARDA.*

NOW my Lady Lombarda was of Toulouse, gentle,
fair, and gracious, and well taught.   And she knew
well to make poetry, and made coblas, and
amorous ones, wherefore Lord Bernart Arnaut,
brother of the Count of Armaias, heard tell of her
goodness and excellence, and came unto Toulouse
for to see her.   And he dwelt with her in great
intimacy, and sought her in love, and was greatly
her friend.   And he made these coblas of her,
and straightway sent them to where she lodged,
and gat him to horse, and without seeing her,
departed into his own land.   And greatly marvelled
my lady Lombarda when she heard tell that Bernart
Arnaut was gone without seeing her, and she sent
him these coblas.

OF LADY MARIA OF VENTADORN.†

NOW well have ye heard how that my lady Maria
of Ventadorn was the most famous lady that ever

* See Mahn, lxxviii.   † See Mahn, lxxix.

was in Limousin, and she that most did good, and most did keep her from evil; and never did her wit forsake her, or folly gain hold over her. And God favoured her with a fair and goodly person, and with grace unmarred by pride. Now Sir Guy of Uisel had lost his lady, even as ye have heard in his song that runs:

> "Si bem partetz mala dompna de vos,"
> (Although I depart from you, cruel lady,)

wherefore he lived in great dole and sadness, and for longtime had neither sung nor made poetry; whence great heaviness came upon all the ladies of that country, and upon my lady Maria more than any, because that Sir Guy of Uisel was wont to sing her praise in all his songs. Now the Count of Marche, the which was called Lord Hugh the Brown, was her knight, and as much honour as lady can show to knight had she even shown to him. And it fell upon a day, that while he was paying court to her, there arose a debate between them, for the Count of Marche said that a faithful lover, when that his lady had given him her love, and taken him for knight and friend, should, while he remained faithful and true to her, have the same dominion and lordship over her as she over him; and my lady Maria maintained that the friend should have neither dominion nor lordship over her.

And Gui of Uisel was in the court of my lady Maria, and she, to turn the matter to song and to sport, made of it a cobla, in the which she inquired of him, if it were meet that a lover should have as much dominion over his lady, as his lady over him. And on this matter my lady Maria challenged him to a tenzon, saying:

> "Gui d'Uissel, bem peza de vos."
> (Gui of Uisel, I am full sorry for you.)

OF AZALAIS OF PORCAIRAGUES.*

My lady Azalais of Porcairague was of the country of Montpellier—a noble lady and well taught. And she became enamoured of Sir Guy Guerreiat, the which was brother of Lord William of Montpellier. And the lady knew to make poetry, and made many a good canzone of him.

[1] **Lady Tibors.** This Lady Tibors, being of Provence, must not be confused with the Lady Tibors who brought about a reconciliation between Bertran of Born and his Lady.

[2] **Fair sweet friend.** The substance of the poem is as follows: "Fair sweet friend, full truly can I say that never am I without desire of thee, . . . and never am I without a mind, fair sweet friend, to see thee often, and never was there a time that I have repented me, and never when thou hast left me in sadness have I known joy till thy return.

*See Mahn, xci.

PEIRE OF MAENSAC AND OTHERS.

End of 12th Century, and first half of 13th.

THE following five Lives, being those of troubadours of little significance, call for no special comment.

OF PEIRE OF MAENSAC.

NOW Peire of Maensac was a poor knight of Auvergne, the Dauphin's land. And he had a brother named Austor of Maensac, and both were troubadours. And they accorded with one another, that one should have the castle and the other the poetry; and Austor had the castle, and Peire the poetry. And he sang of the wife of Sir Bernart of Tierci; and so much did he sing of her, and so much did he honour and serve her, that the lady let herself be stolen away by him. And he brought her to one of the Dauphin of Auvergne's Castles, and the husband made urgent demand of her, aided therein by the Church, and made great war upon him; howbeit the Dauphin so upheld him that he never restored her unto her husband. And Peire was a right excellent man and a merry, and he made canzones that had fair words and melodies, and coblas of great merriment.

* See Mahn, lxxxvi.

OF GUILLEM ADEMAR.*

GUILLEM Ademar was of Gavaudan, of a castle named Merueis—a gentleman he was, the son of a knight that was neither mighty nor rich. And the lord of Merueis made him knight. And he was brave, and good, and pleasant of speech, and a good troubadour; but could not maintain the knightly estate, so became a jongleur. And he was much honoured, and later entered the monastery of Granmont, and there died.

OF HUGH BRUNET.†

SIR HUGH BRUNET was of the city of Rhodez, which is of the lordship of the Count of Toulouse. And he was a clerk that well did uphold learning, and was a subtle man of learning and of native wit. And he became a jongleur, and made good songs, but no melodies, and consorted with the Count of Rhodez, his liege lord, and with Sir Bernart of Andusa, and with the Dauphin of Auvergne. And he loved the wife of a burgher of Aurillac named dame Galiana; but she would neither love him nor retain him, nor do him any pleasure of love, but took the Count of Rhodez for her lover, and gave dismissal to Sir Hugh Brunet; and Sir Hugh Brunet, for grief thereat, entered the order of the Carthusians, and there died.

*See Mahn, lxix.   †See Mahn, lxx.

OF BLACASSET. *

LORD BLACASSET was the son of Lord Blacatz, who was verily the best gentleman of Provence, and the most honourable baron, and the most excellent, and the most upright, and the most bountiful, and the most courteous, and the most debonair. And in good sooth was Lord Blacasset his son in all excellence, and in all valour, and in all bountiful deeds. And he was a great lover of ladies, and much given to poetry, and he was a good troubadour and the maker of many good canzones.

OF HUGH DE LA BACALAIRIA.†

SIR HUGH de la Bacalairia was of Limousin, whence was Gaucelm Faidit. A jongleur he was of little worth, and little went abroad, and little was known of men; yet made he good canzones and made also a good ' Descort,' and good tenzons And he was a courteous man, right excellent, and right well taught.

WILLIAM OF THE BAUX, PRINCE OF ORANGE.
Reigned from 1182-1219.

THIS Guillem, or William of the Baux, is the same prince that has already been mentioned as the protector of Raembaut of Vaqueiras and of Perdigon. He was the fourth Prince of

* See Mahn, xcv.   † See Mahn, cvi.

Orange of that name, his father, Bertran I. of the Baux, having acquired the little State of Orange by his marriage with a sister of the troubadour, Raembaut of Orange.

Allusion has already been made to the intimacy between William IV. of Orange and Raembaut of Vaqueiras, who exchanged tenzons with him, and gave him, though why is not known, the pseudonym of "Englishman." The Ademar, mentioned in the account given below, was a certain Count of Valentinois and Diois, one of whose estates had been plundered by William. Ademar avenged himself, as we see, by causing his fishermen to set on the Prince as he was journeying down the Rhone. Over this misfortune Raembaut of Vaqueiras made merry at William's expense; the Prince therefore replied to him by a tenzon, in which he tells him, that people will now think him even madder than his father Peirol: "Go," he finishes by saying, "Go to the King of Barcelona, and to the others on whom you are casting your eyes; for nothing do you like better than gold, and your wretched raiment.

OF GUILLEM OF THE BAUX.

Now Guillem of the Baux, Prince of Orange, robbed a merchant of France upon his own high-road, and despoiled him of rich goods; and the merchant went and made complaint of it to the King of France. And the King said to him: "I might not amend that which happens in a land so far off from me, howbeit, I plight thee my word that thou shalt have license to help thyself in whatsoever manner thou wilt." And the burgher went and let counterfeit the King's ring, and wrote to my lord Guillem of the Baux a letter,

*See Mahn, cii.

that should be the King's, bidding him come to the King, and promising him great goods, and great honours, and great gifts. And when Guillem of the Baux had the letter he rejoiced full much, and made great preparations for to go to the King; and he departed and entered into the city, where dwelt the merchant whom he had robbed, for he knew not whence the merchant was. And this burgher, when he knew my lord Guillem of the Baux was in the city, caused him and all his fellows to be taken, and he had perforce to restore that he had stolen, and amend that he had misdone. And he went forth poor and despoiled, and went to take an estate named l'Osteilla, held of Ademar of Poitiers. And as he was journeying on the Rhone in a bark, the fishers of Sir Ademar seized on him, and Sir Raembaut of Vaqueiras, who called himself "Englishman,"* made these coblas thereof:

"Tuit me pregon, Engles, qeu vos don saut."
(All men pray me, Englishman, to make attack on you.)

GUILLEM OF BERGUEDAN.

13th Century.

GUILLEM of Berguedan's chief or perhaps sole claim to attention is that of having been in his earlier and prosperous

---

* The custom of friends calling each other by the same name has been already remarked on.

days the friend of troubadours, and more especially, as we have seen, that of Aimeric of Peguillan. His poems, twenty-five in number, have little to recommend them.

OF GUILLEM OF BERGUEDAN.

NOW Guillem of Berguedan was a noble lord of Catalonia, Viscount of Berguedan, lord of Madorna and of Riechs, a good knight and a good warrior. And there was sore strife betwixt him and Sir Raymond Folc of Cardona, who was richer and mightier than he. And it chanced that one day he came upon Sir Raymond Folc, and foully slew him. And for the death of Sir Raymond Folc he was disinherited. Long time his kindred and friends maintained him, until one and all forsook him, because he enticed from them their wives, or their daughters, or their sisters. And in the end none maintained him but Sir Arnaut of Castelbon, the which was an excellent and great gentleman of that country. Good sirventes he made, wherein he spake ill of some and good of others. And he boasted him of all the ladies that suffered his love. And great good fortune did he have of arms and of ladies, and great ill-fortune likewise; and thereafter he was slain by a soldier.

*See Mahn, ciii.

PEIRE PELISSIER.

12th and 13th Centuries.

As was characteristic of an age of curious contrasts and inconsistencies, the much praised generosity and chivalry of the Dauphin of Auvergne did not withhold him from gross injustice towards Peire Pelissier, who, therefore, in the manner of his day vented his wrath in verse, bitterly complaining of the Dauphin's having broken his promise of paying back the money he had borrowed. "Churl courtier," retorted the Dauphin, "ye have squandered what your father left you, and now think to enrich yourself by me. By my faith ye shall have nothing from me. Go and beg like a blind man for alms, and sing if ye will against him who refuses you them."

OF PEIRE PELISSIER.[*]

Now Peire Pelissier was of Marcel, the which is a town held of the Viscount of Turenne, and he was an honourable burgher of great excellence and courtesy. And by his excellence and by his wisdom he rose to so great honour that the Viscount made him bailiff over all his land. Now the Dauphin of Auvergne was in that season the lover of the Lady Comtor, the Viscount's daughter, the which was of great fame for her beauty and excellence. And Sir Peire Pelissier did him what service he would, whenever he came to him, and lent him money. And when Sir Peire Pelissier would recover the money, the Dauphin would not pay him, and refrained from guerdoning him for the services he

[*] See Mahn, cxii.

had done. And the Dauphin left seeing the lady, and from coming to that country wherein she dwelt; neither did he send her message nor letter; wherefore Sir Peire Pelissier made this cobla:

"Al Dalfin man questei dinz son hostal."
(I bid the Dauphin dwell within his house.)

And the Dauphin made unto him a churlish and unjust answer:

"Vilan cortes lavetz tot mes a mal."
(Courtier churl, ye have squandered all.)

PEIRE OF BARJAC.
13th Century.

PEIRE of Barjac, a knight, who, gratuitously insulted and dismissed by his lady, bade her farewell in courteous and forbearing terms, is, as Fauriel remarks, a good illustration of the firm hold that the institutions of chivalry had taken in his time upon the mediaeval mind. While letting her understand that in losing her he has found another lady who will compensate him for the loss, he thanks her for having for a time deigned to accept his love, assures her that though sent away, he will be as zealous as before in promoting her welfare, and that with all his heart he pardons her the sorrow she has caused him.

*OF PEIRE OF BARJAC.**

Now Peire of Barjac was a knight, companion of Sir Guillem of Balaun; and was right skilful, and courteous, and even such a knight as was meet for Guillem of Balaun. And he became enamoured of a lady of the castle of Javiac, the wife of a

*See Mahn, cxiii.

vavasour, and likewise she of him, and he had of her all that pleased him. And Guillem of Balaun knew of their love. And it chanced that upon an evening Peire of Barjac came to the castle with Guillem of Balaun, and held speech with his lady. And it befell that Peire of Barjac parted with her in evil fashion, receiving from her full angry words and a rough dismissal. And on the morrow Guillem departed and Peire with him, sad and sorrowful. And Guillem asked him why he was so sad, and Peire told him the reason thereof. And Guillem comforted him, saying that he would make peace. And ere long they returned to Javiac, and the peace was made. And Peire left her with great joy that the lady had given him.

*PEIRE OF BARJAC'S FAREWELL TO HIS LADY.**

GOOD lady, I am come without disguise
To take my leave of thee for evermore.
Gramercy then, that in the days of yore
It pleased thee to fill my heart with gladness,
Which now it pleaseth thee to change to sadness.
'Tis well thou findest, since our love is o'er,
A knight on whom thou settest greater store,
I'll not complain, nor chide in angry madness ;
Hereafter we will meet in friendly wise,
Nor bitter memories between us rise.

* *Chrestomathie provençale*, page 197.

And since of plighted vows thou tak'st no heed,
True love thus scorned well may bring us woe,
Then let us to a priest together go,
That each the other from the bond releasing,
May serve new Love with ardour all unceasing,
And greater fealty in service show;
And if by any wrong thou hast brought me low,
I pardon thee, and wish thee joy increasing,
And this full truly, for 'tis shame indeed
When pardon doth not from the heart proceed.

Cruel lady, who didst rouse this jealous ire,
To pleasure thee I once was ever fain,
But folly o'er the jealous man hath reign;
He, both in words and deeds all undiscerning,
Endureth pangs untold and heartfelt yearning;
From morn till eve he dwelleth in sore pain,
Nor eke in one place may he long remain.
Behold me from thy once dear presence turning,
E'en so the leper 'midst his torments dire
Would gladly from the haunts of men retire.

GUILLEM DE LA TOR.

13th Century.

THERE is little that is noteworthy in Guillem de La Tor,
excepting the pathetic story of his passionate fondness for his

beautiful wife. His canzones are graceful enough, but of absolutely no originality, and indeed, to judge by the "Life," he was known in his own day rather as a singer of the canzones of others, than as a maker of poems of his own.

OF GUILLEM DE LA TOR.*

NOW Guillem de La Tor was a jongleur. He was of Perigord, of a castle named La Tor; and he came into Lombardy, and knew right many canzones, and loved, and sang full pleasantly. Eke did he make poetry, but when he would rehearse his canzones he was wont to make thereon a discourse longer than were the canzones themselves. And he took a wife at Milan, a barber's wife, full fair and young, the which fled away and was brought by him to Com. And he bare to her greater goodwill than to all the world besides. And it came to pass that she died, whereat he made such great dole that he became mad, and weened that she feigned her dead to rid herself of him; wherefore for ten days and ten nights he left her lying on her tomb. And each evening he went unto the tomb, and uplifted her, and looked upon her visage, kissing and embracing her, and praying her to speak to him, and to tell him whether she were alive or dead; and if she were alive he would have her return to him, and if dead he would have her tell him what were her

*See Mahn, cxvii.

pains ; for then he would have so many masses said for her, and would make such alms, that he would draw her forth from those pains. And the good men of the city came to know of the matter, and made him depart the land. And he went forth seeking everywhere soothsayers, be they men or women, who should tell him whether she might ever come to life again. And a certain scoffer gave him to believe that if, for the space of one year, he should, without fail, read daily the psalter, and say one hundred and fifty paternosters, and give alms to seven poor men or ever he brake fast, she would come to life again, but would not eat, nor drink, nor speak. And hearing this he was right glad, and anon began to do that which had been counselled him, and this he did the livelong year, not one day failing therein. But when he marked that what had been counselled him nothing availed him, he was stricken with despair and slew himself.

FERRARI.

13th Century.

FERRARI, to judge by the following account of him, must have been well thought of in his day, though only one poem of his, a tenzon, has been preserved to us.

NOW Master Ferrari was a jongleur of Ferrara, and he understood the Provençal tongue, and the making of Provençal poetry better than any man that ever was in Lombardy. Withal he was of great learning, and wrote better than any man in the world, and ever did willing service to barons and to knights, and ever abode with the family of Este. And when it befell that the marquises held high court and festival, and that the jongleurs that knew the Provençal tongue came unto them, these all consorted with him, and called him their master. And if any one of them, that was of greater understanding than the rest, questioned him on his poetry or on aught else, anon would Master Ferrari make answer to him, so that he dwelt as a champion at the Court of the Marquis of Este. Howbeit he made but two canzones and one Retroensa;[1] but made right many of the best sirventes and coblas in the world. And he made an extract of all the canzones of the world's good troubadours; and from each canzone or sirvente he took one verse, or two, or three, even those that contained in them the chief matter of the canzones and had the best chosen words. And this extract lies here before me, and in it he would put none of his own verses;

*See Mahn, cxviii.

but he, whose book it is, has written some therein, that it may stand for a memorial of him.

Now Master Ferrari, when he was young, loved a lady named my lady Turcha; and for this lady's sake he made many right good canzones. And when he was grown old he went little abroad, save only that he went to Trevis, to my lord Giraut of Achamin, and to his son. And these did him great honour, and saw him gladly, and gave him hearty welcome and dealt bountifully towards him out of goodwill to him and love of the Marquis of Este.

[1] **Retroensa.** A poem with a refrain, and generally of five couplets, which all had different rhymes.

THE VISCOUNT OF SAINT ANTONIN.

13th Century.

RAYMOND JORDAN, Viscount of Saint Antonin, was a troubadour of little literary merit, hardly indeed deserving mention, but for the following romantic love-story connected with him.

*OF THE VISCOUNT OF SAINT ANTONIN.**

NOW the Viscount of Saint Antonin was of the diocese of Cahors, lord and Viscount of Saint Antonin. And he loved a noble lady, the which was wife of the lord of Pena of Albigeois, a castle

* See Mahn, cxix.

mighty and strong. The lady was gently born, and fair, and excellent, and much praised and honoured; and he full valorous, and learned, and bountiful, and courteous, and good at arms, and seemly, and debonair, and a good poet withal, and men called him Raymond Jordan, and the lady the Viscountess of Pena. Now the love they bare one another was out of measure great; and it chanced upon a time that the Viscount had made ready his harness, and there was a great combat, wherein he was wounded to the death, so that his enemies said he was dead. And tidings of his death reached the lady, and she, for the great grief she had of it, straightway entered into the order of the Heretics. And God so willed that the Viscount recovered of his wound, and no man would tell him that she had entered therein. And when he was whole he gat him unto Saint Antonin; and it was told him how the lady had become a nun for the sorrow she had on hearing of his death; and at this he left all gladness, and merriment, and joy, and was given over to tears, and lamentation, and woe. And he neither rode forth nor went among men, and in this wise did he endure for a year and more, so that all the good people of that country made great moan. Then my lady Elis of Montfort, who was wife of William of Gordon, and the daughter of the Viscount of Turenne, and in whom dwelt youth, and beauty, and courtesy, sent her messenger to him, bidding him full graciously take comfort for love of her. "For I give you" quoth she, "myself, and eke my love to amend you of the misfortune that has come to you, and pray you of your mercy to come to see me." Now when the Viscount heard the honourable and pleasant words of the lady, the sweetness of love began to enter into his heart, and he began to be of good cheer, and to rejoice, and to go abroad again amongst men, and clothe himself and his fellows. And he put on goodly and honourable apparel, and went unto my lady Elis of Montfort. And she made him good cheer, and did him great pleasure and honour. And he was right glad and merry at the honour and pleasure he received of her by word and act, and she right glad for the valour and excellence she found in him, and no-wise repented her of the loving message she had sent him. And well he knew to thank her for it; and he besought her that she should show him so much love, that he might know it was in all sincerity that she had sent him such fair and loving words of greeting, the which he ever bare written upon his heart. And well did the lady show him her love, for she took him for her knight, and received his homage, and gave herself to him with an embrace and a kiss; and for seal and pledge of his faith he gave her the ring from off his finger.

And with this, in great gladness, he left the lady, and returned home, singing and rejoicing.   And it was then that he made the canzone which runs:

> "Vas vos soplei en cui ai mes mentenssa."
> (Towards you, to whom I have given my love,
>   I turn my prayer.)

And ere he made the canzone, sleeping one night, him seemed that Love assailed him in a cobla which says:

> "Raimon Jordan, de vos eis voill aprendre
>   Cous etz laissatz de solatz ni de chan :
>   Ja soliatz en dompneiar entendre
>   Mout leialmen, so faziatz semblan;
>   Eus feigniatz, eus en faziatz gais;
>   Mas aras vei qavetz fenit lo lais,
>   Encolpatz etz si non es qei responda."

(Raymond Jordan, of yourself I would learn wherefore ye have refrained from mirth and song : of old ye were wont to set full faithfully your mind on love-making, or made semblance of it ; and ye bestirred yourself about it, and made merry over it : but now I see that the game is up—Ye will be held guilty if ye answer not.)

GLASGOW : PRINTED AT THE UNIVERSITY PRESS BY ROBERT MACLEHOSE AND CO.